# Gerard Philey's Euro-Diary: Quest for a Life

BRENDAN JAMES

Monday 1st January – Walsall

January 1ˢᵗ again, and same New Year's Day feeling when I woke up this morning: relief that last year is exactly that, followed by sense of dread about the year ahead. Sat on the side of the bed for a minute, staring at the stains on the carpet which started blurring as last year's 'highlights' whirled around inside my head: endless days of tedium, teaching French and German to kids whose mission in life is to flick me red raw with bits of chewed up *Paris Match*; endless nights of marking ungrammatical sentences about guinea pigs and 'mon boy band favori'. The summer hols in Skegness offered some relief, until I slipped on a discarded cheeseburger and apparently created the most hilarious case of groin-strain ever witnessed by Lincolnshire locals. Could just about walk again in time for the September OFSTED visit, on the first day of which the head of languages decides to have a nervous breakdown… Which slowly brings me to Christmas, the season of good will to all men, which Tina, my girlfriend of eighteen months, obviously thinks is code for 'dump Gerard'.

Then I remembered and smiled to myself, as the stains came back into focus. I don't have to look at them any more! It's Bye Bye Black Country Day minus one, and there's absolutely nothing to stop me. I'm twenty-five, with no wife, no girlfriend any more, not even a guinea pig, and a rented room in a house I share with Jan and Phil, whose baby will be terrorising my only peace at night from February… It's nearly time for me, Gerard Philey, to go out and get a life. There must be more than what these last few years have offered. I can become Signor Cosmopolitano - surely. Saw a JFK quote in the paper last week:

"You cannot become what you want to be by remaining what you are".

Spot on. Enough of break-time what-ifs, bus stop musings and bed-time wondering. Am determined this year's diary will not make as depressing (and boring) reading as last year's. There's a big continent out there, and I'm more than ready for it. 1996 and Bruxelles, capitale de l'Europe, j'arrive!!

Tuesday 2nd January - on Eurostar.

Am on my way! First time on Eurostar – marvellous, and
beats the ferry palaver hands down. Spent the rest of yesterday
sorting stuff out and on the phone to British Rail in
Birmingham. Have brought just one case (mainly clothes,
toiletries and the little angel of hope statue Aunty Vera left
me). Broke the news to Phil and Jan who didn't try to dissuade
me. In fact, they got quite enthusiastic about the idea. They
don't mind me storing my stuff in their attic, which is nice.
Still, it's only a few books, jumpers and a chest-expander I used
twice. Think they'll be glad of my room for the baby. Wrote a
letter to the school for Phil to post. Feel a bit bad about
leaving them in the lurch, but what the hell. Plenty of supply
teachers. The thought of another year of it all wrenches my
stomach open.
    Anyway, could hardly sleep last night, so was really tired
when I got on the train in Birmingham. Changed at Waterloo,
and am now travelling through the French countryside. Can't
believe it's doing 186 mph. Can't believe I've actually had the
guts to go. When I think about what I'm doing, I feel a bit
sick. Not met any interesting people yet. There's some sort of
Scandinavian woman opposite me trying to read upside down
so will stop writing now. Cheek.

Wednesday 3rd January

Hotel Henri, Brussels!

Got here last night. Arrived at the Gare Centrale, which is
unbelievably grotty, like some sort of diesel-filled underground
car park. It was only when the arrival of a train from Zurich
was announced in French and Flemish that I was sure I wasn't
in Wolverhampton. Finally emerged at street level, on the
verge of about six lanes of traffic surrounded by nondescript

grey buildings, so wondered again about Wolverhampton. Went into a couple of hotels, quite pricey, but found a reasonable one down a few side-streets, where I performed a fantastic Grade A* GCSE role play at reception. Dumped my stuff on the bed, put the angel of hope statue on the TV, and felt exhilarated by the utter freedom of it all. Thinking about the endless possibilities made me dizzy, so lay on bed for half an hour. After a quick wash and change, felt fine, and let myself loose on the city, feeling as if my life had moved into the fast lane. Had a pizza and wine in an Italian restaurant, then walked around a bit, feeling buoyed up by the dynamic atmosphere - the architectural splendour, the bustle at night, people speaking languages from all over Europe, multi-lingual neon signs. Not a pasty-faced Midlander in sight.

Got up early this morning and went to a cafe nearby for a croque monsieur and coffee, which made me feel very European. Long live the Maastricht Treaty! Have decided to relax for a few days before looking for work, so have done lots of tourist stuff today. Decided to do as much as I could on foot to save money and burn up some calories. Am starting to look a bit podgy round the middle. Anyway, my first time in Brussels for years, so enjoyed viewing the sights - the wonderful Grande Place with its golden gables, the little Mannekin Pis statue, the looming guild houses. Marvellous sauntering down the cobbled streets, earwigging on conversations in French and German, feeling smug. Made a mistake on the Grande Place, though, where I gave into pressure to have a caricature portrait done - cost me an arm and a leg, but thought it was quite flattering in a way. Look like some sort of East End villain, with heavy stubble à la George Michael, solid build and piercing eyes. "Un beau cadeau pour votre copine! "said the artist as I parted with the cash. I smiled politely and thought of Tina. Have thrown it away.

Friday 5th January

Great to speak French to people who don't just stare at me blankly, although so far only in bars and restaurants. Have had some incredible food on the Rue des Bouchers, one long street filled with nothing but elegant restaurants with mouth-watering displays of seafood. Feel a bit lonely eating on my own but picked up a copy of La Rochefoucauld's *Maxims* yesterday while browsing in a second-hand bookshop, so have read that over meals. It's basically a collection of his thoughts, and some ring very true, especially with regard to women (Tina):

"Most women's minds serve more to strengthen their madness than their reason".

Monday 8th January

Spent the weekend sampling Belgian beer in musty bars with log fires blazing away, watching the snow outside, and contemplating how the barmaids manage to switch with total ease between gracious professionalism and supercilious disdain.

Had a hangover-and-a-half when I got up and couldn't decide what to do as everything is a choice now, with no routine to fall back on. Suddenly felt overwhelmed and went back to bed for an hour. Also concerned that I'm spending a lot, so eventually decided to look into some sort of work after all. Was even more concerned when I went into a few job agencies which only seemed to have jobs in IT, plumbing or escort services. Maybe I should retrain in all three and make a killing. Felt quite exhilarated by the idea of becoming an escort. Quite like the idea of living the Richard Gere life in *American Gigolo*. Tina always said I could earn a fortune, don't quite see it myself, but then even she dumped me, so what does she know?

But what the hell, I can work the rest of my life. Have spent the evening chatting downstairs in the bar with Samuel, the hotel barman. He came over from the Belgian Congo in 1954 and didn't get a job till 1963, so I've got nothing to worry about.

## Friday 12th January

Rang mom and dad, told them that I'm on 'study-leave'.
Couldn't be bothered getting into the whole thing, and could
tell they were hardly interested. No news on their part. Also
rang Jan and Phil. He said the school had rung to check I was
serious about the letter, but he hadn't sensed any horror or
panic. Charming! I've slaved away for three years at that
school, and they're not even going to make a bit of fuss about
me going! Makes me glad I jacked it in.

Phil was clearly well impressed by the fact that I was still
away and have no intention of returning. Made up a few
sexploits just to make him jealous. Wish they'd been true.

## Sunday 14th January

Expected to be feeling a bit restless by now, but have surprised
myself. Think I could live quite happily drifting from
restaurant to bar to café, nipping into the odd bookshop,
strolling around. Did quite a long walk yesterday afternoon,
off the tourist track. It's weird, quite a lot of Brussels seems
really run down and dingy, all the more surprising given the
investment that must have gone on here. Went down one
street and saw some woman in curlers with a fag in her mouth
putting a duvet out of the window to air, swearing in French at
a dog that had done his business on an old newspaper lying on
the pavement outside her front door. The door, and the whole
street for that matter, was covered in graffiti. Huge chunks of
plaster had fallen off the walls, and bits of masonry were
strewn among the withering grass patches that bordered the
pavements. And this was only a twenty-minute walk from the
Grande Place. If someone had told me I'd been matter-
transported to West Bromwich, I'd have believed them. But
looking again, I wondered. Grotty as it was, it was Continental
grot, and therefore somehow more exotic and picturesque.
Wonder if a Belgian would think the same in Dudley?

Spent today wandering around again, feeling like an

interesting wind-blown character in a black-and-white French film, analysing the ways of the world. Got chatting to two English Oxbridge types in a bar this evening. They work for the EU here as translators. Felt totally overawed at first, with their plummy accents, and of course we had to go through the usual "so, you're from Birmingham I gather" routine. Turns out that they spend most of their time translating directives pertaining to additives in mushy peas and the like, so felt very under-awed in the end. Eventually they drifted off, thank God, when a posh-looking blond with a big nose and Alice-band arrived.

Tuesday 16<sup>th</sup> January

Met an American student called Gaby in a bar round the corner tonight - I knew she was American before I heard her speak, she was all teeth and hair. Then I heard her trying to get a drink in English (to no avail), so stepped in and did the hero bit. Signor Cosmopolitano to the rescue. Hit it off immediately. She's been 'doing Europe' for two months, but is a media-communications with expressive-dance sophomore (?) back in America. We talked about everything under the sun, and have arranged to meet up again tomorrow night for a meal. I thought about kissing her when we got outside and inviting her back to my room, but decided I didn't want to give rejection a look-in. She sort of hovered silently for a moment and then said "Swell meetin' ya!" and went her way. So that was that.

Wednesday 17th January

Met Gaby in *Le Restaurant Flamand*. She gave me two postcards of paintings she'd got from the musée d'art - two abstract pieces made of gauze and chocolate called 'Les amants' and 'Les secrets du coeur'. Not really my taste, but I was still pleased and wanted to give her a thank-you peck on the cheek, but somehow it all went wrong and I ended up bobbing about, shaking her hand and feeling a pillock. Fortunately the waiter then appeared and took our order - Gaby said she'd have what I had. She's well impressed by my French and says she'll probably do a 'linguistic immersion unit' when she gets back to the USA. Failing that, she might ask her father (a 'presence enhancement facilitator' in Hollywood – I didn't ask) to send her on an intensive course in Paris.

When the meal came (chicken, fancy veg, delicious orange sauce), she hardly touched it. In fact, she just kept moving it round with her fork and smiling at me, while I tucked in. Maybe chicken's not her thing. Later on she started telling me about her boyfriend (Chuck) back in the States, and how she was considering "trading him in for someone with more appealability", having recently met someone that she felt exceptionally attracted to. I didn't ask who it was, and imagined Tina having a similar conversation with one of her friends before Christmas, and then I thought of Chuck tucking into a burger and fries somewhere on his own in America, oblivious. Felt a wave of disdain rush through me. Didn't bother saying anything, and Gaby didn't divulge anything further, so that was that again. She seemed a bit subdued after that, maybe the chicken had genuinely disagreed with her. Reading women is like reading Old Norse with a Dog Latin dictionary as far as I'm concerned.

She told me she's flying back to LA on Saturday, so I suggested meeting her on Friday evening. "That leaves out tomorrow!" she gasped, so I agreed, and she flashed a full set of 98 perfectly formed teeth. How do Americans get teeth like that? Anyway, said good-bye to her outside. She seemed a bit breathy and nervous, maybe she thought I was going to pounce on her, so I ended up shaking her hand again and walking off. Quite fancy her, but couldn't cope with another put-down.

Thursday 18th January

Think the enormity of what I've done is beginning to dawn on

me now. I've completely jettisoned my life as I knew it, bad
bits and good, although some of the bad bits have decided to
hang on in my head, while the few good bits there were are
now jumping round in my mind passing themselves off as
major boons - a regular income, the comfort of routine,
drinking with Phil in *The Blinking Weasel*, the odd laugh with the
A level French class on a Friday afternoon, and until recently,
fun times with Tina. And having got rid of everything, the
only substitute is an extended Brussels break. Wandered
around all morning again, and sat in the cathedral for a couple
of hours this afternoon, mulling over the past and wondering
about my next step. Felt reasonably calm when I came out,
but was then harangued by some Eastern European gypsy in
red and black rags, begging for money. I only had some small
change, which I gladly gave her. If I hadn't been so taken
aback, I could then have learned what sounded like every
Romany expletive going - talk about ungrateful! As it was, I
walked off to the next cash dispenser and withdrew some more
Francs on my visa card, thanking my lucky stars things aren't
that bad for me. Did think about going back and giving her
some cash just to stave off a potential curse, but decided to
risk it and plumped for a Duvel beer in the bar next to the
bank.

Later on, went back to *Le Restaurant Flamand*, but no Gaby.
Sat there on my own again reading La Rochefoucauld, who
seemed wiser than ever tonight, unlike the waiter, who seemed
to have won the outstanding achievement award for services to
smirking and shirking. Why didn't Gaby bother turning up?
Women.

Saw some drunken English tourists on the way back to hotel.
There was a big sign over some shops on the Rue de la Loi,
which said "GREETINGS FROM BRUSSELS, THE BIG
HEART OF EUROPE." They'd knocked the H off HEART
and were just getting rid of the bottom part of the E when the
police arrived.

Friday 19th January

Lay on my bed last night with a pack of Duvels and the angel of hope for company, scanning my Thomas Cook Rail Map of Europe till the small hours, pondering my next destination. Can't see myself in Brussels any longer somehow. The next thing I knew, it was nine o'clock this morning and someone was knocking on the door. Opened it, expecting the cleaner, but it was Gaby! She came in and was over me like a rash, full of "seize the day", "life's too short" and "live for the moment". At nine o'clock this morning, that all sounded a lot more appealing than anything La Rochefoucauld had ever said. But then again, I've never seen him pouting lip-stick and cleavage.

What a perfect day. So intense and complete. Gaby apologized for not meeting me last night - she was falling for me, but knew nothing could come of it with her imminent return, plus she wasn't sure how I felt. Then she decided what the hell. And it paid off. She was amazed I hadn't realized how attracted she is to me. We talked, made love, sipped wine on the Grande Place, the whole day's been strangely intense. Maybe that's the ideal relationship. A one-day affair that can't possibly be extended, that lives like a firework, doesn't allow for changes of heart, humdrum routine, interruptions or arguments, but finishes on a burning high, blazing away, fuelled by a sweet kind of sadness. I thought about seeing her off at the airport tomorrow but decided against it, and was secretly glad she didn't mention it. She kissed me, stroked my face and walked out of my hotel room. I watched her go down the corridor, knowing she wouldn't turn round. I saw the last of her blond hair disappear into the lift, and suddenly realized I might never get a day this good again.

Spent the rest of the evening packing - time to move on.

Saturday 20th January

Train to Amsterdam!

Checked out of hotel this morning, feeling like I haven't felt in ages - looking forward, optimistic, excited and well. Trudged back to the underground diesel trap that is the Gare Centrale and here I am now on the train to Amsterdam, surrounded by people who either have severe laryngitis or are Dutch. Have always liked the sound of Amsterdam. Gaby said she'd spent a week there and reckoned it's not only a fantastic city, but also an easy place for foreigners to find work.

Keep thinking about Gaby. Yesterday was so out of the blue, that's what made it even more perfect. Why didn't we exchange addresses? Keep wondering what life might be like in an alternative universe where I meet Gaby in a place where we both live. Would that intensity have lasted, or would we have ended up buying emulsion at B & Q on a Sunday afternoon? Wonder what La Rochefoucauld would have made of that?

Sunday 21st January

Amsterdam!

Had just stepped off the train when a little tanned blond bloke wearing leather and denim and munching a muesli bar came up to me, and asked me in French if I was looking for accommodation. I pretended not to understand, in case he was a rent-boy or an unconventional mugger, but he asked again in English. I was a bit wary initially but he had an honest face and I like muesli bars, so I admitted needing a room. He said there were rooms at the Van Den Haven Hostel (behind the station), and if I handed in the voucher he gave me, I'd get a 10% discount.

Walked out of the station's rear entrance, facing the harbour. Some hotel boats were moored opposite, a man stood playing a barrel organ and smiled across at me, just as the sun came out. It's going to be good, I thought to myself. Got here in no time, and a burly weather-beaten Dutchman in a woolly jumper rushed me through to a room with two single beds in it, where

I feared the worst for a moment. Not quite the Ritz, but it's warm and cheerful, with pictures of bulb-fields and windmills plastered everywhere. And because it's low season, there's no-one else to share yet. Popped the angel of hope on the bedside table, feels fine for now.

Slept for ages, then went back to the station this afternoon to change some money and get something to eat. Thought about hitting the city, but decided to leave that a while. Spent the evening in the hostel bar downstairs with Joop, the burly jumper, and two Finnish blokes on holiday. They said that Finnish is the most difficult language on earth and has seventeen cases! Thank God it's an obscure language and that I've never had to teach it under the National Curriculum.

Monday 22nd January

Woke up in horror this morning, thinking I'd overslept for 2B's German class. The relief when I realized that's a thing of the past was indescribable.

Got talking to the little tanned blond bloke who collared me at the station when I got here. His name is Frank and it turns out he's German. Apparently, Joop (who owns the place) gives him free lodgings in exchange for encouraging train travellers like me to sleep at the hostel. He and an Irish girl spend the mornings nipping down to the Central Station, intercepting people getting off international trains. Siobhan, the Irish girl, is going back to Cork, so Joop has asked me if I'd be interested in replacing her, as he needs someone with English, French and German. I've said I'll do it, which at least gives me rent-free accommodation in the meantime, and if nothing else, it'll be a change. Give Signor Cosmopolitano an opportunity, see him take it!

Otherwise, have spent time sleeping, chatting with Frank and Joop and discovering the joy of Dutch chips. Have also started suffering from bodily itching, which is a bit embarrassing in public.

Wednesday 24th January

Had a proper walk round city-centre yesterday and fell in love -
gorgeous. Gaby was absolutely right, it's my sort of place -
comfortable, cosmopolitan, historic. Tree-lined canals under
rows upon rows of fairy-tale gables, bikes jostling through
every conceivable gap, boats splashing past under magical
bridges. Marvellous. And then the brothels, the sex-shops, the
neon abandon of it all. Feel really glad to be here, and am
looking forward to getting to know the place properly.

Spent tonight in bar with Frank again, and feel we'll get on
really well. Loads of flamboyant women in tonight. Frank
gave me a list of all the trains we'll be targeting, with platform
numbers, arrival times, number of second-class carriages per
train (no point in approaching first class passengers, he says),
and even indications as to where to stand. We both start at
opposite ends of the second class batch and work our way in.
Feel quite excited about it.

Had quite a good conversation about German theatre, which
Frank is really into. He says there are a few alternative German
theatre groups here, and almost glowed when I said I wouldn't
mind going with him some time or even getting involved.
Who knows, I might become a house-hold TV name in
Oberbrummsteinsauerbach.

Friday 26th January

Up dead early to target first train of the day, from Paris. Then
back every so often for trains from Berlin, Munich,
Copenhagen, Vienna, Milan. Really good fun and quite
invigorating. Felt ecstatic as the trains thundered in from all
over Europe, with Danes, Italians, Poles and Germans spilling
onto the platforms. For a few seconds I just stood there as the
North-West Express pulled in. A huge metallic people and
place connector, bringing together people as diverse as the
places it runs through - different nationalities, happy people,
miserable people; rich and poor; business people and students;

people with plans, people who've no idea what they're having for lunch even. Felt quite overwhelmed.

Rang Phil and Jan later on. Their baby was born yesterday apparently, a couple of weeks early. They've decided to call him Edward - bit old-fashioned. Their only other bit of news was that they've had new carpet in the nursery.

Bit of a scene in the bar tonight when some lager-lout started a fight. Turned out he was with a group of blokes over for the weekend from Essex. Joop said something like this happens at least once a month, and it's nearly always a drunken Brit at the centre of it. When they left, they all piled into a jeep with a GB sticker on the back.

Itching seems to have subsided a bit today.

Sunday 28th January

Seem to have a knack for the old promotional work - the hostel is now full and Joop is really chuffed as it's not even holiday season. The only drawback is that Frank has had to move in with me to free up another room. Don't mind, as we get on well and he's good company, although his aftershave is a bit overpowering.

He was really surprised I hadn't worked out he was gay, although it did cross my mind when he lapsed into rapturous adoration of my angel of hope statue. He filled up when I told him my Aunty Vera had left it me when she died, and how it's seen me through some difficult times over the last ten years. Apparently, his family in Germany gave him such a hard time when he came out that he decided to leave and come to Amsterdam. He hasn't spoken to his parents for ages.

Decided to ring my parents, thinking I should count myself lucky, and also let them know I'm ok in case they were worrying. Dad went on non-stop about some block-paving job he's just finished, mom said she was glad to hear I was all right but would have to go as I'd rung in the middle of Coronation Street.

Wednesday 31st January

Had the last couple of days off, as hostel full to capacity, so no need to recruit extra guests. Walked down the Prinsengracht dodging cobbles, dog mess and bikes to visit Anne Frank's house with Frank, and was very moved. Can't really take in that she was couped up in such a small space, with her diary as her only friend. Amsterdam seems so laid back now, it's hard to imagine it being overrun by Nazis. Frank said he feels ashamed to be German at times, and wouldn't speak German while we were there. I told him I was ashamed to be English at times, thinking back to the lager louts the other evening. He annoyed me then by saying he could imagine. Maybe he's not called Frank for nothing. Anyway, when we got outside, I noticed a woman begging on the corner. She looked like the gypsy I'd seen in Brussels, so I walked over and gave her five guilders, hoping in some way to redeem myself. She beamed with gratitude, then grabbed my hand, scanned my palm and instantly changed her expression. "Careful, careful be!" she gasped at me in broken English. I smiled at her timidly and walked back to Frank, full of foreboding. Don't seem to be having much luck with gypsies - will avoid them in future.

Friday 2nd February

Noticed Frank seemed to be scratching a lot when he got up this morning. He stopped for a second to examine the itching and yelped in horror. Lice!! I examined myself, and sure enough, there were tiny creatures secreted about my body as well! Felt thoroughly disgusting and disgusted. Frank rushed after Joop, who came up to our room with some lotion. Frank said this is the second time he's caught them here. Joop reckons some of the guests' personal hygiene leaves a bit to be desired, and that it's just part of the job. He always keeps a stock of anti-lice lotion for the next time. Frank and I were just kneeling over my bed in our underpants with Joop behind us on his knees, "smearing our backs in wid de stuff", when an

American girl opened the door by mistake and said "This city is just SO perverted".

Monday 5th February

Hostel still full, and Joop has even decided to throw in our meals for free as a reward for our success. The lotion has done the trick with the lice and nobody has turned up from school to drag me back to the riveting world of Keystages 3 and 4. Glory be.

Went to a German theatre workshop with Frank last night. Felt a bit out of place, as I was the only one with a parting and without three earrings in each ear. I also didn't have much of a clue about what was going on. The group was discussing some play in which the characters were all musical instruments that had been abused by careless owners, and now had a range of emotional disorders which affected their orchestral interplay. At some point during the discussion, I understood why *Carry On* films could never have emerged in Germany.

It was even too heavy for Frank, who said he liked the idea, but felt the dialogue was too unnatural, so we went back to the hostel bar, where Joop was in good form balancing two beers and a dildo on his forehead to amuse the punters.

Thursday 8th February

Every night the bar seems to be full of unattached, exuberant women. When I asked Joop what the attraction was, he laughed and said the bar was a watering-hole for the prostitutes from the brothel next door!! What a place! I had no inkling all this was going on right next door. It's just all so ordinary and nobody makes a fuss or seems to mind, which I suppose is fair enough, since it doesn't bother anyone. It's just really weird when you come from a culture where the slightest hint of impropriety heralds the arrival of reporters from *Midlands Today* with a bevy of indignant neighbours complaining about effects on mental health.

Sunday 11th February

Feel really good. Love sharing with Frank. Every night we lie
in bed discussing life into the small hours. He always lights
what he calls 'an evening tranquillity candle'. Last night he was
talking about Kleist, his favourite German writer, whose
central theme is "die gebrechliche Einrichtung der Welt" - the
fragile nature of the world. Plans are always thwarted, things
we hold onto fall apart, our beliefs hinge on the most unlikely
of circumstances. Bit depressing. He also told me how he
ended up in a terrible state after he'd been in Amsterdam a few
weeks. With the emotional trauma of coming out, facing his
parents' disappointment and his lack of direction in life, he got
into drugs and was in a right old situation. A drugs counsellor
helped him through it eventually, and did him the biggest
favour by having a practice a few doors away from the hostel.
Frank wandered in for a drink after a session and got chatting
to Joop. He reckons Joop is the father his own father could
never be.

Wednesday 14th February

A drunken German getting off the Berlin train this morning
landed me one on the cheek as I approached him, knocking me
for six. Amazingly, a bloke who turned out to be a Canadian
wrestler saw what happened and came to my defence, creating
quite a scene on the platform, as he grabbed the German off
me, and held him in an underarm lock till the railway police
arrived, looking about as concerned as if someone had farted
in the buffet car. Frank didn't see what had happened at first,
but was soon there when he saw the commotion. Felt more
embarrassed than anything.

Bill, the Canadian, ended up coming back to the hostel, and
is a really nice bloke. Frank said it's a pity he isn't gay. He
came out for a pizza with us tonight, and then asked us for a
tour of the Red Light District, where we last saw him entering
a brothel at midnight. Felt a bit down when I got back,

realizing I'll just never be the sort of person who could detain someone in an underarm lock on a station platform or walk casually or otherwise into a brothel.

Tuesday 20th February

Have done the art museums over the last few days with Frank. Went to the Van Gogh Museum today. Quite incredible. Fantastic paintings, but so sad to think of the tragedy of the man behind them. Bought postcards of his bedroom at Arles and the Amsterdam drawbridge to stick over my bed. Got the cafe at Arles as well, thinking it'd be a nice gift for Gaby, only I've no way of getting in touch with her. Thought about sending The Crow Fields to Tina, but didn't bother.

Frank and I have decided that it's time we started learning Dutch, so have been to enrol on an evening course at the Van Laren Avondschool which starts next week. It really is a funny old language. I thought speaking German would help, as the written language looks similar, but it sounds worse than the invective from the hacking Transylvanian gypsy in Brussels.

Thursday 29th February

Went to our first Dutch class tonight. Can now say what my name is and the usual stuff about where I come from, etc. The teacher, Henk, looks as though he might have had a wash and a shave at some point during the 60s. He's using the Dutch immersion method, so spends ages miming and prancing about, trying to convey meaning. There was great merriment when Oza, a Turkish grocer, needed the Dutch word for cucumber. This is my life now.

Most of the people in the group are from Romania and Poland, but there are a couple of New Zealanders, Turks and Spaniards. A Swedish girl called Annika sat by Frank and me. She's a walking stereotype of everything called to mind by the combination of the words 'woman', 'Swedish' and 'young'. And more's the pity, she's going out with some Dutch bloke,

as she explained in what sounded to me like native Dutch.
Frank reckons she fancies me, but I didn't get that impression.
Even so, I'm quite looking forward to next Thursday.

Saturday 2nd March

There were seven empty rooms at the hostel yesterday, which
Frank and I managed to fill with guests from today's train runs.
Joop had a drink with us while we had our dinner this evening,
and said what a brilliant job we're doing. He went on to say
he's got a shop not far away, and needs a new sales assistant to
help out. He said we're both "very good in de going around
wid people" and are obviously intelligent (true), so how about
taking it in turns working there? We wouldn't be needed till
noon each day, so would still be able to do the main morning
train runs together. And every other day would mean we still
had plenty of free time. I was a bit worried about coping with
the language, but Joop assured me it wouldn't be a problem.
The money will be welcome too, of course, so we've both said
we'll do it. Only then did he tell us it's a sex-shop. I start on
Tuesday.

Monday 4th March

Went to a party with Frank last night. A gay Dutch artist he
knows called Roel was celebrating his first exhibition. There
was quite a spread laid on, but you could hardly move for
pretension. The exhibition was called 'The fluency of enigma',
which Frank thought was a brilliant post-modern
encapsulation... I asked Roel what he meant by it, but lapsed
into a semi-coma half way through the explanation. Frank
rescued me with a salami sandwich and a hugely made-up
woman from Chile dressed in silver and black. Consuela was
also an artist, and had come over to Holland for a couple of
weeks just to see Roel's exhibition - blimey.
    She said she'd observed me across the room and was
desperate to capture me on canvas. Clearly not right. When I

asked her why, I accidentally spat a bit of salami into her over-sized cleavage, to which she was oblivious, thank God. She said "You have a dark charisma that would be a challenge to channel" and insists I go round to her hotel on Wednesday evening. My mind reeled for an excuse but she was so insistent I ended up agreeing. The next minute she was stuffing her hotel address into my jacket pocket. It's a quirky old thing, life. As La Rochefoucauld might have said better in French, "One minute you're a teacher in the West Midlands, the next you're poised for entry into the Dutch sex industry and modelling."

Tuesday 5th March

Survived my first day as sex-shop assistant at 'Joops Sexmarkt'. I will never ever be embarrassed again. I'd never dared walk into a sex-shop before, but my God! Indescribable. Everything's black, red or pink. Magazines wall-to-wall, covering just about everything you can think of and a few extra things. Toys, DVDs, tapes, underwear, accessories... Felt thoroughly flushed all day. But nobody else bats an eyelid - it might as well be the tinned vegetable section in Tesco's. I tried my best to act casual with the customers as I handed blow-up dolls and bumper mag-packs across the counter, but still ended up asking stupid questions once or twice - "Would you like a bag for the dildo, sir?"

I did relax eventually. At one point, as I stood serving a customer, I turned to the full-time assistant and heard myself saying "Scando-Love-Romp, Sandra, how much?"

What have I come to? On the one hand, I feel slightly seedy and ashamed, imagining what people at home would say. It's the shame of seeing your life condensed on the BBC news as "Former Midlands teacher sells sex". On the other hand, what the hell?

Wednesday 6th March

Decided to keep my appointment with Consuela this evening.

She's renting a luxury suite at the Krasnakovsky. Sumptuous lighting, mirrors, classy paintings on the walls. I'd barely knocked on her door when her cleavage burst into the corridor and I was pulled in. Moments later a Martini was thrust into my hand.

All her painting stuff was assembled in front of a huge pine bed, and after a bit of a stilted chat, she told me to "take away your clothes, take away". She insisted on painting me nude - might have known. And of course, resistance was futile. Stripped before her eyes, wondering once again what I was coming to, and suddenly, there I was, nothing on, lying on the bed, hearing the words "Oh yes, lovely bod, lovely bod". At that point, I was fully prepared for Midlands Today reporters to burst in.

After about two hours of total silent concentration, she shouted "Yes, yes, fantastic, is finished!" and turned the picture round to show me. I looked like some kind of shifty, ageing market trader caught in an uncompromising position, which is exactly what I've become. Just as I was thinking how awful it was, she whipped off her clothes and said "Now it's time for thanks". It was full cleavage time. Richard Gere, eat your heart out.

Friday 8th March

Still on a high since Wednesday night. It's starting to feel spring-like as well, signs of new life emerging here and there - little daffodils poking out of window boxes, nights getting lighter. Feels good. Worked at the Sexmarkt again yesterday. Still can't get over the amount of merchandise that's available. Getting on really well with Sandra. She's a very forthright, direct sort of person, but very pleasant. She's planning to marry her boyfriend, who is "the love of her life", apparently. Went to Dutch again last night. Quite a boring lesson, doing loads of present tense exercises. No Annika either, which was a bit of a disappointment.

Got a surprise parcel in the post today - *The Unbearable*

*Lightness of Being* from Consuela. On the inside cover, she's written: "I not fogret you lovely bod Gerod". Sweet gesture - shame about the dyslexia, though.

## Sunday 10th March

Busiest day yet at the Sexmarkt yesterday. Loads of giggly weekend tourists, leering through magazines. Quite a lot of British tourists, especially the cheeky-chirpy-Cockney-Essex-lad types, who were really getting on my nerves. Turfed one group out for making a scene in the afternoon. I was a bit wary as they were the thick and burly type who'd smack you in the face for looking sideways at them, but decided it was best to get them out before they created any real trouble. A couple of them started shouting things to Sandra like "You're gaggin' for it, darlin', incha?", but they all filed out eventually. Sandra seemed to take it all in her stride. She said there's rarely a weekend in the summer without some kind of scene caused by British louts. She went on about how it's never the Dutch, the Germans, the Italians or Americans, but always the British.

Spent the afternoon sauntering around the canals with Frank – he's feeling a bit fed up. He said he's happy he's found such a good friend in me, which I was quite touched by. He says it's not that he's unhappy with his life in Amsterdam but that he sometimes becomes so acutely conscious of the fact that he's just drifting through it, without a clear goal, that it's hard to be cheerful. The old meaning of life conundrum. I haven't had that feeling since packing in teaching, but it used to be an almost daily companion. Frank asked me if I'd read the French writer, Pascal. Apparently, he reckoned that our natural state is one of misery and futility. The only way to make it bearable is by securing sufficient distractions in life so that we don't get the message too clearly, as it's an unbearable truth....

Just as I was about to throw myself into the canal, some kids, probably about three or four years old, rushed past us chasing some ducks over the bridge, laughing. Frank turned to me and said that one of those kids might turn out to be the doctor who performs his post-mortem on a cold slab in forty years time. No wonder Angst is a German word. I sat there silently, wondering whether suggesting going for chips was appropriate. After a while, he said he'd like to go back to Germany for a weekend to try and make peace with his parents, and would like me to go as well, which is great. We'll just have to sort something out with Joop as regards cover. Then we got some Flemish chips with mayonnaise, onions and curry sauce, and the world suddenly seemed a better place.

Tuesday 12th March

Joop said he doesn't mind us having a few days off, so we're off to Cologne for the weekend on Saturday! Wunderbar!

Wednesday 13th March

Sandra begrudgingly showed a group of people into the back room at the shop this afternoon. A bit later she asked me to take some coffee through to them - I presumed they were suppliers or something. When I walked in with a tray, the last thing I expected was an orgy. A bloke called Frans put his camera down and they all got up to grab a coffee - I was dumbstruck. 'Frans' was taking pictures for a magazine. I couldn't believe how casually they all just stopped. One woman moved away from two blokes as if she was just putting her knitting needles down.

I've been talking to Frank about us getting our own flat, since it's a bit cramped, and it'd be nice to have more privacy. Not sure we could afford anywhere brilliant, as the money from the shop isn't fantastic. But something a bit better. Have decided to have a chat with Joop about ways of increasing our income. I told Frank I draw the line at anything involving cameras and taking my trousers off. Frank said he'd consider nothing less.

Thursday 14th March

The idea of a flat of our own is getting more appealing by the minute. It's great sharing a room with Frank, but I'd be scuppered if I ever wanted to bring anybody back, and it's the same for him. Having our own kitchen and bathroom would be great as well. Practically every time I sit on the toilet, I can guarantee somebody will struggle with the door handle like some kind of frenzied psychopath caught short. Joop's anxious for us to carry on with the train runs, which we don't mind. He said he'll have a word with a few people and see what he can do. The man's a hero.

Good Dutch class tonight. All about going out and making suggestions. Annika was back again and sat by me. Felt my heart racing throughout the lesson. She's got those Britt Ekland eyes and oozes sex appeal. And when she laughs, she grabs hold of you in a strangely sensual way. I could barely concentrate when Henk started on about word order in subordinate clauses, which I thought was a bit much anyway for week three. Later, we had to make up a role play where we made suggestions to meet up and do something in town. We arranged meeting up for a drink, and Annika suggested that we should really do it tomorrow! Maybe Frank's right, maybe she does fancy me.

Friday 15th March

Filled Joop's hostel with arrivals from the Hook of Holland boat train this morning, so didn't do any more runs after that. Really busy at the Sexmarkt. Ran out of dildos this afternoon, as the usual supplier has been affected by a rubber strike in Malaysia. Bet they don't report that on the BBC news. Sandra asked me to go the Amsterdam sex cash-and-carry for forty to tide us over the weekend. It was like a Sainsbury's Superstore except everything was flesh-coloured and made of latex.

Met up with Annika on the Leidseplein. Packed with people, as really mild at the moment, so everyone sitting outside. She insisted on paying for the drinks all evening, saying her boyfriend is super rich as he runs some sort of art business.

She fired questions at me all evening, to the extent that I felt I'd laid myself bare before I'd even had the chance to ask her if she was from Stockholm. While I talked, she'd drink her Martini, her bottom lip sort of massaging the rim of the glass very sensually, before taking a sip. Sometimes she even gives a cheeky wink while she's doing it. Extraordinary. When I said about getting back, she walked with me to the tram stop and started kissing me like I was the last man on earth. After, she said she was sure we have some interesting times ahead of us, and that maybe she could even help me out financially. It's a bit weird. Can't quite put my finger on it. Maybe it's just that I don't know how not to be suspicious when an attractive woman seems to fancy me. Wonder what Tina "you're not good enough for me" Barlow would make of me now.

Sunday 17th Match

Fantastic weekend. Got Euro-City train to Cologne yesterday morning. As soon as I set foot on the platform at the Hauptbahnhof, I knew I was in Germany. The whole place just reeks of solid, stable efficiency (I'm sure that's why every noun has a capital letter in German - to reflect the fact that every THING in Germany is a solid accomplishment, whether it's a loo roll or a motorway.) There's no litter, the railings are polished, everything's made of smoked glass or clean metal. Wolverhampton station this definitely was not.

And everyone's healthy-looking, fashion-conscious and rich. German announcements echoed from tannoys, clear and strong, like genuine amplified voices, as opposed to the muffled waffle you get from the gagged and flagging hostages who do the announcements at British stations. Walking out of the station almost bowled me over, Cologne Cathedral towering above us, massive and imposing, a noun-and-a-half. The number of times I've looked at it in German text books over the years. Amazing. And there it was in real life. Huge crowds gathered on the square below the Dom, pavement artists and buskers swelled their numbers, trains rattled over the Rhine into the station behind us, Mercedes and BMW's raced past in front of us. Suddenly, I realized I wasn't in Holland any more, either. The picture postcard mini-quaintness of Amsterdam was miles away. Around me were the signs and noises of a big country, a massive powerhouse of a country that goes all the way from Holland to Poland and Switzerland in fifth gear.

It was only a short walk to Frank's parents' flat. I felt quite nervous, and noticed Frank looked very flushed. He'd sent a postcard warning them we were coming so that it wouldn't be a massive shock. My heart was going ten-to-the-dozen as we stood in the hallway waiting for the door to open. And open it did, revealing a sturdy collection of solid wooden furniture. Frank's parents were overjoyed to see him and hugged him to death, crying uncontrollably, as was Frank, and even I got dragged into the hugging business. Made a few sniffing noises just to fit in.

His parents, both glowing images of health and portliness, pleaded with Frank to come back to Germany and settle down. The discussions went on for ages, during which time the phrases "Aber bitte Frank!" and "nein Mutti!" were frequently used. In the end, his parents conceded that they were happy the falling-out was behind them, and that they were friends and family again. Made me feel a bit homesick, which is quite ironic really. If I went back home, I'd never get a reception like that. However long it's been between visits, it's always as casual as if I'd just nipped to the loo in the break during Emmerdale.

After all this, the pampering began in a serious way - coffee, cake, cream, the full lunch situation with more types of meat, bread and Wurst than can be good for you, followed even later by dinner, which gave new meaning to the phrases 'large portion' and 'trapped wind'. To say nothing of beer, wine, and more cake and coffee. And the day ended with me flopping into one of those super-soft massive quilted pine beds, in a clean, homely bedroom. Marvellous.

Today followed much the same pattern food-wise,

interspersed with all sorts of anecdotes from Frank's youth: how he won a glamourous baby competition in Wuppertal (I didn't say anything), how they all laughed when he managed to undo his nappy at church in front of the priest, and the time he peed on a Jehovah's witness at the front door. I asked if he was in the habit of exposing his privates to strange men, but everybody went quiet at that (shouldn't have said anything).

Then it was time for red-faced, tearful but happy good-byes, and I really felt quite sad to be going. His mother rubbed my cheeks and said I was a good boy and that she could tell I was a good influence on Frank. Then she winded me with an industrial-type Hug with a capital H. Felt quite morose on the train coming back, which Frank noticed - I just said I was just having a bout of what he'd had the other day, especially with my birthday coming up soon. He just put his arm round me and told me not to worry. Oddly enough it really did the trick, and as we walked back from the Central Station, with our arms round each other as two friends, I felt really great. Some drunken yob with a Manchester accent leaning on a rubbish bin shouted "Bloody woofters!!" as we walked past.

Tuesday 19th March

Joop got back to us tonight on how we could boost our finances. I could tell it wasn't going to be anything conventional by the glint in his crinkly eyes and the way he was twitching his walrus moustache. And sure enough I was right - escort work! And to think I'd shied away in Brussels. A friend of Joop's runs an escort agency for international business people. He assured me before I could protest that sex is not part of the deal. Sometimes it's to accompany them to functions, sometimes to break the tedium of evenings alone, but the sex is purely discretionary, and apparently this is clearly stated in the contract we'd sign. Quite like the idea, now I've digested it, and the money sounds really good. Very useful for getting somewhere better to live. Frank thinks it's a brilliant idea, especially as it's mostly evening work as and when suits.

Joop says he'll introduce us to his friend, but that I'll have to invest in some smart and modern outfits. That means wearing garish colour combinations to the Dutch, who feel naked if they're not wearing green, red and blue all at the same time. Will have a look in C & A later in the week. Keep eating your heart out, Richard Gere. Signor Cosmopolitano is coming.

Thursday 21st March

Will be glad when the escort business starts. The more I think about a place of our own, the more impatient I get. The chance to set up a proper base, my base, with my things, not a room in somebody else's place.

Dutch class again tonight. The theme was work. I mentioned I was a qualified languages teacher, everybody seemed well impressed. Annika there again, this time more tactile than ever. We had a quick drink afterwards in the 'Hallo Bar'. As we were leaving, she followed me to the toilet, and we ended up reenacting a scene from *Nine-and-a-half Weeks* by the urinals! I can hardly believe it – anyone could have walked in! I kept imagining Tina strolling in, shocked, and me saying: "So, not good enough for you, eh? As you can see, I've moved on".

When we got outside, a square-framed bruiser with shocking blond hair and a black leather jacket came over to us - Annika's boyfriend, Ben! He shook my hand, which was really trembling now, and said he'd heard all about me. Then he said he could put some occasional work my way - delivering paintings to clients now and again. He said something about the paintings occasionally being involved in tax situations somehow, so there was nothing really illegal going on, but it's better to have a non-involved deliverer. Sounds well odd, but he said I'd get fifty guilders per delivery - which would be dead handy for a flat. Annika, having flung herself devotedly around Ben by that point, said she was sure I wouldn't refuse and winked at me. Not quite sure I like all this, but the money sounds good.

Friday 22nd March

Been in a funny mood all day after last night's incident.  Don't really like the idea of getting involved in dodgy goings-on, although the money is good and I could always plead ignorance if anything went wrong.  I also feel strange about Annika.  She's an unsettling person, and I don't like to think she was implying she'd drop me in it with Ben if I refused his offer.

Frank, as ever, has been Mr Supportive today (when he hasn't been meditating).  He reckons I should just "ride it for a bit", "chill out in the meantime", and enjoy "the cash when it comes rolling in".  His knowledge of English idiom staggers me sometimes, and yet he didn't know the word 'palaver'.  I could take it as my specialist subject on Mastermind.

Saturday 23rd March

Had a terrible dream last night, involving *TV Quick* readers who were campaigning for my release from prison.  Reporters from Midlands Today were queueing up outside to interview me, and I could hear them chatting to journalists about whether the best headline was 'Let's Go Dodgy Dutch With Midlands Rembrandt' or 'Sexcort Double Life of Midlands Art-Perv'.

Monday 25th March

Spent tonight in the bar with Joop, Frank and Joop's escort connection, Albertus.  The man is the total and utter embodiment of dodge.  Seventies man revived - hairy chest, jewellery, velvet jacket, big moustache.  Chewing ten to the dozen and over-jovial.  Couldn't say that I didn't like him, though.  He slapped Frank and me on the back and said we had potential, but that I needed to do something about the clothes.  I told him I'd only bought what I was wearing (casual jacket and jeans) this week, but he scribbled down an address of a shop in the Red Light area, and said to say Albertus sent me.

Joop kept pouring out the drinks, and assured Albertus we can turn our hand to anything. Albertus laughed and said we'd probably have to, which worries me. Frank didn't say anything, just sat there looking flushed.

Apparently, 90% of the clients tend to be American businessmen and women purely after male conversational company. The rest are usually Eastern European men, often Russian, he reckons, eager to practise their English. Very odd, really. He guarantees us at least four 'dates' a month, which we have to honour. Extra meetings are optional, and the monthly rate is 500 guilders - unbelievable! God knows how they can afford that. We signed a proper contract, and will hear from him soon via Joop. Getting a flat is now well and truly on the cards. I can't believe how interesting life has become. JFK, you were a wise man.

Wednesday 27th March

Major embarrassment today in the Sexmarkt. Henk, my Dutch teacher, came in wanting change for the video cabin! He'd asked me before he realized who I was, and I could see his mind reeling as he tried to place my face. When the penny dropped, he turned into Mr Fluster, and said he'd just realized he was late for an appointment! Sandra reckons he's one of the regulars. "How awful to live without true love in your life", she said.

Thursday 28th March

Henk must have still felt a bit awkward in Dutch tonight. He was over-friendly in a sort of seeking approval way, and kept telling me my answers were 'fantastisch', even when I'd only said "Ja, dit is een glas bier". The subject tonight was talking about your hobbies. Maria, a Spanish woman, asked him what he did in his spare time - he just laughed, looked sheepishly at me, and said he collected stamps.

Annika was in a very odd mood, strangely business-like and curt. After the class, she said Ben wanted a chat, which put the wind up me. I said Frank and I had arranged to see a German play, but she said it wouldn't take long. Frank came as well, just in case there was any funny business. Not that he'd have been much use in a fight wearing a pink shirt and hair gel. We went back to the 'Hallo Bar', where Ben was waiting. He at least seemed quite friendly, though he didn't beat around the bush. He gave me a card with an address on it, and said to be there to pick up a painting tomorrow morning at eleven. He then produced another card out of his top pocket, like in a naff magic trick, and said to take the painting to that address. He then produced a fifty-guilder note, smiled, and said not to mess up. After that, he and Annika stood up to leave. He refused to divulge anything further, saying that was enough - and if his name or Annika's was ever mentioned, I was to say nothing.

Frank took an instant dislike to Ben, and it's rare for Frank not to like anyone. Frank says he has an aura of moral darkness about him; I think he's probably just a bit of a git. I feel very unsettled by the whole business, as though Annika's blackmailed me into this, but Frank said not to worry too much - it's money for old rope after all, and if things get complicated, he reckons Joop has some 'heavy' contacts who'd help me out. God knows what we'd do without Joop. The man is a star.

Friday 29th March

Another very disturbed night. Had a terrible nightmare involving Paul Daniels, Van Gogh and Philip Beardsmore from Midlands Today. Frank said I gasped in my sleep several times. Up at seven as usual to meet the first train in from Paris. Felt absolutely exhausted.

Mission accomplished with the painting business. The first address was on the Kloveniersburgwal in the Red Light area. A toothy woman with scraped back hair and no make-up thrust a wrapped painting into my hands as soon as I rang the bell. There was a dodgy moment on the tram on the way back, when a kid who was breakdancing at the back where I was standing nearly put his foot through it. He had one of those jackets on that look like lagging off the hot-water tank. The next address was near the Concertgebouw, where a scrawny woman with too much make-up took it off me without saying a word. Felt quite exhilarated afterwards, and wished Tina "Oh you're just so routine-centred, Gerard" Barlow could see a snapshot of my life now - Signor Cosmopolitano peering into gangland.

Frank's on his first escort assignment tonight and spent two hours exfoliating and cleansing in the bathroom before he left.

Saturday 30th March

Finished reading *The Unbearable Lightness of Being* waiting for Frank to get back last night. What an absolutely fantastic book. Probably even better in Czech. He eventually got back at 2.00 a.m., looking exhausted. His 'assignment' was Doug, an American computer consultant, desperate for company. Apparently, he lectured Frank for five hours on software applications, before moving on to his involvement with the church back home in Tennessee. Still, for nearly two-hundred guilders, you can't complain.

Normal sort of day otherwise today. Suffering a bit from the approach of the Birthday Blues. No doubt I'll be uttering the Birthday Maxim on Monday night again: "it came and went without event."

Monday 1st April

I take it all back - what a thoroughly brilliant birthday! None of the usual messing around with the few in the know pretending to have forgotten and then saying April Fool! Joop and Frank put a big sign up in the bar, saying "Happy Birthday, Gerard!" Loads of people have wished me happy birthday.

Frank bought me *The Book of Laughter and Forgetting* by Milan
Kundera. Inside, he's put: "To my dear, dear friend, Gerard,
whom I'm so glad to be knowing." Joop gave me a really flash
black leather jacket (no doubt got it 'through a contact') - not
the sort of thing I'd normally go for, but as I tried it on, it felt
as if I was slipping into a different skin, a different person.
JFK, there you go again. When I went to the Sexmarkt this
afternoon, Sandra had made a cake for me - I was really
touched. She'd even iced novelty genitalia on it, as a little
(Dutch) joke. She'd also got me a book on healthy eating,
which was quite thoughtful, as she'd obviously remembered us
talking about it the other day. Even the customers seemed a
bit jollier and more well-meaning than normal.

Tonight has been phenomenal, though. When I got back
from the Sexmarkt, Joop and Frank had put on a really
fantastic spread, and invited all the current residents (mainly
American, Danish and Italian), who likewise wished me Happy
Birthday. Joop caused great hilarity teaching them all to sing
the Dutch version of Happy Birthday to me. For the first time
in years, it's felt like a proper celebration. At one point when
everybody was singing Happy Birthday, raising their glasses to
me and cheering, I felt totally overcome, and could hardly
believe I was the toast. Started filling up, no doubt partly
down to all the alcohol, and felt really stupid, but Joop just
grabbed me round the neck and rubbed my face in his jumper,
which made me start laughing and everyone else cheer more
loudly.

Just when I was thinking I couldn't remember a better
birthday, Joop gave me an envelope. Inside was a key - to the
back flat above the Sexmarkt!! Apparently, the current tenant
has just moved out, and Frank and I can rent it for four-
hundred guilders a month! Fantastic is not the word.

Had a card from my parents, saying "Hope you're keeping
well." Also from Jan and Phil, who go on about the baby for
ages, and finish with, "Remember the laugh we had about
those mushroom rings at The Blinking Weasel on your last
birthday?" No recollection at all.

Wednesday 3rd April

Spent the last two days sorting things out at the flat. Hope to
move in tomorrow. Extremely handy with it being above the
Sexmarkt.

A man called Dik - yet another of Joop's contacts - owns a
second-hand shop on the Van Dingelstraat where we've
managed to get some basic stuff like a coffee-machine, plates,
cutlery, and even a couple of chairs, settee and things.

The flat itself is a bit dingy, but much better than the hostel.
Definitely an improvement. There are two small bedrooms, a
bathroom/toilet and kitchen/living-room, which is small, but
luxury compared to what we've had so far. And in Central
Amsterdam, you can even see the St. Nicholas Church if you
stick your head out of the window. What we'd do without
Joop, I don't know. Joop's happy because he knows we'll be
reliable tenants, and by moving out of the hostel, he'll have an
extra room to rent. Don't think I've ever felt so happy.

Thursday 4th April

Up early to move the last of our few possessions to the flat
before the train runs this morning, which were quite hard-
going for once, as there seemed to be literally hundreds of
people getting off the trains - Easter weekend tourists. There
were so many that we could hardly move amongst them to
hand out the vouchers, but we managed. The hostel is now
fully booked until the middle of next week, which is great, as
we don't have to do any runs till next Wednesday.

Getting things really sorted at the flat. Got some pictures
from the market on Waterlooplein. I got two gorgeous prints -
one of a sunset over an Alpine forest, the other was a
reproduction medieval map of Holland. Frank got one of
those arty black-and-white photos of a muscular-buttocked
male nude, and something modern with lots of red splashes by
a Dutch artist. Caught my thumb on the hammer knocking
nails in the wall, and dripped blood onto Frank's painting on

the floor. When I tried to wipe it off, it just smeared . Later on, Frank said he thought the painting looked even better now it was hanging up.

Dutch class again tonight. All about the home, furniture, rooms and stuff, so very useful vocabulary. Annika seemed back to her normal non-aloof self, but the attraction has died on my part - just don't know where I am with her. She gave me two more pieces of paper with addresses on them, and said to be at the first address by 9.30 tomorrow morning. She squeezed a fifty guilder note into my hand and told me not to worry about her telling Ben about the sex thing: "Ve don't vant to upset him, do ve? You vouldn't like him ven he's upset". "Is he the Hulk?" I asked.

Good Friday - 5th April

Had a wonderful time with Frank last night, languishing in the privacy of our own flat for the first time, before retiring to our individual bedrooms. Brilliant. Frank lit a karma candle "to invoke calm and love into our well-being", while I unwrapped a Mars Bar, contemplating my angel of hope statue, now given pride of place on the table, and wishing once again that I could video my life right now and send a tape back to England.

Walked over to collect painting number 2 from an address on the Damstraat this morning. This time a Grant Mitchell look-alike almost threw it at me without saying a word. The second address was on the Apollolaan, so had to get the tram again. The recipient there was an oily bloke in a dark suit - God knows what it's all about.

Albertus rang while I was working downstairs in the Sexmarkt this afternoon - my first escort assignment tomorrow night! An American businessman will be waiting for me in the Hilton bar at 8.30. Hope he's not as boring as Frank's was.

Sandra came up tonight for a meal after finishing her shift. Cooked Chilli Con Carne, following one of the recipes in the book she bought me. It's brilliant making our own food after weeks of eating what other people have prepared. We chatted and chatted about everything under the sun, and had a really good laugh. She tends to go on about her boyfriend, but suppose that's how it is "when you're in love", as she keeps saying.

I can't believe I had the guts to leave in January - it already seems like years ago - another life-time. Thank God I came away. In my third home of the year now, so reckon it's third time lucky, in spite of what gypsies would have me believe.

Saturday 6th April

Felt on tenterhooks all day waiting for tonight. Got to the Hilton Hotel far too early, so hung around outside for ages, until a dodgy-looking bloke wearing jeans he'd been poured into came up to me and told me to clear off his patch! Cheek.

Went to the bar and waited with a Cinzano, wearing my leather jacket. After a bit, a good-looking dark-haired bloke came over to me and said my name with an American accent. He smiled, revealing super-white teeth and said his name was Tom. He's been in Holland a week, and is here for another two months or so. He said he couldn't divulge his line of business, which intrigued me, but said it didn't involve socializing, hence the need to make social contact in this rather unconventional way. Then he said he was engaged to be married, no doubt to dispel any fears of sexual shenanigans.

All that out of the way, we had a really great evening. He riveted me all night with stories about New York, his philosophy and his girlfriend, and seemed genuinely interested to find out about me, what I was doing, etc. He'd even heard of Walsall, as he once spent a month in Birmingham, and got stuck on the M6 there. The drinks came one after the other, and at the end of the night, he said he'd really like to "enjoy my company again", and would be in touch with the agency to arrange it. It all suddenly felt a bit weird and squalid. Selling my company almost seemed worse than selling my body - neither of which had particularly generated much interest till recently - but the moment passed, and he shook my hand, saying "You're a terrific guy, Gerard", with the stress on the second syllable. Actually, I much prefer that to the normal pronunciation.

Frank was all ears when I got back. Thought he might have been a bit miffed that I've had such a good time after his experience, but not a bit. There's not an ounce of malice in the man. Lying here on my bed, in my own room in my own flat in the heart of Amsterdam, thinking of all that's happened recently, I feel absolutely blessed yet again.

Easter Sunday - 7th April

Frank wanted to go to church this morning. I felt I ought to go as well, as somebody up there has definitely been looking out for me so far this year. Not that we could follow much of the service. So I sat there, thinking about things, thinking about how last year I felt completely trapped in crap, and how easy it seems in retrospect to have extracted myself from it all. Weird.

Went over to see Joop tonight. We were welcomed like two long-lost sons. Albertus ("Call me Bertus") was there too, medallions hanging out. He said the leather jacket does wonders for me. Sandra called in with her boyfriend, Jaap, who seems quite a pleasant bloke. He's a plumber, and I managed to converse quite well in Dutch with him, until he got onto the intricacies of calibrated boiler conversions.

Later on, I asked Joop if he was involved with anyone. He looked a bit lost for a second, then explained that his wife had died of cancer three years ago. I noticed a bit of a tear come in his eye, and wanted to put my arm round him, but didn't. Just then, Bertus reached forward for his Heineken and accidentally farted out loud. It's a funny old world.

Tuesday 9th April

Done two days in a row downstairs in the Sexmarkt, as Frank's come down with a really bad cold. An English bloke came in this afternoon and said he could sell us a video with Nazis, nuns, animals and kids in it. Just as I was thinking what a perv, he produced a copy of *The Sound of Music*!

There's also been more porno filming going on in the back today. It's right underneath Frank's bedroom, so he's been subjected to the exaggerated groaning and moaning all day. I don't know how they keep it up. It doesn't half keep the fat off them, though.

Wednesday 10th April

Frank's feeling a bit better today. He said he'd rather work than lie in bed listening to women having orgasms anyway. Just as well, as he was able to help me with the train runs. Bertus rang again this afternoon - telling me to meet Tom at the Hilton tonight.

Another really pleasant evening. This time we went out for a Thai meal. Over dinner, Tom asked me what I planned to be doing in ten years' time, and how I planned to achieve my goals. What a question! So hard to answer - I'm not particularly career-oriented, and now I'm out of teaching, I wouldn't fancy going back in. But I would like to be well regarded, have some position of authority, my own place, maybe a family. I also envy the supreme and casual confidence that people like Tom seem to have, and would like that as well, but I didn't tell him.

After the meal, he suggested going back to his room for a nightcap. I suddenly felt a bit wary, and remembered watching a documentary which said that most serial killers seem perfectly charming on a day-to-day basis. He must have read my mind, as he went on to say "I'm not gonna eat you, you know, Gerard, and I'll certainly be leaving my pants on!" Felt stupid then, so went back and had a couple of whiskeys. He told me all about his forthcoming wedding to Bonnie, and asked me if I was involved with anyone. I told him I'd ended a fairly long relationship last Christmas, with someone who was completely routine-centred, and basically not good enough for me. Not sure he was entirely convinced.

Friday 12th April

Have been painting the living-room with Frank, in between
train runs, Sexmarkt and everything else. I wanted magnolia,
Frank wanted garden-rose, so we've compromised on lemon,
looks very fresh.

Dutch last night, bit boring. Loads of grammar exercises.
Henk would never be able to get away with teaching like that
in England, although it does drill it into you. Annika handed
over more addresses and cash, while reminding me not to
upset Ben, so I collected and dropped off another painting this
morning. Nearly didn't make the scheduled delivery time, as
the number four tram got stuck on the Utrechtsestraat, so had
to run the last part of the way. Dripping in sweat when I got
there. When I told Frank, he asked me if I'd thought about
joining a gym, as I might need to make a quick get-away one of
these days. Then he said cutting down on fast food wouldn't
be a bad idea either. I asked him how much he normally
charges for personal training consultation, which he thought
was hilarious. Germans either seem to have no sense of
humour whatsoever, or find everything funny. Still, I know
which type I prefer.

Frank's out on escort business tonight. Too tired to cook, so
brought back chips and a kebab from the take-away. Felt
guilty afterwards, in case Frank said anything, so hid the papers
in the bin outside on the street. Then felt ridiculous, so went
back out and fetched them in on principle. A gorgeous-
looking elegant blonde appeared from nowhere as I was fishing
the papers out of the bin, like some sort of wino, so felt even
more ridiculous in the end.

Sunday 14th April

Frank out till 4.00 a.m. on Friday night. This time he was with
a Russian businessman who got him totally drunk on vodka,

and then took advantage of him - or at least he thinks he did! He was so drunk when he got back, he couldn't even get his key in the door. I had to carry him up to bed and undress him. He spent the rest of the night throwing up. Feels totally awful about it now.

I met up with Tom again last night. Thank God he's such a reasonable person, just hope future 'assignments' will be. After meeting at the Hilton, as usual, he said he'd got an invite to a party. Apparently, some 'contact' had invited him, and he was only going out of politeness. It was over on the Willemsparkweg, quite a posh area. Loads of people there, including - of all people - Ben and Annika, who totally blanked me! Couldn't believe it. They made it obvious that contact was out of the question, so I assumed they were there in connection with the paintings malarkey. Tom noticed me gesticulate to them, and asked me who they were. He seemed abnormally interested.

He introduced me to a few people as a good friend of his. Everybody we met talked pretentiously about art. Tom kept leaving me on my own as well, mingling like nobody's business for someone who was only being polite, so I had to put up with listening to a load of tosh about the quality of light in Holland and neo-pointillism in the modern age. Still, easy work I suppose, and there were some incredible vol-au-vents doing the rounds. Ben and Annika must have left quite early, as I didn't even glimpse them after my initial sighting. Afterwards, went to a bar with Tom, who seemed a bit preoccupied. He said it was just tiredness when I passed comment, and soon suggested calling it a day. I was back by midnight. Funny old evening.

Dead busy again in Sexmarkt this afternoon. Spent ages price-stamping a new batch of vibrators. Wouldn't normally have taken so long, but the on-off switches were faulty, so they kept going off while I was sticking the prices on. Sandra caught an American trying to slip a copy of 'NetherRegions Weekly' into his bag. He was totally mortified and bribed her with a hundred guilders not to pursue the matter. Sandra said it's pointless anyway, the police are never interested in tourists.

Frank feeling more human tonight, so went over to Joop's for a drink. He said he's heard of a good gym on the Singel, so might see about calling in this week.

Monday 15th April

Surprise visit from Annika and Ben tonight. Ben grilled me on everything to do with Saturday night, what I was doing there, who Tom was, etc. Felt like a naughty kid, caught doing something I shouldn't have been doing. Frank, who was mixing up a herbal remedy for a rash, butted in, asking what it had to do with them. Ben, who's about a foot taller than Frank, went over to him and said "Shut it, you gay German bastard!" He handed over another couple of cards with addresses for a delivery on Thursday, and told me to watch it. As I was about to risk telling him that I wasn't interested any more, he pulled out a knife and said: "Be grateful – dis is a job for life – dat's a good thing deez days". He left on that, Annika in tow. She didn't even look at me.

Tuesday 16th April

Slept really badly last night, kept waking up with it all on my mind. Had three low-fat rusks at 4.05 a.m, heeding Frank's advice about healthy eating  Funny how only babies eat rusks in England - here in Holland everybody eats them. Couldn't sleep much after that as had terrible indigestion. Keep wondering what the real story is behind Ben and these paintings.

Wednesday 17th April

Whatever next?  Just as I'd come downstairs for my afternoon shift, who should I see rifling through the Beefy and Buxom Section, but Mr Jones from next-door-but-one to my parents!! And sure enough, within seconds he was over at the counter, presenting me with a copy of Benelux-Boobs and a twenty guilder note. He cowered back the instant he recognised me, then got all flustered, said it was just a laugh, and then got all indignant and asked me what I was doing here anyway.

I said I was just helping out, and that he could rely on my discretion. He looked massively relieved, sighed, winked and then said "Nice to see you again, Gerard", as he left the shop. Don't suppose he'll mention it to my mom and dad. Mind you, even if he told them I was working as Europe's hottest live porn star, they'd probably just say: "Well, I'm glad he's keeping well, how's Mrs Jones going on with her bunions?"

Saturday 20th April

All go in the Sexmarkt today. Sandra was convinced there was a bees' nest in the store room, so she got the pest control people in just in case. Turned out to be a batch of those faulty dildos going off on their own again. When the bloke went through to the back, dressed in full bee-keeping protection mask and gear, a customer came over from the 'Kinky Corner' and asked me how much for a session with him. Honestly speaking.

Sunday 21st April

Went for a long walk around the city this afternoon. Walked for miles along the canals, down by the Amstel, and back, stopping off now and again for a beer on the odd terrace. Been a glorious afternoon. Have decided definitely to suss out the gym business this week. Walking past a shop front, I glanced in the window and noticed a distinct thickening round the waist in my reflection.

Went round to Joop's tonight with Frank. Bertus was there as well - he is SO uncouth. When we arrived, he was doing his hide-the-guilder-in-his-foreskin routine for some American tourists. They could hardly contain themselves, unlike Bertus, who could contain enough for a small lunch. He started doing the trick as a teenager apparently, and managed to dodge fares on the trams and buses for years, claiming it was the only loose change he had on him, which of course none of the drivers would touch with a barge-pole. He reckons this helped him save enough over the years to start up his first business at seventeen. You don't get stories like that on *The Money Programme*.

Tuesday 23rd April

Constantly doing the train runs is starting to give me itchy feet, seeing people coming in from all over Europe every day. Have picked up some leaflets from the station. Frank also quite fancies a break.

   Finally got round to calling in at the gym this afternoon after working downstairs. It's called Slimbods, which I think is really naff, but the Dutch think giving anything an English name does wonders for its image. I was shown around by a bronzed poser called Frans, who automatically made me feel like Mr Lard, especially when he took me into a cubicle and measured my fat with a pair of calipers. Him apart, the place seemed all right, and wasn't too busy. I'll have a 'personalized training programme' worked out next time I go. Had a kroket and chips on the way back.

Thursday 25th April

Had a surprise phone call from Tom yesterday. He's going back to America, but gave me his address so we can keep in touch. Quite pleased to hear from him. Otherwise not much to report. Went to Dutch again tonight and signed up for the exam in June. Really fancy going on a journey somewhere. Must get something sorted out.

Friday 26th April

Went to gym this morning. Frans demonstrated all the

machines to me and filled in a card showing me how many sets I need to do on each one. He kept saying things like "Dis vill optimize quality mooscle on your bodyparts," which sounds great, but I'll believe it when I see it. Felt a bit out of place at first, until I realized that everybody was so obsessed with themselves that they didn't have time to notice me.

Sandra kept bursting into tears in the shop this afternoon. Apparently, it's all over with her boyfriend, the plumber. She'd noticed he seemed to be getting more and more emergency call-outs in the middle of the night and started to get suspicious. Last night she decided to follow him, and, to cut a long story short, caught him trying out a very novel version of pipe-lagging, so she's thrown him out. The things people get up to.

Saturday 27th April

Every bit of me aches today after all that exertion yesterday. Stiff as a board. Endless source of amusement for Frank, who's lapsed into fits of laughter each time I've bent down or moved too quickly. I got quite irritated at one point, and said I thought it was typically German to be so amused by something not even worth half a smile, but it just heightened his amusement: "Gerard, you are really sutch a von," he said. "Shut your face, you daft Kraut", I said, but under my breath. Went and had a beefburger later while he went into a solarium to top his tan up. For someone who spends ten minutes checking for E numbers before he buys anything, he doesn't seem to mind a bit of radiation.

Round to Joop's tonight. Had quite a good laugh, as always. Bertus was quite pleased to see me, as he's got an escort assignment for me tomorrow night - a Hungarian. Meeting him at the Krasnakovsky at 9.00 pm.

Joop said he'll be going to Prague at some point to pick up some 'merchandise', and that it'd be nice to have some company on the way. Frank's dead keen, and so am I - never been anywhere in Eastern Europe before. He said he'll let us know in advance when he'll be going.

Frank and I discussed our own travel plans over a bottle of wine when we got back. Frank's got a friend called Thomas (where would I be without other people's friends?) who works at the German School of Milan. He hasn't seen him for over two years, but reckons it'd be no problem for us to stay with him. Frank thinks Italy is probably the best country on earth, and from what he says, it does sound appealing. He's ringing Thomas tomorrow. Hope we can stay with him - really fancy Italy - thousands of years of history, culture and the arts. Bound to be my sort of place.

Sunday 28th April

This escort lark really is sod's law. It sounds vaguely exotic and naughty, but in fact is about as thrilling as hanging around in a bus shelter in West Brom - at least, it was tonight. This Hungarian bloke, Gabor, is into 'goulash product marketing'. He's over here gleaning information on how best to prepackage authentic Hungarian meals-for-one for sad Western Europeans. Dare say I'll be buying them myself before too long. He was basically after an English lesson and a bit of company. Wouldn't mind, but my packaging vocabulary is quite limited, as are my views on culinary marketing. People get really sucked into their jobs as though it's the be-all and end-all, doesn't seem to matter what line of work people are in - Gabor was genuinely excited about the possibilities of vacuum-packaging; people at my school used to break out into a sweat (and probably still do) when a new packet of flashcards arrived. Maybe I just can't be professional, even Tina said I lacked ambition.

Anyway, the good news is Frank rang Thomas, who says we can go any time we want. Now that I *can* get excited about! As long as Joop can arrange cover, we'll leave next weekend!

Monday 29th April

Didn't need to do more than two train runs this morning, as loads of tourists streaming in now, so managed to fill Joop's rooms dead fast. Decided to revisit gym, since want to look as fit and appealing as possible for Italy. Took my time and felt incredibly fit afterwards, until I saw two blokes in the changing rooms with carved pecs and washboard stomachs. What do I have to do to get like that? How many bars of chocolate do I have to resist? How many times do I have to work out?

Went into the mixed sauna afterwards with my trunks on, thinking it was the right thing to do. Should have known better, of course. Nobody had a stitch on, so I managed to arouse mass attention by presenting myself as a covered-up prude. And then I made it all worse by deciding to take them off, thinking I too can be liberal - everybody just stared even more and made me feel like some kind of seedy flasher, which did nothing to enhance my genital magnitude. Sat there for three full minutes, feeling mortified, but then the heat overcame me, so went and sat on a deckchair outside the sauna. Earwigged on a conversation between two Dutch women wearing thongs about where to get the cheapest saucepans in Amsterdam. It was all getting too much, so pushed my way through the biceps for a quick cold shower and went straight to the shop.

Normal sort of day after that, apart from Sandra bursting into tears when a Japanese tourist bought a copy of *Plumber-Lover Pipes It Up*.

Tuesday 30th April

Dutch national holiday today, 'Queen's Day'. The whole of Amsterdam has been filled with cheapskates trying to flog stuff from their attics on stalls which people are allowed to set up everywhere. And those who weren't flogging were bargain-hunting. Frank said he's never been anywhere where people are so obsessed about saving the odd cent. Even in the Sexmarkt, you can tell the Dutch customers, as they're the ones making a beeline for the 'Second-*Hand*' section.

Wednesday 1st May

Can't believe how fast this year's going. May already. Went to
the gym again this morning after train runs. Fairly quiet.
Decided to have a quick sauna afterwards, so went in with not
a stitch on, only to see four people all with bathing costumes
on - typical. They all gave me funny looks, so I just kept my
towel around me. Frans came up to me as I was leaving and
said he'd have a chat with me about diet next time I go. Dare
say he'd been thinking what a podgy git I am, so felt totally
deflated when I walked out.

Went and got train tickets for Milan this afternoon with
Frank. We catch the 'Holland-Italy-Express' at 18.15 on
Saturday night. Marvellous.

Otherwise, normal sort of day. Did Dutch homework with
Frank tonight. Getting pretty good now - even know how to
split pronominal adverbs in subordinate clauses.

Thursday 2nd May

Went to gym again. Frank thinks I'm overdoing it now. Was
going round from machine to machine quite happily when
Frans rushes up to me on the pec-deck, saying my technique's
all wrong. I was then forced to perform a set under his
supervision, with him watching my every gasp. Felt stupid,
panting away self-consciously in my old T-Shirt, him standing
there in his lycra sports vest bulging with finely honed muscles.
Git. Finally managed to perform to his satisfaction, praise be,
so he left me alone for a bit. And sure enough, as I was
leaving, he's straight over with the promised diet lecture. All
sensible advice, I'm sure, but I can do without being patronised
by bronzed blonds who see carrots as a mouth-watering snack.
Anyway, good-bye chips and chocolate, hello salad, chicken
and tuna. Will this pleasure never end?

Dutch went quite well tonight. Lots of activities based on
the perfect tense, which Frank and I have no trouble with.
Should sail through the exam. Annika quite friendly again,
only because she had another 'job' for me. Usual ritual with

the handing-over of the cards.  Not really bothered, as just keep thinking about Milan on Saturday.

Frank went out escorting straight after Dutch, so have spent a quiet evening reading *Health and Fitness Monthly* (borrowed from Frans).  Highlights included 'deltoids in tandem', 'barbell blitz' and 'ultimate abs', all written by people who see Mars Bars as demonic manifestations.  Got up and looked out of window at one point, could see canal lit-up at end of street, tourists and cyclists passing below.  Then turned round and surveyed the scene inside - and felt thoroughly happy.

Friday 3rd May

Usual routine with painting exchange business this morning, but all sorted eventually.  Anyway, better start getting clothes washed for Italy, then see about working in the Sexmarkt this afternoon.  God knows when I'll fit in a salad sandwich.

Saturday 4th May

On the Holland-Italy-Express

On the way at last!  Very busy in Sexmarkt yesterday afternoon. Filming going on in the back again, and loads of tourists buying all manner of things from clockwork genitalia to talking dildos (why?!).  Sandra said she was going to miss me, which I thought was nice.

Got everything sorted out with Joop this afternoon.  He shoved a hundred guilder note into my hand as we were leaving and told us to make sure we have a good time.  Made a pile of sandwiches for the fourteen-hour journey – no boiled eggs, so as not to be anti-social in the compartment. And here we are, on the train at last.  Train is now leaving Arnhem station, so will be in Germany shortly.  Only two other people in the compartment - two Dutch women in their fifties, short grey hair, scrubbed Germanic faces - who started shelling hard-boiled eggs straight after Utrecht - that's the Dutch for you.

All you need on a 14 hour train journey. Frank is snoozing. Will write more later.

10.30 pm.

Now well into Germany, and heading down the Rhine valley. Bit of a scene earlier when the two Dutch women started criticising German architecture for being bombastic. Typical for the Dutch - fanatical travellers abroad, but incessant critics. Anyway, Frank took offence, and said it only seemed like that to them because there's nothing of any grandeur in Holland, which started a bit of an argument, into which even the boiled eggs eventually got dragged. Couldn't resolve it, so the women huffed off to the buffet car about an hour ago. Will get the couchettes sorted in a minute.

2.00 a.m.

Still awake. Both the Dutch women are snoring. Train is now in Switzerland, at Basle Station. Never been to Switzerland before. Shame we'll be going through some of the world's most stunning scenery in the dead of night. Am writing this with the aid of my individual nightlight. Will read a section of *Health and Fitness Monthly* to try and induce sleep. It's very hot and stuffy, and someone in the next compartment keeps farting out loud, prompting raucous laughter and cries in German of "Oh nein, Hans, not again!" The joys of international travel.

Sunday 5th May

Milan!

Eventually managed to get off to sleep last night. Woke up in Chiasso on the Swiss-Italian border. Glorious sunshine, marvellous views of cypress hillsides, elegant villas and flamboyant villages set against a blue sky. Glanced at the two

Dutch women, and suddenly they looked really out of place - imports from an alien northern world. The train pulled into Milan at 8.30. Unbelievably imposing station - huge monument of a building, apparently built under Mussolini. Wonder what the Dutch women made of it.

Anyway, Thomas was waiting for us in the station hall. Smashing bloke. Nothing's too much trouble for him. One of those Germans with shocking blond hair and less body fat than a low-calorie celery drink. Can't help but like him, though. He took us straight back to his apartment not far from the station, and had already set the table for breakfast - salami, cheese, bread, tomatoes, eggs, etc. It's that ruthlessly efficient German hospitality that just seems second nature to them. Bugger the diet.

Had a bit of a kip to revive ourselves - Frank and I have to share a bed, but no problem there. Spent rest of day strolling round. I've never seen anything like the cathedral - huge, elaborate birthday cake. Felt immediately at home here. Gorgeous weather, fantastic-sounding language, phenomenal food. Sat outside on a bar terrace tonight, watching the world go by, feeling totally cosmopolitan as people with more natural style than is good for you whizzed past on vespers. Have the feeling it's going to be a great holiday.

Monday 6th May

Thomas had left for school by the time we got up, so had a leisurely breakfast and went off to explore. Roasting weather. Sat drinking cappuccino in a bar for a bit. Frank was virtually champing at the bit ogling Italian men - he reckons they're the most gorgeous in Europe. I fell in love about six times with women I passed on the street. Later on, we got some shopping from a supermarket nearby, where I fell in love again, this time with the checkout assistant, and then went back to make a meal ready for when Thomas got back.

Spent the evening in a bar with some of Thomas' Italian friends, who were all gay. Frank immediately hit it off with a little curly-haired bloke in leather called Giuseppe, who turns out to be a salami butcher, but very pleasant. They disappeared after a bit, no doubt back to Giuseppe's pad, so don't expect he'll be back tonight. Had a really good chat with Thomas and a bloke he introduced to me as his fitness instructor, Gianne, who was instantly more affable than Frans. Anyway, picked up some very good tips on stomach reduction. Gianne reckons regular jogging should soon see it off, although he then said he liked guys with a little bit to play with, poked me in the stomach and said something in Italian which probably meant my luck would have been in if I'd been that way inclined.

Tuesday 7th May

Frank got in first thing this morning, all messy-haired and bleary-eyed - what a tart! He's totally smitten with Giuseppe, but I reckon it's just a holiday romance type of thing. Had a nice relaxing day wandering around the Castle and its grounds. Had three ice-creams. Would have been four, but Frank told me I'd only feel guilty. Went back to supermarket for more food for tonight's meal. Still the same dark, gorgeous stunner on check-out. It said 'Maria' on her name-tag. I'd told Frank what I thought of her yesterday, and he knew I wouldn't have the nerve to approach her, so he deliberately got chatting (she speaks English) and started to explain about us being on holiday, etc. In the end, he said he had an appointment this evening (with Giuseppe, of course), and wondered if she could entertain me - amazingly, she said she'd be happy to!

Met her in the bar next to the supermarket tonight at 9.00. Could hardly eat a thing beforehand. And sure enough, there she was at a table when I walked in. Out of her supermarket apron she looked more gorgeous than ever. Thought I was going to be tongue-tied at first, but she had loads of questions, and was pleased to be practising her English, she said. Turns out she's a graduate in marketing but hasn't been able to get a better job yet, so she's working in the supermarket to earn money. She smoked her way though a packet of cigarettes and prefaced every question with "Eh Gerardo, tell me...". The more she spoke, the more obsessed I became by her hand movements, soulful eyes and glossy black hair, and my mind was racing ahead to the stage where we'd settled down and were bringing up three children on a Tuscan farm, the sex industry a thing of the past.

And then she brought up her boyfriend - devastation. I knew it was too good to be true. He's doing his military service in Calabria, and she misses him terribly - typical. It took all my effort to appear unmoved and casual while she talked about him, when actually I felt as if my whole raison d'etre had been wiped out. Sounds ridiculous, but that's how it felt.

Got back at midnight, and let myself in with the spare key. Thomas already in bed, Frank still out. Sat on the bed with two packets of crisps and a bottle of warm lager from my rucksack, contemplating an alternative universe where self-delusion never gets a look-in.

Thursday 9th May

Frank woke me up at 11.00 yesterday morning when he got back from Giuseppe's looking exhausted but all sparkly-eyed. It must be love for him, the git. He cheered me up even more by telling me I looked terrible, but I couldn't take offence. If it hadn't been for him, I'd never have got any further forward, so would have been wondering for months, if not years, how things might have turned out if I'd had half a nerve. At least I know now.... Not sure that's a good thing actually, now I think about it. Anyway, both of us felt a bit jaded yesterday, for different reasons obviously, so we hung loose on the piazza, Frank no doubt more than me. Shelled out a fortune for cappuccinos and baguettes, but past caring.

When Thomas got home, we went to a trattoria and spent a pleasant evening just the three of us. Giuseppe was apparently having to work late on the sausage-packing line at the salami factory. Didn't bother commenting on that. Thomas had us in stitches with tales about the problems he's had with Italian bureaucracy since he moved here, it was hilarious, he's so witty (for a German). God knows why I don't loathe him, he's just got too much going for him. Anyway, the bureaucracy stuff worried me a bit, since I've never even thought about registering with the police in Holland, and I'm not officially on any systems, as the money I get is all cash-in-hand. I'll ask Joop what he thinks when we get back.

Frank was spending today with Giuseppe, who'd got the day off in lieu of working last night, so I decided to get out of Milan and take the train to Florence. Shared a compartment with three nuns who kept looking sideways at me, clutching their bags as though they recognised me from Italian Crimewatch. Felt quite affronted.

Anyway, got there fairly early. Quite amazing. Teeming with tourists, desperate to see all the splendours. The cathedral, the palaces, the Uffizi, Giotto's bell tower. Strolled along, and there it was - the statue of Michelangelo's David, in the square outside the Uffizi. Stunning. Every day for four years I'd glanced at that very picture in the language lab at Walsall Comp, feeling trapped, limited and dull, imagining the splendours of living or being somewhere like Florence. And there I was - right in front of the real thing. Overwhelming moment. As I stood looking up at the statue, I suddenly had a strange feeling in my trousers. When I looked down, I saw a kid's hand leaving my pocket clasping my wallet. The git then dived through the crowds before I'd even had a chance to bring my jaw back up.

Thank God I'd left most of my cash and passport back here. As it was, I lost the cash I'd taken for the day and my return ticket! I thought of the nuns, who'd maybe had some sort of premonition when they looked at me. Anyway, decided to report it to the police, but needn't have bothered. When I eventually found the police station, it was like arriving at NYPD on a bad morning, except everybody was speaking Italian, and showed about as much interest as if I'd turned up trying to flog British Rail memorabilia. Tried to make myself understood in English, French, German and words of Italian, which meant I eventually got handed a plethora of forms, none of which I could understand. Was overcome by the pointlessness of it all, especially as it seemed very unlikely they'd be putting out a task-force to nab the kid and reclaim my wallet, so just walked out in the end, fighting back tears of frustration.

Hitch-hiking seemed my only hope, so set off for motorway straight after. Took me a gruelling two hours in baking heat to get there, but good exercise, no doubt. Kept thinking of the stomach reduction value to keep me upbeat. Then spent another two hours with my thumb up, as the queue of hitch-hikers was whittled down. Finally a lorry pulled up. Hauled myself on to find a huge-bellied sweaty-vested wrestler type smiling at me. Here we go, I thought. Turned out to be a gentle giant. He only spoke Italian, but could understand French, so I managed to explain what had happened. During my explanation, he tossed his head from side to side, tutting profusely, and then started gesticulating at the glove compartment area, got me to open it, and said "Prenda, prenda, prenda", which I could work out meant 'take'. There were rolls galore and bottles of water. What a hero. People like that restore my faith in humanity. Then it was "Prego, prego, prego", as I swigged away.

He eventually dropped me off at a service area near Milan, where he smacked me on the shoulder and thrust a handful of coins at me, saying "Per telefonare, telefonare, amici, capito?" Funny how the worst in people and the best in people is often seen back-to-back. Anyway, thank God Thomas is in the phonebook. Rang him and he drove out straight away in his black VW Golf. He was really sorry to hear what had happened, and pampered me with sublime efficiency when we got back tonight. Meal, wine, soft music and a ready ear all at the drop of a hat. This man must have some flaws, he's starting to unnerve me. Frank still out with Giuseppe, of course. Definitely time for bed. Just hope I don't sleep-walk and shove a few Mars Bars down Thomas' throat.

Saturday 11<sup>th</sup> May

Basle

Frank turned up at 10.00 yesterday morning. He was horrified
to hear about the Florence fiasco. Decided to have a relaxing
day, so we just pootled around the streets, stopping off for
cappuccinos and lunch. Avoided the supermarket. Got Joop a
bottle of Amoretto and Sandra a box of chocolates. Bought
Thomas *The Unbearable Lightness of Being*, as a thank-you. He
said the other night he'd like to read it some time. He was
really thrilled and thanked me profusely, which somehow made
me want to force-feed him full-fat chocolate cake even more.
Spent the evening with him and friends in bar down the road.
Everybody in good form really, except Frank and Giuseppe,
who sat draped around each other all night like a couple of
tranquillized chimpanzees.

Up early this morning to catch train to Basle. Thomas and
Giuseppe saw us off. Frank and Giuseppe all watery-eyed.
Thomas hugged me against his super-hard body and said how
much he'd enjoyed having me. If he goes up any more in my
estimation, and if my present luck with women continues, I'll
be wishing it was true. Once we'd left, Frank went on for ages
about how wonderful Giuseppe is. I listened attentively, but
just felt peeved. I'm glad for him, but would love for
something to work out for me just once in a while, other than
the odd night of passion with a Chilean sex fiend, and un-
extendable flings with homeward bound Americans. Maybe if
I can get into the old fitness game my 'appealability' will
improve.

Anyway, decided to spend the night here in Basle and return
to Amsterdam during day tomorrow. Very sophisticated town,
full of bankers and business types from all over Europe
wearing £100 shirts and sunglasses. Went out this evening to a
restaurant overlooking the Rhine. We talked about the last

week, and somehow I already felt gripped by a sense of nostalgia for it, even though we only left this morning. Funny really. In spite of my ridiculous disappointment with Maria and the Florence incident, I've really enjoyed this last week. Frank is already saying it's been one of the best weeks of his life. He called the week a celebration of friendship, a bit gushing maybe, but he is a gay German and I do recognise the sentiment. He also said how great he thought I'd been not to get jealous of him paying so much attention to Giuseppe, and hoped that I hadn't felt neglected. As if! It's fair enough, I wouldn't even have been there without him. And Thomas and everyone, even the lorry driver, was really so kind.

We took our time walking along the Rhine back to the hotel, the river beautifully illuminated. Frank said he's glad to be going back to Holland, and I must admit, I'm quite looking forward to getting back as well. First holiday in years where going back home doesn't fill me with the dread of tedium to come.

Sunday 12th May

Home in Amsterdam

Well, back again. All seems unreal now, somehow. Got EuroCity this morning from Basle to Amsterdam. Uneventful journey, apart from a group of Romanians being turfed off at the border for not having Dutch visas. They were manhandled off and told to go back to Bucharest to get them. I was really shocked but nobody else batted an eyelid. It felt wonderful getting off the train at the Central Station, even Frank seemed to have overcome his pining for Giuseppe, until we heard the announcement for the Holland-Italy-Express, and he filled up again. Everything fine back in the flat. Home sweet home! Popped into the Sexmarkt to see Sandra. She was really pleased to see us and flung her arms round us both. Just a normal week, she reckoned, apart from the BBC calling in to do some filming and interviews! Apparently they were doing some research for a programme on British sex tourists. Trust me to miss my televisual big break!

No post whatsoever waiting for me. Just a pile of the free local papers. Must write more letters. Don't know who to, though. Have lost touch with everyone from school and poly, and am glad to see the back of 'former colleagues'. Anyway, time for bed. Frank went about an hour ago, but I can hear him playing his Italo-Hits 95 compilation and sniffing every time a ballad comes on.

Monday 13th May

Could have done with a lie-in this morning. Just time for a bowl of low-fat Brekko-Bites and then straight back into the train runs, and over to Joop's with the recruits. Joop was out when we got there, very unusual - only Rita the cleaner about. Went back to shop, where Sandra was in a flap, as someone had just made off with an unpacked bumper box of porn mags from Stockholm which the courier had left outside. Whipped it into a van just as Sandra was about to fetch them. Frank was also transformed into Mr Fluster, so I thought I'd better go and report it.

Went round to the police station on the Damrak, and was dealt with by a Detective Van Arlen - big, square head, overpowering aftershave, no sense of humour. On the way there, I'd decided it might be best to lie and say I was on holiday, staying at a friend's place, with not being registered, and pretended not to speak Dutch so as not to arouse any suspicions. As it was, I made myself look extremely suspicious - why was I reporting it instead of the shop assistant, did I get a look at the thief or the car, what was I doing there at that time in the morning? I said the assistant was too upset, and heard myself lying that I'd gone in asking for directions and had seen a tall dark man getting into a small green car. Then he wanted full details - the man's build, hair colour, height, the make of car, the registration. Now I started to feel like Mr Fluster, and felt a cold sweat breaking out. I told him I couldn't say more than that, but he just stared sceptically at me, and asked me to fill in a few forms. Came out and it was still only 9.30!

Frank's turn to work downstairs this afternoon, so I went back to bed. When I got up at 5.00, I picked up last week's local freebie paper and a loose sheet dropped out - it was a note from Ben that must have lodged itself between the pages. It was dated 8th May, and asked "Where the hell are you?," as he'd got a painting job for me that he'd have to get someone else to do now. It ended with "Will contact you soon - you'd better be there". Frank said again about Joop's 'boys' (whoever they are), who could sort things out if there was any trouble. Don't really like the sound of all this.

Wednesday 15th May

Had Ben round yesterday morning. He wasn't as aggressive as I'd feared, but not exactly chummy either. He said I should let him know if I'm not going to be around. I told him I couldn't when I had no way of contacting him, but he just snarled and handed over a couple more cards for an exchange on Friday. His hair was greasy, and I noticed he'd got a fading bruise on his jaw. He mumbled off without even the decency to say good-bye.

Good fun working in the Sexmarkt yesterday. Joop's having some new video cabins put in, so there were workmen in and out all the while. One of the more subtle ones kept winking at Sandra and flashing his spirit-level, but it didn't amuse Sandra one bit. I thought it was quite funny, though.

Turns out Joop's run into a bit of trouble as well - the tax people are onto him. They've done a spot check and have worked out he hasn't been declaring all his income. Poor bloke. He says he'll have to start getting his paperwork sorted, and about Frank and me registering with the police. He'll have to show that we're properly on the books, which'll mean him having to pay more contributions and things, but will get round it by paying us less 'on paper'. Sounds a nightmare.

Bertus was saying in the bar over there tonight that they'll land Joop with a huge fine. I asked Bertus if he could get into trouble about the escort business, but he reckons it's all above board. Joop himself seemed totally unaffected by it all, and was knocking back the gin no problem. He seemed more bothered by a fire started in one of the rooms by a couple of Americans experimenting with drugs. No massive damage, but it's scorched the wallpaper apparently. I volunteered Frank and me to redecorate it for him. It's the least we can do under the circumstances.

Friday 17th May

Busy couple of days. Train runs, painting over at Joop's, working in Sexmarkt. Sandra's invited me over for a meal tomorrow night. Dutch last night - normal sort of class, hadn't missed much at all. Henk as boring as ever. Only nine people left in group now, including Frank and me. No Annika, which I was actually quite glad about. Also been back to the gym, so feel as stiff as a board now, what with all the painting as well.

Did the paintings job for Ben. Irritating though it is, between the Sexmarkt, the escorting and the deliveries I'm really not too badly off. Went over to police station and got the registration sorted out. I'd hate to have been from a non-EU country. As it was, anyone would've thought I was a Colombian drug lord trying to claim benefits for a family of twelve, going by the surly faces and gruff questioning. Anyway, it was all sorted out eventually. I now have a one-year residence permit. Walked past Detective Van Arlen on the way out. Hoped he was going to ignore me, but he wanted to know what I was doing there. When I told him he looked even more sceptical than the last time, even though I was telling the truth this time.

Saturday 18th May

Letter from Jan and Phil today. The most exciting thing they had to say, apart from riveting stuff about the baby's digestion, was that they're having their upstairs windows replaced with white PVC ones.  This time last year that might have been the highlight of my weekend.

Giuseppe's rung about five times.  He's coming up to stay in a week or so.  Starting to get on my nerves a bit as every time he rings, I feel obliged to give Frank his privacy, so keep disappearing into my bedroom.  One time he was on for fifty minutes, so felt trapped.  Tidied up my underwear draw, feeling resentful.

Went round to Sandra's tonight for meal.  Lovely evening. Turned out to be just me and her.  She'd prepared three courses and had loads of make-up on, which she doesn't normally bother about.  Kept on about how glad she was now that she'd got rid of Jaap, and about how they could never really talk about things.  She also said how much she enjoys the days when we're both working.  Felt quite flattered and appreciated.  About three hours later I had to carry her through to the bedroom after she'd passed out from the wine. She obviously feels very relaxed with me.  I stuck to two glasses, as read in *Health and Fitness Magazine* this afternoon that wine is extremely calorific.  Just before she passed out, she said what a wonderful bloke I am in Dutch.  I thought of undressing her and putting her into bed, but didn't really like to, so just struggled her onto the bed and left her a note, saying "Thanks for a lovely evening, hope you feel better tomorrow".

Sunday 19th May

Been back from Italy a week now, so decided to get properly back into the fitness lark.  Went to the gym and decided to look at as few people as possible, as the sight of finely honed bodies only seems to demotivate me.  Had only been there five minutes when Frans bounds over, looking more bronzed and bicepped than ever, his little vest clinging onto him for dear life.  "Whad about de cardio-vascular work?"  Apparently, that's what I should be concentrating on at the start and end of every work-out. I told him I was well aware, and lied that I go jogging regularly, as advised by an Italian fitness instructor I know (partly true). He marched me straight up to the jogging machine and watched me till it was nearly time to call for the paramedics. And every twenty seconds he'd ball out "knees up!", "posture!" or "pace!". After what seemed like an hour, but was only six minutes, he let me stagger off. And to think I pay for that. Will jog along the canals in future, which will also be less boring.

Normal sort of day otherwise. Bertus rang with escort details for jobs for both of us on Tuesday night. He assured me there'd be nothing physical involved - some Finnish businessman for me. Frank got us tickets for a Bertolt Brecht play in Utrecht this evening. On balance, think I'd rather have discussed the merits of PVC windows, but didn't let on to Frank, who was well impressed by the actors' deployment of alienation techniques. Still, kept his mind off bonking Giuseppe, I suppose.

Monday 20th May

Sandra back to her normal self in Sexmarkt today. She apologized for getting so drunk, but said she just hadn't realized how much she was drinking. Said she'd had a wonderful evening, and that it was just a pity I hadn't taken advantage of her, given the state she was in! When I joked that I had, she blushed and put down a dildo she was just gift-wrapping. I said that I was only joking, the Dutch never being quick to latch onto irony, and am sure I heard her mumble the Dutch word for "what a pity" under her breath. Then she just carried on with the dildo and gave me a red-faced smile. Very odd.

Jogged down to the Munt Square and back early this evening, but never again. Far too many British tourists fancying themselves as comedians. Did my self-esteem no good at all, not sure it even did my body any.

Tuesday 21st May

Up early for a jog before we went to the Central Station. Best time of day to do it - nobody about and a lovely sunny morning. Saw Detective Van Arlen getting on the train to Amersfoort while we were waiting for the Danube-Waltzer-Express from Vienna. You'd think he'd have a car, but that's the Dutch - environmentally obsessed. I smiled at him, but he just blanked me, which is also typically Dutch - surly gits. At moments like that I wish I was in England, where people have at least got the civility to acknowledge you, even if they can't stand you.

Frank's had his hair cut really short. Makes him look quite a hard case. Might have the same done to mine, but don't know that it would suit me.

Both of us out escorting tonight. Frank had a wail of a time with some vodka-swigging financial bisexual from Gdansk. I asked him if he was faithful to Giuseppe, which got him chortling. Yet another instance of the humour divide. "I am faisful in my heart, that's the only place you can be faisful", was his answer. I couldn't be bothered arguing, and suppose he's got a point somewhere.

The Finnish businessman turned out to be an engineer from the north of Finland. He must have been about seven feet tall, with white hair and white skin. I'm sure it must be due to the lack of sunlight half the year - just like plants growing all white and spindly when you grow them in a cupboard in biology. Am beginning to find it less stressful at the start, and can almost fall back on the same questioning routine every time to keep the conversation going. Suppose I'm gradually coming to see it more as an unusual sort of 'service' job, and less as a seedy transaction. Especially easy tonight, with Hakka being quite a well-balanced bloke, in fact. He's over here on some two-week project, and fancied an evening's company for a meal (Chinese and fairly low-fat), a drink and a sauna to break the evening monotony. Apparently Bertus' agency was just included in the hotel information. Bertus is obviously quite a shrewd businessman. Had a very pleasant evening and got paid to boot - can't believe that a year ago I'd have been marking sets of exercise books or popping down the Blinking Weasel with Tina.

Thursday 23rd May

Only six people in Dutch tonight. No wonder, when we only started a few months ago with "Hello, my name is blah, blah", to discussing a passage about drainage techniques and dike erection tonight. Don't know how Henk gets away with it. Ben was waiting for me outside when we came out with a few more cards up his sleeve. He handed them over in the usual way, and the only thing he said was to Frank: "Like de haircut". He looked even worse than the last time I'd seen him. Frank just swore in German under his breath. God knows what's become of Annika.

Friday 24th May

Busy afternoon in Sexmarkt. The new video cabins are a real puller. Can't believe how people just come in and use them. There's a toilet roll holder and a little bin inside each one - gross! Absolute goldmine, though - more people in and out than the toilets on Birmingham New Street Station.

Sandra looking very flushed this afternoon. Also very tactile. Every time she had to get past me, she put her hand on my shoulder or bum. Must be finally starting to ooze a bit of sex appeal. Went over to Joop's tonight with Frank. He's counting the days now till Giuseppe gets here. When we walked in, Joop and Bertus were all over two Swedes I'd taken round this morning. Bertus ended up doing his hide the guilder routine, not long after which he went upstairs with the taller of the two. All in all, a very sexual day.

Saturday 25th May

Jogged to station this morning. Frank jogged with me, and actually really enjoyed it. He reckons he can see it making a difference now. When we got over to Joop's with today's recruits, Joop was in the middle of rather complex manoeuvres with that Swedish girl on the counter. Anyone else would have been mortified, but as it was, they just moved along a bit, leaving Frank and me to show today's tourists up to the rooms. God knows what they must have thought. Even Frank was taken aback. He says someone told him there's no word in Dutch for embarrassed. I'm not surprised. What a fantastic facet to be lacking. Maybe if I stay in Holland long enough I'll be farting out loud in saunas whilst telling all and sundry about my itchy bum and not batting an eyelid.

I was almost more surprised that it was Joop. Still, good luck to him. Anyway, did painting business after that for Ben - no hitches. Usual odd characters, no questions asked.

Went to Rotterdam with Frank on train this afternoon for a change of scene. Very impressed. Went up Euromast, round shops (got a new lamp for flat), and to an art gallery with loads of b's in its name (Frank's choice). Lots of people in there hanging around in front of canvases which looked like they'd been sneezed at in colour. One bloke was blabbing on to some woman about "the restraints of artistic abandonment" and "the chaos of the cosmos" as reflected in the painting, when he walked backwards into a Persian vase, causing a bit of a scene.

Had a lovely Indonesian meal this evening. Frank can hardly contain himself now with Giuseppe only days away. I asked him if he could see himself moving to Italy if things developed. He said he could, but would really miss me, Joop, Amsterdam and the rest of it. Experienced a moment of total depression at the thought of Frank leaving, but suppose time will tell.

Sunday 26<sup>th</sup> May

5.00 a.m.

Woken up at three o'clock this morning by Frank, screaming hysterically. Put the light on, and had the shock of my life - he looked like the Elephant Man. His face was hugely swollen, his lips were all red and puffy, and his eyes had almost disappeared between his swollen cheeks and eyebrows. When I saw him first, I screamed as well, thinking some lunatic weirdo had broken in, until he spoke and I realized it really was Frank. He'd got up bursting for the loo, and nearly died when he saw himself in the mirror. Bit of a panic then, while I looked through the phone book for an emergency doctor, who came after about fifteen minutes. While we were waiting, Frank was inconsolable - he was dying, he'd got AIDS, he'd never be able to go out in public, couldn't work, would have no sex life, Giuseppe wouldn't want to know him, would I look after him, etc. He was sobbing into my lap when the doctor arrived, leaving my pyjamas soaking round the groin. God knows what the doctor thought.

Anyway, he took one look at Frank and smiled. "Been to an Indonesian restaurant?" was his first question. Apparently, it was a common and temporary allergic reaction to some kind of small fish that's often used in Indonesian cooking - nothing to worry about. So I made us a cup of herbal tea and have just put on clean pyjama bottoms. Hope I can get back to sleep now.

Monday 27th May

Had a totally relaxing day yesterday, after all the trouble in the night. Spent hours in a cafe in the Jordaan with Sandra, who rang up and suggested meeting. She was really chatty, going on about her parents and family, and how she'd like to get a job in an export company, especially as her parents disapprove of her working in a sex shop. I'd agreed with Frank that we'd do our Dutch homework together at 5.00, so left at 4.30. She gave me a really intimate kiss as we left, and I don't know whether I was more surprised or excited. Afterwards, felt a bit weird. I like Sandra, but don't know that I'd want a relationship with her.

Can't work it out really. Frank thinks I'm probably scared of commitment. Maybe I am. It'd also be very awkward if it didn't work out, working together and all that. Frank's face is totally back to normal now.

Anyway, things were all right between us at the Sexmarkt this afternoon, although she was in her tactile mood again. Went to the gym afterwards and had the equipment virtually all to myself as everybody else was crowding round some Neanderthal type who'd dropped a weight on his head. Eventually it got a bit busier after he'd been carried out on a stretcher. Have decided to monitor my weight loss to motivate me. Weight today - 83 kg.

Wednesday 29th May

Had a letter from Jan and Phil today - did I have the room to put them up for a weekend in the summer? They're desperate for a break, have never been to Amsterdam, and would love to see me again (I'll bet) so they wondered if I could help out. Frank said he doesn't mind. At least they won't be bringing the baby - Phil's mother will look after it. Wrote back tonight and said it would be ok. At least they've kept in touch.

Sandra actually groped me at a quiet moment this afternoon. Again, I was amazed - one minute we're talking about some job she's thinking of applying for, the next minute she's touching me up. Then she said she'd really enjoyed Sunday and that she'd have to cook for me again. Just at that moment, someone stuck his head out of the video cabin asking for a toilet roll- I left Sandra to deal with him. Some people really have no shame. That would have been the height of humiliation for me, but for the Dutch it's just like dropping your specs in Tesco's.

Went for a jog tonight and found an envelope on the mat when got back. More cards with addresses and instructions from Ben, also the cash. Frank's out escorting, so have enjoyed an Italo-hits-free evening.

Friday 31st May

Did nothing but exam practice in Dutch last night. Spent half
the class doing a test, and the other half going through it with
Henk. Totally dull, but it did make me realize how much I've
learned since I started. Living here makes a difference, of
course. Exam only two weeks away now. Doubt if Annika
will ever come back, especially now she's missed partitive
article splitting.
  Had a good session in the gym this morning. Still can't see
any difference, but it feels as though it's doing me some good.
Finished off with a sauna, but left after five minutes, as two
women with the biggest breasts I've ever seen came in. Is it
necessary? Sandra all over me again this afternoon in shop,
and for once I found myself happy to oblige. Am convinced
she must fancy me.
  Spent the whole of this evening giving the flat a thorough
clean with Frank. Partly because it desperately needed it, partly
because Giuseppe's coming tomorrow. I'd have been happy to
give it a quick dusting, but Frank insisted on thoroughness.
Had a bit of an argument when I said the Germans are
obsessed with cleanliness, and Frank said the English are "filzy
fish-and-chip eaters". Didn't last long, though, as I couldn't
take him seriously wearing an apron and waving a duster, so we
both ended up laughing. Funny that I ended up doing the
heavy duty polishing, though. Frank borrowed the hoover
from the Sexmarkt, and was very impressive with the
attachments. Place now looks super smart. Am absolutely
exhausted, though. Must be about 25 degrees, even though it's
gone midnight.

Saturday 1st June

Had one of the worst nights of my life last night. As if the
heat wasn't bad enough, I was plagued by mosquitos from hell
all night long. Even after I closed the bedroom window, there
was no let-up. Each time I managed to let the heat lull me

close to coma, there'd be an almighty buzzing straight in my ear-hole, which had me sitting bolt upright every time. I'd then spend five minutes standing on the bed, slipper in hand, trying to spot the git. Occasionally I got one, but there must have been hundreds of them hiding. Consequently, I got up feeling bog-eyed and knackered, and looking like someone with a severe skin disorder because of all the bites. Frank was really shocked, and thought I'd come down with something. He's knocked up some sort of herbal concoction for me, but I'm sure it's only made it worse.

Anyway, his major concern was picking up the salami wonder-boy from Milan, who finally arrived this morning. He jumped off the Italy-Holland-Express like an energetic gnome with diarrhoea heading for the loo, covered in shiny black leather and gelled curly hair. Frank was on him like magnet. I'd told Frank I'd take any hostel recruits on to Joop's myself, giving him the chance to get Giuseppe back to the flat. As it turned out, there were no takers today for some reason, so no problem really.

Wanted to give Frank and Giuseppe a bit of privacy afterwards as well, so decided to go to the cinema this afternoon. Had intended to see the new Richard Gere film, but must have gone through the wrong entrance (multiplex cinema) and ended up seeing a Swedish hard-core film with subtitles (not many, and in Dutch). Was too embarrassed to get up after it'd started, besides which I was soon rivetted. Not by the film so much as the surreptitious mass-groping going on all around me. Incredible. When the lights came on at the end, a woman sitting one seat away yelped when she looked at me, drawing everybody's attention to my swollen face. Charming, after I'd been sitting there for ninety minutes, the soul of decorum!

Decided to go over to Joop's this evening, which was another mistake. Ended up being the brunt of Bertus' disparagings about my face, which is still covered in red welts. I sat at the bar listening to him going on about Frankenstein with acne, trying to amuse the punters at my expense, until I could feel tears welling up. Everybody was staring. I had to get up and leave. Joop rushed out after me and stuck his arm round me - he said it was just Bertus' way, and not to take it to heart. I made out I was just feeling a bit under the weather and needed to get back anyway. Came back via the all-night chemist where I got some mosquito repellent and even more funny looks. Got back to total darkness in the flat, except for the light coming from under Frank's door. Have just covered myself from head to toe in the mosquito stuff, while listening to all manner of noises and groans from Frank's room.

Monday 3rd June

Miserable day yesterday. Didn't dare venture out of the flat, not wanting to provoke national horror. What a country - you can have someone reading a porno mag next to you smoking pot, and nobody bats an eyelid, but have the odd mosquito bite on your face and it's front page news. At least the repellent stuff works, so have managed to sleep all right.

Spent the day revising for Dutch exam and exchanging the odd word with Frank and Giuseppe, as and when they emerged from his room. Honestly, I don't know how they manage it.

Facial swelling gone down considerably today, so fortunately not had to suffer any stares or comments. Joop was very conciliatory when we took over this morning's train recruits. He told me to take no notice of Bertus, and I felt stupid about overreacting, but there you go. Normal sort of day after that. Sexmarkt busy again. Sandra invited me over for a meal on Wednesday night. She's hoping it'll be a celebratory meal, as she's got a job interview on the afternoon.

Tuesday 4th June

Face more or less back to normal now. Went over to Joop's tonight, as Frank and Giuseppe have taken themselves off somewhere for a change. Bertus was in the bar, and looked genuinely pleased to see me. I was a bit cool with him at first, still feeling hurt at the remarks he'd made, but didn't keep it up for long. It strikes me the Dutch are just genetically deprived of tact and sensitivity, so when they are rude, they've got no way of knowing they might be overstepping the mark. He cheered me up by telling me he's had some very good feedback about my escorting. Apparently they fill in a 'service questionnaire' after the evening, so that Bertus can 'monitor quality'. I was bracing myself for more criticism, but I always come out as 'extremely sociable and pleasant', he reckons. I didn't dare ask him what the other questions were, and am only surprised that he didn't give me a warts-and-all analysis, but saw Joop pulling funny faces at him.

Wednesday 5th June

Went round to Sandra's tonight. She did one of those meals where there are lots of bits of meat which you fry on an individual tray over the course of the evening. Very Euro-cultured, very me really. Sandra was beaming, so I knew it must be good news as soon as I walked in - she's got the job. She starts next month as an office manager with some marketing company near the Rijksmuseum. She'd still got her interview clothes on, and looked really smart for once. In fact, it was the first time I've seen her looking really attractive. Her jeans and shirt had been swapped for a blue skirt and blouse, and her curly hair was smartly tied back, fully exposing her rosy freckled cheeks, making her look a picture of health. She'd also got make-up on again, lots of blue round the eyes, emphasising their colour and somehow her blond-red hair as well. And whereas she normally just looks sturdy, she looked solid and sexually powerful tonight - it was almost like meeting a new person. She was on a high as well because of the new job. She says her parents are over the moon, as they never liked her running a sex shop. Anyway, as we chatted, ate and drank, I found myself getting more and more attracted to her, and I could tell it was mutual. Thank God my facial welts had gone down. As soon as we moved over to the couch, it was inevitable. I was making Richard Gere look like an extra in Last of the Summer Wine, she was Julia Roberts on love steroids.

Brilliant as it was, I didn't want to spend the whole night there - nothing like my own bed, and I felt I needed to get my head round it all. Sandra wanted me to stay, but I said I had to see to a couple of things, and would have to be up really early for the first train run anyway. She didn't argue.

When I closed her flat door behind me, and walked out into the street, I felt fantastic. I walked back along the canals, kicking a can, my jacket flying open in the breeze, my hair passion-ruffled. Amsterdam was still buzzing with people- a group of Spanish women wolf-whistled me from across a canal, I just waved and smiled. This is what it's all about.

Thursday 6th June

Floated through this morning. Had breakfast in cafe on other side of the canal with Frank and Giuseppe after early train runs. They both noticed I seemed different, and couldn't stop smiling when I told them why. Giuseppe asked if it was love - I said I think it could be - whatever it is, it feels pretty big. Frank hugged me and said he was pleased for me. It's so strange, really. I bought some roses from the florist's stand on the corner and took them into the shop later on before it opened. Funny moment at first, as there was the 'old' Sandra behind the counter, jeans, no make-up. But when she looked at me, I saw the new one again. There was a funny sort of awkwardness for a few seconds, but it disappeared when I produced the roses. She was thrilled, and started crying - she said she thought I'd left because I regretted sleeping with her. When I told her she couldn't be more wrong, she just grabbed me, and soon enough, we were in the store room, acting out things that surrounded us on front covers.

Couldn't see each other tonight, as she'd been invited over to her parents for a meal, and was going to give them the good news about her job. Had to go to Dutch anyway, as last lesson before exam. Giuseppe came along as well. He kept laughing, saying the language sounds so stupid, which didn't endear him to Henk, who finished the lesson fifteen minutes early, and didn't even bother to wish us luck for the exam.

Could have gone out for a drink with Frank and Giuseppe afterwards, but didn't want to. Came back here, where Ben, of all people, was waiting outside, looking scruffier than ever. He didn't realize it was me at first for some reason - am sure he's on drugs. Then came the ritual handing over of the address cards and the cash for a job on Saturday, and he was off. Miserable sod.

Have spent the rest of the evening with half a bottle of wine and my thoughts. Is it just infatuation, novelty, sex? Is it love, is it a good idea? Keep thinking about how good it felt when Tina and I first started. Things obviously settle down, but I never thought she'd ditch me. At least Sandra and I won't be working together if it does go wrong. Wonder what Joop will do about replacing her. Anyway, whatever happens, it certainly feels good now.

Saturday 8<sup>th</sup> June

Up early for painting delivery. Picked it up no problem, but nobody was in at the address I'd got from Ben, so left it inside at the bottom of the stairwell. Hope it's all right. Lovely warm day, so everybody's been outside packing the cafe terraces - marvellous. Went to the station with Frank to see Giuseppe off tonight on the Holland-Italy-Express. They'd had some kind of argument in the night and must have woken me up at least twice. Couldn't quite hear what the problem was, as the bottom of the glass was too thick. Will ask Frank when the moment's right. Whatever it was, they seemed to have made it up, as they were both streaming with tears, Frank on the platform and Giuseppe out of the train window, as it pulled out of the station. Even I felt quite tearful with the emotion of it all. Poor old Frank. He wanted to be left alone afterwards with some Greta Garbo video, a bottle of wine and a box of tissues. Suited me fine, as I was meeting Sandra. Met her in Bar Scorpio, she was already there when I walked in. She had a tight black leather skirt on and had already had a couple of glasses of wine. She looked fantastic. I was really bowled over. Anyway, we had a couple of drinks and then went back to her flat, where she'd got the bed made up with black satin sheets borrowed from the Sexmarkt! Afterwards, she started asking me about the future - what I want to do, did I want to stay in Holland, how did I feel about her... Something a bit unsettling about being asked those types of questions. Made me realize that I've deliberately been putting off thinking about things like that - bit too much to cope with, somehow.

Anyway, Sandra had to leave to do the late-shift at the Sexmarkt, so I was left to self-scrutiny as I walked back to the flat. It's nearly half a year since I left now. I suppose it is time to have a good think. On the way back, I noticed all the Amsterdam 'types', people who came here years ago, in the Sixties probably, and have drifted through the years, getting by very easily with a bit of part-time work, a bit of sex, and usually a bit of dope. They're all a bit sad, somehow. Or maybe they only seem that way when you've been brought up with the old work-ethic stuff. Maybe they've got it exactly right.

Got back feeling loaded down by thoughts. Frank was the worse for wear for wine and Greta Garbo on the sofa, and we had one of those deep and meaningful chats that I used to have when I started at poly, about love and life. Don't think it helped anything. Turns out he and Giuseppe had been arguing about giving up their relationship, as long-distance affairs usually fail in the end. Giuseppe's idea, apparently, but in the end they decided to give it a bit longer. Frank reckons Giuseppe will dump him eventually, and kept bursting into uncontrollable sobbing. He asked me how I would feel if Sandra had said the same in a similar situation. The awful thing is that I wasn't sure. He asked me if she does for me what Maria, the Italian check-out girl, did for me... Can't take any more self-philosophy now, am going to bed. No wonder people like Descartes never got up.

Monday 10th June

Spent yesterday in a bit of a stupor, trying to digest and process everything. I seemed to be turning it all over in my mind all night long, so hardly had any proper sleep. Didn't get up till one o'clock as a result, Frank was even later than me, but in just as much of a state. Nothing like someone in a mess to cheer you up a bit, though. We had dinner in the snack-bar down the canal, which cheered me up even more, and spent the evening watching TV - a film about some bloke coming to terms with disability in the Australian outback. Not a good idea on reflection. Sandra was spending the day with her parents, so didn't have to see her. Feel a bit guilty that maybe she isn't the big love of all time, but maybe that doesn't matter.

Anyway, knew it wasn't going to be a good day today when I got up with toothache. Keep ignoring it, hoping it will go away. Had only just got back from train runs, when Ben turned up, spitting blood. Apparently, the painting was never found - somebody must have made off with it! I felt really bad, until he called me a stupid bastard, grabbed me by the shoulders and shook me, calling me everything from fat to prat. I was speechless. Totally shocked. He was deranged. I asked him what else I should have done, but he just kept ranting on. I kept saying I was sorry, but in the end he pinned me against the wall, his hand around my throat, and warned me: "I expect more commitment ven I give somebody a job for life".

Frank got back just as Ben was leaving. When I told him what had gone off, anger seized me. What a bastard. I keep going over it in my mind. Frank reckons I should talk to Joop about it and see if some of his 'boys' can't teach Ben a lesson. I wouldn't mind, but I want to do something myself. Must put my mind seriously to revenge. I've got to do something.

Went over to Sandra's tonight, still seething. Started to tell her about the whole episode, but all she could say was that I should've taken the painting back, and anyway, she wanted to see some Dutch chat show on TV. She stuck a glass of wine in my hand and patted me on the head, which really rubbed me up the wrong way, although I didn't say anything - which bugged me all the more. I tried canoodling a bit during the chat show, which, as far as I could make out, was an interview with some Dutch TV celebrity who's landed a part as a psychotic Nazi dwarf in a Hollywood film. Sandra was totally uninterested in my advances, and ended up pushing me aside, saying she was trying to watch the TV!! And this is our first week as an 'item'!! Couldn't be bothered making a scene, so came back after it'd finished. Being set about by an angry lunatic, and found less interesting than a Nazi dwarf is too much to cope with on the same day. Tooth ache not gone away yet either.

Wednesday 12<sup>th</sup> June

Still plagued by thoughts of revenge on Ben. Have had really vivid dreams the last two nights, involving me, Ben, dark streets and a couple of chain saws. Woke up early and went for a jog before train runs.

Went round to Joop's with Frank tonight. He seemed a bit subdued, and kept twiddling his moustache. I noticed he had really pronounced bags under his eyes as well. I asked him if he was okay - turns out he's due in court on Friday for all this tax business, and he's worried about what'll happen. Bertus, ever the stirrer, wasn't helping by talking about being banged up in prison, or 'bonked up', as he put it. Apparently, it's not uncommon in Holland to be sent to prison at weekends for financial offences. Joop wasn't going to let Bertus get him worked up, but I could see it was playing on his mind. Poor bloke. In a feeble attempt to cheer him up, we invited him round for a meal next week. Oddly enough, he seemed quite buoyed up by the idea.

Anyway, he got onto to Sandra leaving the Sexmarkt, and needing someone to take over. Then he drops the bombshell -

what about me? He'd asked Frank before he took Sandra on, so knew he wouldn't want the full-time commitment of it all. I was flabbergasted! And flattered, but not sure I could cope with running the place on my own. All three of them - Frank, Bertus and Joop - said I was being ridiculous - of course I could. And the more I thought about it, the more I liked the idea - turning sex industry professional. Sex retail manager. Definitely me. More money, more prestige, and a solid career focus for once. No more early morning train runs. Joop says he's got big plans for the shop, and is confident I'll be up to the job. In the end, I said I'd do it, which got the three of them cheering, and Joop got another round in. Joop said we'll sort out the details next week. Good stuff. Might tell Ben to stuff the painting jobs as well. Maybe I'll just smack him in the face the next time I see the git. Still can't get over him talking to me like he did, let alone shaking me. I'll have him somehow.

Bertus wanted to know what Sandra was like in bed, as he's always had his eye on her. Joop slapped him on the back, laughing, telling him to mind his own business. I wouldn't say anything, but he just came up with a few suggestions of his own. Hadn't noticed before that he's got a gold tooth to match his necklace. Frank screwed his face up, said it quite turned his stomach.

Anyway, quite a day, one way or another. Must do some revision now for Dutch exam tomorrow. Tooth ache seems to be subsiding.

Thursday 13th June

Exam seemed ok, apart from bloody tooth aching like Hell all the time.

Went out to Bar Scorpio with Sandra tonight. Told her about Joop suggesting I take over from her, which somehow seemed to peeve her a bit. She didn't think it was a good idea, and says I should try and get a more 'acceptable' and better-paid position somewhere else. I argued it'd be a good experience for me, but she said I should think about getting something else anyway, as we'd need more money to get a bigger flat together in the future!! I was gob-smacked. Bit presumptuous of her after one week. Anyway, came back here to my room, where she was all over me like a sex-beast. Actually, she was a bit too rough, and caught my throbbing cheek with her knee at one point. When I told her to be careful, she jumped up and got dressed in a flash - touchy or what! I couldn't be bothered trying to smooth things over, as my face was really throbbing, so she just stormed off. Is it me?

Saturday 15th June

Joop's been fined for non-payment of taxes. He wouldn't say how much, but is acting like somebody who's just come into money, not lost it. When I walked in this morning, he was as cheerful as I've ever seen him - no doubt the relief of not going to prison.

Things all right again with Sandra. She apologised for storming off, and said that we just keep misunderstanding each other. She made me promise to speak my mind if she was bugging me, and she'll do the same with me. That way, we'll be forced to talk things through and sort them out when they happen. That's the only way we'll build a solid future, she said. Whenever she says something like that, the hairs on the back of my neck stand up. Don't know why I react like that, as I like her, fancy her and we get on. I suppose I panic a bit that she's rushing me. Why do women always seem to think ahead, instead of enjoying the relationship as it develops? Anyway, I'm invited to her mother's birthday party next week. Apparently, her parents are dying to meet me.

Frank's laid-up in bed with one of those awful summer colds. He's dosing himself with lemon drinks, herbal candles and Italo-Summer-Hits. Wish Ben would come round so that Frank could breathe germs all over him. No, that's too mild. Must try and think of a suitable revenge. My blood still boils every time I think about the other day. If I knew where he lived, I might go and chuck a brick through his window in the dead of night.

Had a letter from Phil and Jan, thanking me for mine. They'll be coming over on 12th July for the weekend. Not sure how I feel about them coming, really. Still, they've always been all right with me.

Only notice tooth problem when I chew on the left now.

Monday 17th June

Frank seems to be having trouble shifting this cold. Giuseppe only rings him every four or five days now, so things must be cooling off. Poor Frank. Seems really down in the mouth. Decided to stay in tonight to keep him company, as he was totally fed-up - couldn't even be bothered to play his Italo-hits, and all his meditation candles have burned down. I spent the whole of last night at Sandra's. In between bouts of passion, she kept explaining different things about the Sexmarkt to me - how often I should ring the suppliers when I take over, the rates for back-shop filming sessions, etc. Fell asleep in the middle of the night while she was filling me in on how to price-tag dildos so that the label doesn't fall off. Her first words to me this morning were to remember to match the despatch notes against magazine deliveries from Hamburg, as Karl-Heinz is always trying it on. Was glad to get away in the end, but everything was okay again when we were together in the shop this afternoon.

Anyway, Frank's been saying he hasn't got anything to look forward to - the Giuseppe thing doesn't look promising, his life lacks direction, he has no ambitions. It's funny how you sometimes see your life for what it is, and it just doesn't seem to amount to much, even though you might not be desperately unhappy. I told him he'll feel better when he gets over this cold. He's decided he should do a course of some kind to get a job. What with Sandra moving on, me taking on the Sexmarkt (gulp!),Joop and Bertus with their fingers in every pie going, and even Ben the git raking it in with his dodgy doings, he says he just seems to be drifting along between the hostel train runs and the odd afternoon in the shop. I suggested we ask Joop about us both running it, but he said it'd be better all round for him to develop independently.

After a bit, he said he was tired of thinking about it all, and wanted to be left alone with the cucumber from the fridge!! I went to fetch it for him, my mind boggling, but he just cut it up with his Swiss Army knife and stuck the slices on his forehead to cool him down. Maybe I should think twice about working full-time in the Sexmarkt.

Wednesday 19th June

Frank feeling a lot better, which was just as well with Joop coming round tonight.

Things still going okay with Sandra. She went through some paperwork with me this afternoon downstairs. Stomach churns a bit when I think about having to shoulder all the responsibility myself from July. She's started writing down everything she does, so that I'll have checklists to refer to when she's gone. What a wonderful woman she is, really. When I mentioned I was worrying about it, she rubbed my face and told me I'd be fine. Fingers crossed.

Anyway, Joop over for meal tonight. Spaghetti, salad and red wine. Extra lean mince, as still trying to watch my weight. Had a good chat about things. Frank was talking about how he feels he should get some practical qualifications so that he stands a better chance of getting a full-time job. Joop reckons it's a good idea, and revealed his plans for the shop. The whole sex business is getting onto the Internet these days, apparently, which means that there's a massive world-wide market to be tapped into from the shop. Joop thinks this could mean big-time profits. He's going to get Bertus (who turns out to be well into the software malarkey) to get the shop set up on-line. He'll need someone then to create Sexmarkt web-pages, and to look after incoming orders, etc. If Frank can get up to speed with computing by August, the job's his!! Frank thinks it's a brilliant idea, and I could tell the prospect of having something to get his teeth into had bucked him up.

Friday 21st June

Longest day of the year.  Can't believe it was only six months ago that I was sitting in my room at Jan and Phil's in Walsall, pre-empting the tedious Christmas routine and dreading New Year.  Amazing.  Even Brussels seems years ago.

Ben came round yesterday.  Looked a bit smarter than of late.  I was terse with him.  I didn't say a word as he handed over the cash and the addresses.  Would love to know what's really going on behind all this, but knew it was pointless asking.  For some reason, I found myself asking him about Annika.  "De bitch is lying low for a vile.  Caught her having sex vid anudder guy, so had to teach her a lesson – get my meaning?" I certainly did.  Then he said: "Don't foul up dis time or else you really get it".  I waited till I heard him close the door downstairs, then rushed down to see where he was going.  I decided to follow him, keeping my distance all the time.  Followed him for about fifteen minutes to the Van Den Bonkengracht, where he got into a red jeep (of all things), registration number GI - 00 - T Z outside number 66, and drove off.  So at least I now know where he lives.  Now all I need is to perfect the revenge plan.  Did the delivery job this morning - no hitches this time.

Frank's already enrolled on a computer course, and seems much perkier than I've seen him in ages.

Out to the cinema with Sandra tonight.  She looked really gorgeous again, I could hardly concentrate on the film - a Dutch comedy about a sexually-repressed butcher who poisoned collaborators with dodgy sausages during the war - from what I could make out.  Sandra came back here with me after, and had a couple of glasses of wine.  Before she left, she gave me a really passionate kiss and her parents' address in Utrecht, where she's spending the 'birthday weekend' with her mother.  I'm invited over on Sunday afternoon.  After she'd gone, I noticed she'd written something on the back of the address - what I should take (flowers) and wear (my navy jumper, white shirt and jeans). Then she'd drawn a heart, around which were the words: "I think I'm falling in love with you, Gerard". Felt very flattered, but suddenly became acutely aware of my tooth aching.

Sunday 23rd June

Got train to Utrecht this afternoon, and walked to Sandra's parents' place. Lovely detached house - all dark wood and interesting paintings. Sandra rushed to the door to meet me, looked me up and down, saw that I was wearing what she'd said to, and then winked at me, saying well done! Felt really pathetic - this is not what JFK had in mind for me. Then she introduced me to her parents and relatives. Her mother was really chuffed with the flowers.

Everybody was sitting in a circle round the room, making stilted conversation about football, holiday plans and how nice the cake was. They were all grinning inanely. Sandra's mom and dad - Piet and Rina - look like they've been magically lifted off the front of a knitting pattern. After they'd asked me where I came from, and subsequently run down the Midlands for being industrial and dirty (cheek), her mother started on about how I should think about getting a more respectable job, as working in a sex-shop was no career for her future son-in-law!! She said Sandra had told her what a loving person I am, and how keen she is on me. Her dad then chipped in, saying they can't wait for the day when grand-children are on the cards, at which point he winked at me and scratched his crotch. My mind was reeling, the only words I'd spoken since I'd walked in were "near Birmingham", I was struggling not to choke on my first piece of cake in ages, and already my whole life was being mapped out by some smug git in a golf sweater and a Laura Ashley disciple. When I managed to swallow the cake, all I could do was smile back inanely, and say how nice it was. Sandra rescued me at that point, and gave me a tour of the house and garden (actually very nice, with lots of furniture from that Norwegian DIY place). She told me not to take too much notice of her parents, saying that they mean well. I'll bet they do.

When she showed me her room, she grabbed me and told me she loved me. Was I shocked? I said I was really flattered, then she wanted to know how I felt about her. I said I felt the same - (maybe I do, I don't know). It must have been the right answer anyway, as she hurled me onto the bed for a bout of passion. As we lay there afterwards, there was a knock on the door, after which her mother came in with two more cakes and coffee on a tray!!! I was mortified, and started mumbling something about not feeling well and having to lie down, but Sandra just said "dank je, moeder" and marched over to the cream slices, naked breasts a-bobbing. It's another world. But do I want to live there?

Tuesday 25th June

Think I'll be all right taking over next week. Sandra's been brilliant again, showing me what I need to look out for. There's a hell of a lot of stuff involved. Joop at least gets the books done, so I won't have to worry about the accounts side of it, which is just as well. The main things are:

1. Getting regular print-outs of all items sold to see what needs reordering;
2. Making sure all DVDs on loan are back by 7.00 pm each night;
3. Keeping appointments with reps to order latest mags, DVDs, toys, lingerie, sex CD Roms and computer games;
4. Emptying the video cabins regularly - money and waste-paper bins (gross!)
5. Making sure people aren't bunging stuff in their pockets;
6. Price-tagging all merchandise when it comes in;

7.      Making sure there are always DVDs, mags and
        computer games constantly in stock under the main
        categories: straight, gay, bi, oral, bums, boobs, SM,
        kinky, trans-sexual and inter-racial;
8.      Checking off all deliveries against the delivery notes;
9.      Making sure the alarms are switched on at closing time
        and that the panic button is always working;
10.     Providing 'actors' with regular refreshments during
        filming, and making sure that payment is received for
        use of premises.
11.     Keeping a good stock of plain brown paper bags.

At least I'm well used to handling customers and the till by
now. Quite looking forward to the authority of it all.

Sandra's getting a bit nervous about starting her new job, but
I'm sure she'll be all right. She took the afternoon off to get
some new clothes, and came back at 5.00 pm with a new pair
of jeans (!), a smartish black jacket and an appointment for me
at her dentist's for next week! I can't face that on top of
everything else, besides which the pain seems to have subsided,
so I got her to cancel it. Sent her into a huff, of course, but
she came round in the end.

Bertus nipped over tonight with an escort assignment - first
in ages - for Saturday. Sandra was here, and seemed cool with
him, I thought. Bertus was quite the opposite with her,
however, and kept flashing his gold tooth again. Funny how I
never noticed it before.

Thursday 27th June

Still can't think of a good way to get my own back on Ben.
Frank thinks I'm becoming obsessed. Couldn't sleep last night
thinking about it all again, so decided to get up and jog over to
where he lives. Picked up a bit of a brick on the way, thinking
I might shove it through his windscreen. Got there at about
3.00 a.m., and kept jogging up and down the street. Sure
enough, the jeep was there, and felt confident I'd get away with

it. Just as I was about to chuck it and run, a police car came round the corner, so legged it back to flat. Crept back in, to find Frank in an orange thong brandishing a bottle of ketchup over my head, shouting "Halt!", thinking I was a burglar. He almost seemed disappointed when he realized it was me, but shocked to see me with a brick in my hand. I said I'd taken it in case anyone attacked me while I was out for a run. Don't think he believed me.

Sandra in a bit of a funny mood tonight. Turns out she doesn't like Bertus, so she doesn't like me working for him, especially escorting. I told her sex didn't come into it, but she just said she didn't like the whole thing and wanted me to stop. I said it was a pleasant and easy way to earn good money, and was none of her business anyway. At first I thought she was about to do her usual huff-and-up routine, but instead she suggested dropping the subject and going to bed. Afterwards, she said "You're so masterful, Gerard."

Saturday 29th June

Beautiful summer's day again. In and out of clothes shops all afternoon with Sandra, until I couldn't take it anymore. Sat out on a terrace on the Leidesplein drinking beer after that. Felt very relaxed and tranquil somehow, both sitting there in the sunlight, watching tourists strolling round, admiring the city. Felt overwhelmingly positive - sunshine, a 'new' job on Monday, a girlfriend by my side, relaxing in Amsterdam, a great flat that I share with a great mate. Marvellous. Sandra was equally chirpy, quite excited now about starting her new job. Walked back to the flat for a glass of wine with Frank, who was setting up a computer he'd brought over from Bertus's ("Knocked off de back of a truck") to help him with his course. He's well into it all now, and so even he was chirpier than of late, which is amazing really, as Giuseppe hasn't rung for days. He kept going on about uploading, mega RAM and drives, and using all the computer lingo everybody seems to know these days.

The only thing that spoiled it all was Ben turning up with another delivery job for tomorrow - a Sunday of all days. Frank and Sandra just ignored him. He was wearing his black leather jacket, even on a day like this! He looked at us all as though we were a bunch of divvies, and had a silly smirk on his face. I wanted to land him one more than ever, but just took the addresses and money off him without saying anything. He then picked up a glass, helped himself to wine, swigged it back, then smashed the glass on the floor. Bits of glass went everywhere. We were all too shocked to speak. He then turned round and said "I don't vant to cramp your style, folks", laughed and walked out.

Sandra cleaned up the mess, Frank said we really ought to speak to Joop, as it's getting out of hand now. I'm not sure. I don't like it, but don't want it escalating. All this excitement, and now I've got to get ready for my escort assignment - am supposed to be meeting a Russian called Viktor at the Marriott at eight. And to think Cilla Black's Blind Date used to be the highlight of my Saturday nights.

Sunday 30th June

What a night last night! Viktor, a Russian doll manufacturer, turned out to be the Soviet equivalent of Bertus, complete with gold medallion, bracelets and perm. Had a brilliant meal in hotel, although a little more fat and carbs than I would have liked, but extremely delicious.

Very easy company, as he chatted ten to the dozen, pausing only occasionally to ask me for a grammatical explanation or some obscure carpentry term - palmed him off more than once just to shut him up. "How are you calling the measure of wood curving the shape of a lath?" After I was told "Think, think, you must know!!" for the fourth time, I told him it was a 'lummock'. By the time I was eating my fruit salad, he was talking about lummocks, the difficulty of finding good quality spiggets and the importance of fuff-plopping.

After dinner, he wanted a tour of the Red Light Area, so no

problem there. City was throbbing with summer tourists, so we could hardly move down some streets. His eyes kept popping out as we walked past brothels with women in the windows. He obviously thought I was a total expert, as he kept asking me "This one a good one, no?" In the end, he told me to wait, and decided to go in to have his wicked way with one of the prostitutes. Not the best of places to have to wait for someone, but he was back out five minutes later, tucking his shirt in and smiling ear to ear.

Then he wanted a massage, and wanted me to have one as well. Never had one before, so quite happy to give it a go. Went into the parlour opposite the flat. Marvellous stuff. Must do it again. Within minutes, we were stripped off lying on two slabs, our backs and bums being pummelled in semi-painful pleasure. The only thing to offset it all was Viktor going on about phrasal verbs and possible sales outlets in England for Russian dolls.

Got up late this morning, as Joop's already got someone else to help Frank out with the train runs - the son of one of his mates, a lad called Hans. Did the painting delivery this afternoon - no hitches, but couldn't stop thinking of Ben all the while I was out. I need to think of a good revenge strategy as resentment, rage and indignation keep clouding my mind.

Over at Sandra's tonight. She spent an hour ironing her clothes for the coming week, while I watched a quiz show on TV - some fat bloke bet he could pull a lorry by his teeth, which came flying out just after he'd started. Anyway, when I left she gave me a massive hug and wished me luck. I did the same. Then she said how lucky she was to have me, and how wonderful our future together will be. I smiled and said I'd see her tomorrow.

Well, should get to bed now. Big day tomorrow.

Tuesday 2nd July

Well, so far so good. Opened up yesterday at 1.00 pm. Stood in the shop and looked around. Felt great. A year ago, there I was looking forward to two weeks in Skegness and some temporary relief from the tedium of teaching the West Midlands' most disinclined. One year later, here I am, managing a sex shop in Europe's sex capital, and loving every minute of it. I suddenly realized how I don't count the days any more - I was always counting the days and weeks to the next holiday, putting my life on hold, somehow. No looking back now.

Yesterday was quite busy, like most Mondays. Frank came on in the evening, tonight as well. Joop's sorting out somebody to work alternate afternoons/evenings with Frank, but might take a while yet. Today was less busy, which gave me the chance to get on with pricing some inter-active CD Roms that arrived from Copenhagen this morning. Good job Sandra told me about checking the delivery notes, as there were ten copies of Technodiks Skanderaktiv missing. Rang Steen (the Danish supplier) straight away - blamed the computer, of course.

Not finished till 10.00 each night, but time seems to fly by. And only have to walk upstairs and I'm home - can't be bad! Sandra just rang - she's getting on fine as well. Everybody very friendly and work very interesting. The firm exports fibre-optic cables, and Sandra processes incoming orders. Would bore me stiff, but there you go. Said I'd call in tomorrow night.

Thursday 4th July

Went round to Sandra's last night. Candle-lit dinner waiting for me when I got there. Barry White on the radio. Table beautifully laid, candles. Thought she'd given me a dirty serviette at first, and was about to throw it away, when she screamed at me, and told me to read it. She'd written on it in black felt tip. It said: "Gerard, you're such a wonderful boyfriend, and we're going to be so happy together!" I felt a bit embarrassed, quite honestly, but she just beamed at me, giggled, and brought the soup in. Never really know how to respond to gushing sentiment - not that it's figured largely in my life.

After we'd finished, she brought the coffee in on a tray, with a card for me, on which she'd written: "When you've found the right person, you want to keep him - Gerard, let's get engaged!" Total internal turmoil, complete disbelief, but ended up saying yes before disappearing into the loo to regain mental composure.

When I came back out, she asked me if I really thought it was a good idea. I'd managed to think up a response in the loo, so said that I did, but just that it seemed to be going really fast - what's the rush? She said she's tired of being messed about by blokes, and has decided that things will work with me, so why not give a little extra commitment? I said I'd also been messed about, and needed time to consider things carefully before deciding - I said it was only out of concern for her that I wanted to make sure we'd be doing the right thing. Fortunately, she understood, and so we've said we'll see how things look in six months. Been chewing the whole thing over all day, can't really fathom why I'm so hesitant. Frank says it's natural and is so glad to be gay.

Saturday 6th July

Couldn't sleep after all on Thursday night, still mulling it all over, so ended up going for a jog, and drawn once again to the Van Den Bonkengracht. Sure enough, Ben's jeep parked outside number 66. Felt really aggressive and vengeful again, so was about to scratch my key over the bonnet, when another bloody police car comes round the corner! This time it pulled up alongside me. Thought I was on the verge of a heart attack. A typical smarmy type with a moustache leaned out of the window and asked me what I was doing at that time of night. I said I was jogging, which he just laughed at. He wanted my details, and ended up taking me back to the flat in his car so I could prove I had residency, etc. While I was sitting in the back, he suddenly asked me what I charge for 'hand help', as he called it! The nerve! A police constable! Think he could tell I was shocked, as he didn't say another word till we pulled up outside the Sexmarkt, and he followed me in.

Frank wondered what on earth was going on, and came out of his bedroom rubbing his eyes and wearing pink pyjamas. As if the whole thing wasn't bad enough. The policeman winked at me, assuming we were together, looked at my passport and permit, then wished us both good night, winking again. Frank told him he was welcome to stay for a drink, but the policeman just said "Anudder time, eh?" and walked out. This place really takes the biscuit at times. You'd think they'd be out there trying to prevent crime rather than trying it on with innocent passers-by.

Anyway, some good news. Had result of Dutch exam - passed with top marks! Another thing to add to my CV. Also had card from Sandra, saying "Love is taking time and being understanding." Bit daft, since I was seeing her tonight anyway. Can do without the sentimentality of it all, but suppose she means well. Went out for a pizza with her, as Frank said he'd do night shift in Sexmarkt. She started asking me about my past, and I realized that she's hardly ever asked me anything significant about myself before - strange really, given that she wants to get engaged. Avoided the Tina story, and got on to talking about Phil and Jan coming over next weekend. She says she's looking forward to meeting them.

Sunday 7<sup>th</sup> July

Sunday shift at Sexmarkt only 6.00 - 10.00 pm, so went over to Joop's afterwards. Blinding night - first time we've had a 'lad's night out' in ages - Frank, me and Bertus all hogging the prime seats at the bar, Joop serving and entertaining as usual. Quite a lot in, including a couple of American women that we got chatting to. Bertus was straight in there, talking about his friends in Texas, New York, Chicago, etc, and asking them what they liked about Holland. They said they liked the openness and tolerance, which is what everybody says, and is

Bertus' cue to sound them out on their views on sexual tolerance. Thirty minutes and half a bottle of rum later, the spare room is occupied and the video's running! Don't know how he does it - he's just total brazen confidence. Joop says Bertus works on a statistical basis - if you try it on often enough, you'll always get a degree of success. Amazing. And then he's back down an hour later offering me a video for fifty guilders – unbelievable. In the end, he got two-hundred for it from some fat German bloke. Really wonder what sort of company I've got in with at times. Anyway, didn't have to pay for a single drink all night. Must open a bank account, as Joop wants to set up direct transfer every month now I'm full time and on books, etc. Money also building up under mattress, which is a bit daft.

Walked back here with Frank. Lovely balmy evening. Just as Frank was sticking the key in the door, a police car slowed down, with 'Officer Hand Help' from Thursday night at the wheel. "Efreeting okay boys?" he shouted up. Frank waved back like a teenage girl, but I told him to get inside. "Oh, Gerard, you're so masterful," Frank said. Am sure someone else said that to me recently.

Tuesday 9th July

Opened bank account yesterday morning with the BUMRO Bank. Silly name for a bank, really, but you see the sign everywhere. Thought they were sex-shops at first, but then most Dutch words sound a bit dodgy. The woman who took my details was called Mrs Van Der Poop. Anyway, that's a good thing sorted now, so have cash-point card and cheques, or will have when they come through. Very handy.

Ben round last night with another job. He said he thought he'd seen me the other night on the Van Den Bonkengracht - I made out I didn't even know where it was, which he seemed to believe. Will have to be very careful when I do finally work out my revenge. Anyway, found myself asking him again what the game is exactly with these deliveries. He just laughed, ran his hand through his hair, and said it was none of my business! Then he helped himself to a handful of peanuts out of the bowl on the table, farted, wiped his greasy hand on the wall, leaving smears all over it, then left without saying good-bye. This man's nerve knows no bounds.

Bit of an incident in the Sexmarkt this afternoon. A bloke got stuck in one of the video cabins when the knob on the bolt snapped off, so he couldn't let himself out. He started shouting and moaning, which I ignored at first, as some people do tend to get a bit over-excited, but then he started screaming, so I knew something was up. I eventually managed to force it open with a screwdriver. When the bloke came out, he was all sweaty and red-faced - very unpleasant. Then he shoved 25 guilders into my hand, and asked if I could lock him in again next time – I tell you....

Joop just came round - he's got someone to help me out part-time - her name's Mariska, she's twenty-six and single, apparently. Felt quite excited when Joop told me. He said she's used to working in shops, so should be a big help, which is quite good, as she can relieve me a bit this weekend with Jan and Phil coming over. Wonder what she'll really be like? Sandra rang after Joop had gone, but I didn't mention anything to her. She didn't have much to say, apart from something about a new supermarket opening up round the corner from her. Whatever next, I thought.

Frank is turning into one of those computer boffins. He's already not washed his hair for over a week. He seems to be on it night and day, only stopping to attend his course. Still, as long as he's happy. He's not heard from Giuseppe for a good while now. Suppose it's therapy for him.

Thursday 11th July

Absolutely boiling at the moment. Must get some more comfortable summer clothes. Don't really like wearing T-shirts, as they tend to accentuate my stomach. Must try and get back into a proper jogging routine and lose some belly.

Everywhere I look at the moment, I seem to see finely sculpted muscular bodies, tanned and scantily clad. A bloke came into the Sexmarkt yesterday afternoon, looking like someone off Gladiators. For a moment or two, I struggled with the desire to maim him for life with the pricing-gun.

Met the mysterious Mariska. Not quite how I'd imagined her. Apparently, she narrowly missed out representing Holland in the shot-put at the last Olympics, due to an elbow injury. She told me this within the first two minutes of meeting her, which struck me as a bit odd, and I thought for a second she was going to shed a tear at the reminiscence, but then she just scratched her backside and asked me what needed doing. Quite like the idea of being the top dog. She didn't bat an eyelid when I asked her to go down to the wholesalers for a box of crotchless knickers, which have been going like hot-cakes in this weather. The shot-putting experience showed itself to full effect later on when a bloke started making a nuisance of himself in the Kinky Corner - she sent him packing no problem. Think we'll get on fine.

Frank still obsessed by the computer. Am amazed how he's so absorbed by it. All I can hear now is him pressing the keys, and then every so often he lets forth a stream of expletives in German when he gets stuck.

Spent last night at Sandra's. She wanted to cook a meal on Saturday night for all of us, but I said we might as well just eat in a cafe and save the hassle. She got all funny about it, saying she thought it would be a nice idea. Had to do the full pampering bit then to win her back over. All you need after a hard day flogging porn. Jan and Phil just rang to say what time they'll be arriving off the boat train from the Hook of Holland. Knew already, of course, because of the train runs. Can't believe they'll be here this time tomorrow night. Tooth been hurting off and on again today.

Friday 12th July

Am writing this on the sofa, where I'll be sleeping for the next two nights, as have given Jan and Phil my room. Funny seeing them getting off the train at the station. Always thought they were so sorted somehow, they always seemed to know better, know what to do, how to be. But there they were suddenly, this time looking like two wet fish out of water. Blimey, and I thought my fashion sense needed improving!! Jan was wearing a cardigan under a light-weight anorak, with brown sandals. She's had one of those awful home perms which does absolutely nothing for her. Phil waddled down the platform in his tweed jacket with elbow patches, lifting his greasy hair out of eyes. I went to put my arms round them but they just raised their hands and shook mine as though it was covered in some sort of questionable lubricant. Walked back to the flat, which neither of them passed any comment on. Jan just said "Mm, so this is what you've come to, living over a sex-shop." She totally disapproves of the whole sex thing.

Took them both down into the shop to meet Frank before we went to the snack-bar. For somebody who disapproves of it all, Jan managed to eyeball every magazine and item as though she was on the Generation Game conveyor belt, whereas Phil just looked hot and bothered. When I introduced them to Frank, anyone would have thought he was Satan himself, judging by Jan's expression, while Phil just said "How d'you do", keeping his hands firmly clasped together over his buttocks. Felt awful. I told them Frank was a wonderful person and friend, and that I hoped they'd be polite towards him as it's his flat as well. Phil nodded, but Jan just said "I don't know how you can live in the same place as a queer, it's not natural, I hope he's never slept in the bed we'll be sleeping in." I ignored it, not wanting to create a scene on their first night, but it really bugged me.

And when we got to the snack-bar, they sized the place up like a couple of hygiene inspectors, before settling for hamburger and chips twice. All Jan could say afterwards was "They're not like *our* chips, are they?" After that and a few hundred anecdotes about the baby, Jan went to bed. Phil apologized on her behalf, and said he was quite envious of me, which amazed me, as he normally only ever has suggestions on where I'm going wrong. Then he got all red-faced again, and asked if he could nip down to the shop, which staggered me. Apparently, "things not going so well since the baby was born," was all he would divulge, and then asked what coins he needed for the video cabin - and not to mention anything to Jan! At least he had the decency to apologise to Frank for Jan's behaviour when we went down. I had a chat with Frank while Phil was in the cabin. Frank said he couldn't imagine that I'd ever had anything in common with them. Funny really. After about ten minutes, Phil emerged, redder than ever, and rushed off upstairs. All in all, not the best evening I've ever had. Hope the weekend is an improvement.

Saturday 13th July

Thank God they'll have gone this time tomorrow night. Can't be bothered to write any more at the moment.

Sunday 14th July

Back in my own bed, peace at last! What a nightmare. How did I manage to live with them for three years? I've never been so irritated in all my life. First of all, they drove me mad harping on constantly about money. Don't know whether it's because Phil's a maths teacher, but every single thing they bought, from a postcard, to a sandwich, to the entrance fee at the Van Gogh Museum was subject to a five-minute financial discussion and analysis of whether it was really value for money.

When we finally got it sorted, Jan trotted out her usual "Well, it's not like that in England, is it?" Having a coffee on the Leidseplein: "They're not like *our* espressos, are they?" In the van Gogh Museum: "He never did the nice landscapes like you see in *our* museums, did he? Never seen the appeal of sunflowers anyway." Walking down the Prinsengracht: "They're not like the canals round by *us*, are they?" Was ready to ram a marrow down her neck by the time I went to bed.

As if all that wasn't bad enough, she kept on about how disgusting it was living somewhere surrounded by sex and sleaze - Phil never said a word, he obviously just wanted to keep the peace. After a bit, I couldn't be bothered arguing. In fact, I started laying it on thick, going into detail about some of my escort antics and tales from the Sexmarkt. Her face was a picture. Phil said again how jealous he was of me when Jan went to the toilet at one point - "They're not like *our* toilets, are they?"

When we met up with Sandra at the cafe, the atmosphere seemed to improve, as the conversation turned to the baby yet again. Sandra was well interested in all the domestic anecdotes, and Phil and I left them to it for a bit as we stood at the bar. Felt quite sorry for him, he basically means well. Saw myself in him in a way, same old boring job teaching the disaffected and dysfunctional, no prospects of a change... And he's got the added handicap of Jan. He said things just seemed to go downhill after I left (which I thought was nice of him to say). Having the baby didn't seem to improve things between them, and neither has coming away, which is what he was hoping. "Neither of us have ever been to Europe before," he said, and once more I was amazed at how superior I felt to him, struggling with his coins all day, looking left and right fifty times before he crossed over, looking blank when waiters spoke to him in Dutch. And less than a year ago, he was so sorted in my eyes - he was the one with a wife, he had a mortgage, he was second in maths, "This is what you want to do...". Funny how things get knocked upside down.

When we rejoined them, Jan was filling Sandra in on how service has improved at The Blinking Weasel in Walsall since it's been under new management, and how they even do onion rings now as a starter. Almost more worryingly, Sandra seemed genuinely interested. After eating, we strolled back to the flat, Sandra and Jan walking ahead of Phil and me. They got to the flat ahead of us, and as we approached them, I could see Jan was agitated again - some bloke had apparently come up to her and asked how much she wanted for a 'B-job', as she called it. Phil and I both burst out laughing, which did nothing to help things.

Saw them off this morning at the station. Phil shook my hand firmly on the platform, and whispered he was really sorry about the way Jan had behaved at times, but that it'd been great to see me, and see me doing so well at that. Felt quite touched, as he's never been much of a one for a compliment or expressing his feelings.

Spent the rest of the day pottering about. Frank's been working on a spreadsheet project all day, so dare say he needed a laugh.

Tuesday 16th July

Totally knackering day yesterday, felt exhausted after the weekend. Not too busy in Sexmarkt, fortunately, so was able to get on with things fairly quietly.

Tooth started hurting again, so finally decided to do something about it, as it's obviously not going to go away on its own. Rang dentist this morning and have made an appointment for Thursday morning. Dreading it. Sandra rang to see if I wanted to go round tonight but I said I was too exhausted. Frank's been brilliant, cooking dinner and generally being a soothing influence. On his way back from his computer course this afternoon, he bumped into that policeman again. His name is Arnold, apparently, and he's asked Frank out to a club! Frank took his number and said he'd confirm it with him.

Thursday 18th July

Just got back from dentist's. Thank God it's all over. Have finally been and got the whole business out of the way. Hardly slept a wink last night, and when I did drop off, I kept seeing Laurence Olivier bending over me in that awful scene of dental torture from The Marathon Man. Anyway, totally restless night, and couldn't even manage my Brekko-Bites this morning. Stomach like a knot. Walked over to the surgery, just round the corner from where Ben lives, which was an alarming coincidence, and got there far too early.

Anybody would've thought I'd just been conscripted, judging by the receptionist's gruff interrogation - what my mother's middle name was, what my line of work was (retail manager, I said) what I'm allergic to, how often I brush, what I do in my spare time, what childhood illnesses I've had, etc - thought she was about to stick her hand down my trousers and ask me to cough at one point. When she'd done, I had to leaf through endless copies of CIAO BELLO! and SUNSHINE WEEK, reading articles such as "genital warts - the tell-tale signs" and "living with a small penis". God knows who writes these things, or buys these magazines for that matter. Fascinating article on stomach firming, though. Must get to grips with diet and exercise again.

Anyway, after what seemed an eternity of angst and self-scrutiny, not to mention the full-blown face-ache, I was called through. The dental assistant looked like somebody off Baywatch with a white coat on, the dentist looked alarmingly like Laurence Olivier. Had to answer all sorts of stupid questions with a prong in my mouth, which did nothing to enhance my self-image in front of Pamela Van Anderson. Also conscious of having bad breath because of having no breakfast, but must be a run-of-the-mill hazard for dentists. How anyone can want to make a living from poking around in people's mouths is beyond me.

After a bit of prodding around accompanied by the "2, 3, 4, left" dental-speak, the lecture I'd anticipated about neglect followed. He'd got a strange Dutch accent - think it was probably quite posh - so could only understand the gist, which was maybe just as well. Not really in a position to argue either, so just kept nodding with that caliper type thing still wedging my jaws open. Then he said the tooth would have to come out, and set about extracting it - without an injection!! Had to almost beg him for one, otherwise he'd have taken it out just like that! He kept on about the health benefits of a natural extraction - what a nutter.

The actual extraction wasn't half as bad as I'd thought. Was also distracted by the dental assistant whose cleavage seemed fixed in view above my head, obscured only occasionally by the hand-held implements she kept on passing over me to the dentist. Felt jubilant when it was all over. The assistant smiled at me as I left, revealing a set of perfect white teeth, of course. I smiled back, and felt saliva dribble onto my neck - but at least I could smile. Rushed out after that, and had to pay 150 guilders! Anyway, at least it's not hanging over me any more.

11.30 p.m.

Normal sort of day after dentist. Mariska helping out in Sexmarkt again today. Thought she was a bit whiffy, until I realized I'd forgotten to empty bins in video cabins. Not one of the nicest aspects of working in the sex-retail business, but there you go.

Sandra round tonight. Mentioned the article I'd been reading at the dentist's about stomach firming. Turns out she'd read it as she has SUNSHINE WEEK every week. She then spent the rest of the evening drawing up a day-by-day health plan for me, writing down what and when I should eat, go for a jog, etc, which got right up my nose. She annoyed me even more when she said there was an article about 'knobs' (her words) in last week's that I might be interested in. She annoyed Frank as well by telling him to shush while he was on the phone trying to make himself understood with one of Giuseppe's flat-mates in Milan. That's the third time Giuseppe hasn't returned his call - doesn't sound good.

Saturday 20th July

Went to The Hague with Sandra on the train this afternoon. Invited Frank as well, but he was too busy messing with his floppy yet again - talk about an obsession. Was quite looking forward to going as never been before. Seems to me that everywhere in Holland looks exactly the same, though - little-bricked houses, fancy gables, bit of a canal knocking about somewhere, and everywhere dead flat in between. Sandra whizzed me round the historic bits, including parliament (quite impressive) and then on to Madurodam, where they've reconstructed Holland in miniature - as though they needed to! Loads of people there, but not really my cup of tea. At some points you couldn't move for Dutch brats running round, laughing raucously and generally being obnoxious. Sandra told me it's one of her favourite places in Holland.

Then it was off to the shopping centre. Sandra had decided it was time for me to extend my wardrobe. Saw some nice corduroy jackets, which she just scoffed at. After about two hours of trying things on and off, I ended up buying a bright red jacket and four Jean Picardet short-sleeved shirts in bright green, blue, yellow and mauve. Not sure it's me, but Sandra assured me it was.

Got back to do busy Saturday night shift. Frank still hard at it on the PC. Databases at the moment. Managed to get him off it long enough to have a chat. I told him we should see about going to a German play again soon - feel I've been letting things slip a bit culturally of late, and would also be good for my German. Only use it in the Sexmarkt with German tourists these days, to say where the Big and Buxom Section is, and say "Ja, das Toilettenpapier ist in der Kabine". He seemed quite keen. Am sure he's just throwing himself into the computer game to distract himself from Giuseppe.

Must get to bed now, really busy tonight, what with the hot weather bringing out the salacious side in people, and the summer tourists. One American bloke with a moustache and tight T-shirt winked at me and asked me to let him know if I needed a hand. Frank suddenly materialised at that point, saying assistance would be most welcome. Another world.

Monday 22nd July

What a day, yesterday. Frank decided to try Giuseppe yet again, this time he was there though. And sure enough, the inevitable news followed - he's going out with some bloke he met at a bus-stop (why have I never met anybody at a bus-stop? - must have spent at least five weeks of my life waiting on the Birmingham Road for the X 51 over the years), and is moving in with him. Frank was totally distraught when he came off - couldn't get back to his spreadsheets even. He howled and blubbed until his eyes were red-raw, and said that this is how it'd be for the rest of his life - "a string of relationships that buzz for the first five minutes and then dissolve". I told him that he should write it all down, get it off his chest but he just flung his head into the cushion and shouted "Gerard, oh why, it's all so futile!" This went on for about two hours. Am sure he just enjoys going through the full German forlorn angst routine. Kept throwing his hands up in the air between bouts of sobbing and shouting "Ach, warum, warum?" And then suddenly he stopped quite abruptly, in a way that shocked me - there was an air of manic calm about him. He looked at me intensely and said: "But life must go on, Gerard, and I must draw on inner strength". He got up and walked into the kitchen, so I followed him, wondering what on earth he was about to do - turns out he was after his address book, which he quickly leafed through for a phone number - and then rang 'officer' Arnold to arrange a date! Half an hour later he was telling me things were looking up, and was back on his databases, meditation candle lit.

Went over to Sandra's tonight. Boring evening watching TV with her. When she's watching TV, there's really no distracting her. Came out of her kitchen at one point with a choc-ice, and she leaned over and slapped my hand! All she said was "Don't forget your health plan!" and carried on viewing. I was so infuriated. And when the film had finished (boring Belgian drama set in a launderette near docks in Antwerp), she thought she'd make use of my body. I told her that she can't just expect to use me at her convenience - I'm not just a human sex-machine. Then she patted me on the head and said she needed an early night anyway! Couldn't be bothered having an argument, so decided just to go. As I left, she said: "That yellow shirt really suits you, Gerard". When I got outside, a bird crapped on my shoulder. Some nights are just a total wash-out.

Wednesday 24th July

Had a letter in the post today from Phil, thanking me for my kindness and understanding, and apologizing for Jan's behaviour again. Apparently he'd told Jan he thought they should think about divorce, but she wouldn't hear of it, so he's agreed to try and give things a go, as they say. Ordinary sort of day otherwise. Sandra round tonight to invite me to her brother's birthday cake and coffee evening. I said what a fantastic social highpoint it would be for me. Sandra said she was looking forward to it as well, and asked me to wear my blue shirt. Sometimes I feel we're on different planets.

Frank seems to be bearing up incredibly well after the Giuseppe split. Officer Arnold was round earlier to pick him up before they went out to a club. Frank was still getting ready (i.e. plastering himself with Celsius 100 and squeezing the blackheads on his nose) when Arnold arrived. He's not the world's greatest conversationalist for a gay policeman. All he said was "Been out for any more midnight jogs lately?" and then laughed uncontrollably for about three minutes, as though he'd just come out with the joke awarded 1995 best witticism, before becoming totally serious again and leering intensely at me until I gave my response: "No". This prompted further hysterics on his part. Thank God Frank emerged at that point, sparing me any further hilarity. Maybe it was just first date nerves, I don't know. Frank had jelled his hair up so that it was spiky, and he smelled like somebody who'd come a cropper in a perfume factory. His nose was all red and blotchy. He greeted Arnold by saying "Hallo sweetie" in German, which prompted even more hysterics. I was glad when they'd both gone out. Still, nice to see Frank away from the computer screen.

Thursday 25th July

Frank got back at 2.30. He seems well taken with Arnold, "who's really nice when you get to know him". Am always suspicious of people that that remark is applied to. Plus he's got a funny sort of rat face, not helped by his moustache which looks like an elaborate set of whiskers. But maybe I'm not giving him a chance. And Frank wouldn't be bothered by or probably even notice his lack of humour either, which could well be a blessing. Sometimes I feel having a British sense of humour is a curse, as it sets us apart from those that don't share it, and can seem like an unbridgeable divide, which makes me feel a bit lonely at times. Maybe that's more of a barrier than the language one.

Sandra rang tonight and insisted on coming round. Was eating a Mars bar when she walked in, which sparked off a massive row about self-neglect and a lack of discipline. Tried to explain that I needed a bit of comfort after the day I'd had, but might as well have talked to the wall. Didn't care either, as she looked particularly raunchy this evening, and was very physical. Afterwards she started harping on about not seeing enough of each other, so had to palm her off with vague suggestions. Blimey, is it worth it? Glad when she went, which sounds awful. Maybe I just need my own space.

Joop just rang. Wants us to meet up to talk about Prague next month! Brilliant.

Friday 26th July

Went to Utrecht on train with Sandra, to 'celebrate' her brother's birthday. What a pointless evening. Edwin, her brother, is one of these students who intends to be earning millions as soon as he's got his degree in business administration. He'll probably end up in tele-sales, though, like everybody else seems to. When we got there, everybody was sitting in a circle round the room, just like at her mother's birthday party, wolfing cake down and making the same inane conversation. I say conversation, it was more one-way than that. I listened to one of his neighbours telling me about the best sea-food restaurants in Cyprus, including details on prices and speed of service; Sandra's mother told me everything I didn't want to know about her mother-in-law's incontinence; and Sandra's brother launched into a tirade about how awful it must be living in England, how we've got no sense of style, awful houses, a disgusting class system, filthy cities, lousy pubs, no terraces,.... He only stopped when his mobile phone went off, heralding his retreat into the kitchen. What a git. Nothing worse than having a foreigner criticise your country. Height of rudeness.

Sandra was well away, absorbed by family anecdotes, in between ferrying nibbles around. She scrutinised every crisp I ate, until she decided I'd had enough, when she actually grabbed a salt-stick from my mouth. Coming back on the train, she said what a wonderful evening it'd been. I couldn't bring myself to respond. Then she said how nice I looked in my blue shirt. When she noticed I seemed quiet, I just said I was feeling tired. Was glad when we arrived back at the Central Station and she got her tram. Walked back to flat wondering what on earth I'm doing with her. Apart from the physical side, am beginning to think it's fairly pointless.

Sunday 28th July

Busy weekend in Sexmarkt. Mariska extremely helpful. She just gets on with it all and never seems to waste a minute, from making drinks, cleaning out the cabins, pricing new stock, serving, etc. Bit on the quiet side, though. Asked her what she does in her spare time. All she could say was, "Oh, you know, this and that. Quite like the tele, really".

Anyway, went round to Joop's last night with Frank. Really good night, as haven't seen him for ages. Bertus was there of course. He apologised for the lack of escort work of late, but I said that I can't manage too many evenings anyway, with working full-time in the Sexmarkt now. Joop wanted to know all about Frank's course, as he was keen to go on-line over the next few weeks if possible. I've got to give it to Joop, he really does show an interest in us. Reckon I'll look back on my life one day and see him as one of the people who moulded me. If I ever got on This is Your Life, he'd be the person who comes on at the end.

A dodgy-looking bloke in a dirty leather jacket turned up half way through the evening. Joop just looked at him and gesticulated "round the back". He obviously understood, and was followed instantly by Bertus. Frank had never clapped eyes on the bloke before either. As far as I could see through the bar, there was a bit of a kerfuffle, with Joop roughing the bloke up, after which the bloke handed something over to him. Very odd. The bloke went out the back way, and Joop and Bertus came back in, looking quite serious for once. Frank asked if everything was ok. Joop said "No problem", and changed the subject. Very odd.

Anyway, good news about Prague. He needs our help with some 'merchandise', as he called it. Some porno supplier he's got in touch with has loads of stuff for him to bring back. It'll be a bit of a whistle-stop tour, apparently. We'll drive over next week, load up with 'the merchandise', then drive back the next day. Frank and I can share the driving with him, but can't really see that he needs us to go with him. But then that's Joop - what a decent bloke.

Frank out with Arnold tonight. They arranged to meet in town, so I was spared having to interact with him. Not seen Sandra all weekend. Phone going like mad tonight, but didn't answer it, as was convinced it'd be her. I just sat there and ate two Mars bars in defiance as the phone rang out. Can't face her at the moment, not sure I'm being fair. The doorbell went at 10.30 tonight. Looked out of window, expecting to see her, but it was Ben. What a time to call round. He was his usual self. He'd got another painting job for me, and handed over the addresses, plus cash. As he helped himself to some peanuts from the dish on the table, he noticed my angel of hope statue and asked if it was valuable. As he walked over to pick it up, I replied that it was to me. Having examined it from every possible angle, he dropped it "accidentally on purpose". It smashed into hundreds of pieces. "Oops!" was all he could say, before adding that I could get back to playing with myself now he was going. I was too upset to be angry at first. Ever since I was a kid, I always felt things would be ok as long as I saw that statue regularly at Aunty Vera's, in a semi-religious/superstitious way. Words really fail me this time. Brushed up the pieces in tears, can't bring myself to throw them away.

Tuesday 30th July

Been exhausted the last couple of days. Not been able to sleep properly, too full of hateful thoughts about Ben. The more I think about him, the more I detest him. Have been visualizing all kinds of dreadful tortures. Did the delivery job for him yesterday morning all the same, seething with anger every step of the way, feeling that I was prostituting myself. Maybe I should just refuse to do any more jobs, suffer the consequences and then draw a line under the whole business. But then again, what would the consequences be?

Sandra round last night, couldn't put her off any longer. Had to rush to hide a Mars bar before she came up - totally ridiculous. She wanted to know where I'd been - over at Joop's, I said. Then she started on about how I shouldn't have so much to do with him, and how I should try and extend my circle of friends, and how we should try and do more things together to make joint friends, and on and on and on. Talk about an ear-bending. I said I wouldn't hear a word against Joop, as good as he's been to me. She looked a bit strange at that point, as though she was about to tell me something, but then didn't - probably just as well, as she was really getting on my nerves. Went to a bar on the Leidseplein - I wanted to walk there, on such a lovely evening, but she said we might meet more people if we took the tram - as if!! Anyway, we took the tram, and spoke to nobody. Sat on the Leidsplein nursing a couple of drinks, while Sandra went on about some bloke called Pieter breaking the photocopier at work, and other such fascinating escapades.

Went to see Brecht's *Mutter Courage* tonight with Frank and Arnold in the Cafe Deutsch. Very interesting, if not a little over-intellectual. Am sure it was over Arnold's head, as he kept laughing in all the wrong places. Frank didn't seem too bothered by it, though. The whole place was full of Germans smoking and wearing tiny black-rimmed glasses. Got chatting to a gorgeous woman from Berlin who was over visiting her boyfriend - worst luck. She said my German was excellent, which was nice. Arnold was really surprised as well, but insisted he could hear my English accent underneath. I turned to him, and asked him in German how effectively he felt Brecht had exploited the alienation techniques in the second scene - that shut the bugger up.

Wednesday 31st July

Well, the end of another month, my first month as manager of a successful Amsterdam porno outlet, and the figures look very good indeed, so Joop tells me. He rang tonight. Feel that I'm holding my own very well. Video sales been particularly good. The cabins alone generated 7000 guilders - unbelievable. Joop wondered whether we couldn't maybe push some of the sex toys a bit better, so have spent the evening drafting a couple of multi-lingual eye-catching posters, along the lines of "50% off dildos with any two sex CDs!" and "Buy any two latex plugs and get a free Skandapump Mag free!" Quite like the creative side of the job. Frank out escorting tonight, so invited Mariska up for a drink after closing time, feeling a bit sorry for her. While I was in the kitchen, she answered the phone - a woman, apparently, asking for me, but she hung up - very odd.

Friday 2nd August

Sandra over last night. Bit of a funny evening. Seemed offish
with me, but I'm past trying to interpret her moods. In the
end, I told her I felt exhausted and wanted to get to bed, so she
just got up and left in a huff. When I got to bed, I couldn't
sleep a wink - thinking about everything - the stalemate with
Sandra, wondering what I'll be doing ten years from now, my
broken statue and Ben, the bastard. Once I started thinking
about him, that was it. I reached that middle-of-the-night
fever pitch, and decided it was time to do something. Put my
jogging stuff on, took Frank's Swiss army knife, and off I
jogged to the Van Den Bonkengracht. Casually, so as not to
arouse any suspicions, but hardly anyone about anyway. Soon
enough I was outside the git's house, and approaching his jeep.
Looked around swiftly, and then swooped down, pretending to
fiddle with my lace. And then I did it - plunged my knife into
his front tyre. Felt totally empowered by the experience,
pathetic though it is as an act of revenge, but jogged away
triumphantly. Would have loved to be there and see the git's
face when he went to get in. A flat tyre is the very least he
deserves.

Saturday 3rd August

Sandra round in floods of tears this morning - wondered what
on earth was up. Turned out she thinks I'm having an affair -
apparently, it was her that rang the other night when Mariska
answered, and apparently she rang in the middle of the night
last night when I was out vandalising Ben's car. Frank had
answered the phone apparently and told her I wasn't in my
bed. And Sod's law, of course, haven't seen Frank since then
as he got up extra early today to go camping (no pun intended)
with Officer Arnold for a few days. Had to go through the
whole rigmarole of reassuring her to shut her up and stop the
tears. All I needed first thing on a Saturday morning. Not sure
I've totally convinced her, but she stopped accusing me
eventually.

    She left this afternoon when I had to start downstairs. Really

busy today, tourists flocking in. Loads of blokes on stag
weekends from all over Britain. Some jokers from Lancashire
started getting a bit out of hand, leafing through magazines and
collapsing into fits of raucous hysteria, saying things like "Ay
up, Kev, this un 'ere's a dead ringer for your Madge we'out the
donkey, mind!" Had to go over to them when one started
messing about with a pair of crotchless knickers and a dildo.

Went over to Joop's after closing up for a drink before going
to bed. Knew he'd still be open. Just as I walked in, the same
dodgy-looking bloke I'd seen the last time was just leaving. He
looked really haggard, and I noticed he'd got a black-eye. Very
strange. Not many in the bar, but Joop was pleased to see me,
and got me a drink straight away. Bertus was just leaving with
some blond woman in a leopard skin top who looked as if she
needed help removing some melons which had mysteriously
got trapped in her clothing. Dare say Bertus would be of
service.

Joop looked exhausted, and I noticed his shirt had a rip in it -
strange, as he's normally quite well turned out. Didn't stay
long. We'll set off for Prague on Friday morning, so I'll have
to sort out covering the Sexmarkt with Mariska. Can't wait.

Monday 5th August

Sandra round last night with some clothes she'd picked up
from some sort of bargain shop on Saturday. Frank and
Arnold had just got back from camping in the sand dunes (the
lengths the Dutch have to go to for a bit of scenic variety!), so
they sat there and watched as I was forced to try on assorted
T-shirts and sweaters. Both of them sat there, tittering like
schoolboys and getting on my nerves. Arnold didn't stay long,
and Sandra left just after him "to sort out her ironing for the
week". Frank said they'd had a wonderful time, and that
Arnold is so sensitive. I said "I'll bet he is, after three days in
the sand dunes", but it was lost on him.

Normal sort of day today. Sorted out the weekend cover
with Mariska. A friend of hers will help out as well. Frank's

very chirpy, in spite of having his computer exams later on in the month.

Wednesday 7ᵗʰ August

Frank's birthday

Got him a collection of men's toiletries and Brecht's biography. Sandra got him a blue and red T-shirt with logos plastered all over it. Officer Arnold got him a season ticket for the Concertgebouw - wouldn't have minded that myself. Joop gave him a wad of cash, not sure how much, while Bertus gave him a video called "Hot boys, hot nights". His parents sent him a parcel with everything in it from marshmallows and cakes to gloves and socks (in August!).

Sandra, Frank, Arnold and I went for a meal at the Argentinian Grill and then on to Joop's, where there was more present opening and jollity. Definitely got the feeling that Joop is not that keen on Arnold for some reason, as Joop is not his normal boisterous self around him. In fact, he disappeared for about an hour at one point, and got back looking all flustered. Reckon there must be something going down, as they say. When Arnold nipped out to the toilet, I overheard Joop tell Frank to keep quiet about the details for the Prague trip. Frank nodded and winked, he obviously knows better than to land Joop in anything.

Anyway, quite a good celebration. Alcohol flowing freely, Sandra was knocking it back like nobody's business, so had to walk her back to the flat. I'm trying to cut down my calorific intake, so limited myself to five beers. As I got her into her bedroom, she started going on about how much she loved me, how I must never leave her, how we should look for somewhere to live together, and then eventually drifted off into a drunken stupor. At least I didn't have to bother responding.

Got back about half an hour ago, had a hamburger on the way, regretting it now. Called in to see Mariska and close up

Sexmarkt. No problems. Frank and Arnold gone on to a club. Might as well go to bed.

Friday 9th August

German motorway!!

Am writing this in van, as we speed down the Autobahn! Got to bed at a reasonable time last night, since had to get up at five to be over at Joop's for six. Made the mistake of reading up on Prague in bed, so too excited to sleep when I eventually put light off. Pathetic really. Was still awake when Frank got back from escort job at 1.30. Feel totally knackered. Frank and Joop as fresh as buttons. They're sitting in the front, I'm lying down on a sort of mock-up bed in back. Not bad really, although a bit bumpy now and again. Drove over border into Germany about half an hour ago.

Later.

Slept solidly all the way to Nuremberg. Frank woke me up for a break, as needed to stop for more petrol and something to eat. Have just indulged in a German motorway cholesterol fest, so feeling a bit guilty. Frank and Joop had bread and soup.

7.00 pm - on the A 240 in Czech Republic

Amazing. We are now in the Czech Republic, following signs for PRAHA. Can't believe it! Bit of a delay at the border, lot of messing around with forms and stamps, and little blokes in green uniforms with guns who obviously love their job. Thought we were going to be ages, but then I noticed Joop handing over what looked suspiciously like a 'wad', and minutes later he was back at the wheel. I've just finished a Mars bar and third packet of crisps today. Really weird looking out of window and seeing forlorn villages and signs with loads of zcd's and zksch's. Lots of green interspersed with the depressing-looking grey blocks I'd expected. More later, as don't think it's too much further to Prague now.

11.00 pm

Unbelievable. Joop drove into centre of Prague as if he'd lived here all his life, Frank directing with the map. And what an entrance - brilliant evening sunshine illuminating Slavonic-style spires. As we got into the centre, with Prague Castle beaming down from the other side of the Vltava River, I realized I'd seen Judith Chalmers here on The Travel Show some time last year, and can remember resenting her. Frank directed us into the 'New Town', which looks even more medieval than the 'Old Town', and soon enough we were where we needed to be. Some very austere-looking block tucked away behind other blocks. Huge official entrance, covered in signs with loads of cszd's and zsk's again, all with exclamation marks after them.

Joop hadn't actually said anything about where we were staying. Frank looked at me and raised an eyebrow, obviously thinking it all looked dodgy too. Only turns out to be one of Prague's prisons! Trust Joop to know the best people. After Joop knocked, a grid shot back, Joop mentioned what must have been somebody's name, another wad of cash was handed through the slot, and the door opened. We were led through endless corridors, one of which led past a row of inmates - like in *Silence of the Lambs* - pressing their faces to the grids, some of them screaming in Czech and banging with their fists - very worrying. For one terrible second, I was convinced that Joop had concocted a terrible plot to sell us into the sex trade, and that any minute I'd be pushed into a cell and end up learning Czech the hard way. Fortunately, though, we finally went through into some sort of annex, where a bloke called Tomas greeted us in his office. Relaxed immediately then, as I could tell he was just like Joop - he even looked like him, with walrus moustache, heavy build, and beaming grin.

He took us into the old town and gave us a tour of the sights - Wenceslas Square, Charles Bridge, St. Vitus Cathedral - absolutely stunning. It really was like being transported back to medieval Central Europe, the cobbles, the dim light of evening, the gypsy fiddles in the distance. Frank had tears in his eyes as we walked over the Charles Bridge, looking up at Karlstejn Castle. Very poignant. Looked across at Joop, and noticed him ogling some woman with huge breasts who'd just dropped an ice-cream down her cleavage. Tomas was obviously incredibly proud of being Czech, and his eyes became watery every time we said how beautiful it all was.

In the end, he took us to a bar where it was fat-fest mark two, plus beer. Joop had obviously never met Tomas before, as they kept referring to "our mutual acquaintance". Very pleasant evening, all in all. Only midnight now, as Joop didn't want to make it too late with driving all the way back to Amsterdam tomorrow. When we got back to prison (!), Tomas showed each of us into our own 'cell'. Am writing this by the light of a bare 30 watt bulb. There is a vague hint of urine, and constant coughing in the background. Frank said he's often had thoughts about spending the night in an all-male prison. Never ever crossed my mind before.

Saturday 10th August

Motorway in Bavaria.

Already on way back. Totally exhausted. Up at crack of dawn, after lousy night, kept awake by noises. If I didn't know better, I'd have said I'd spent the night in an asylum, judging by the wailing and groaning going on. Needed the toilet at one point, so went in search - nowhere to be found. Ended up having to use commode-type thing in cell. After that couldn't even think of dropping off. What a night. Was glad to "be released" at 7.30 when Tomas knocked on door and threw a couple of rolls at me - bread rolls, that is, not toilet. He grabbed the bucket and made off with it. Could've died with embarrassment.

Frank and Joop emerged after a bit, Joop looked bleary-eyed as well. Eventually, he brought the van round to the back, and we started loading what must have been about two-hundred boxes of various sizes, which we had to keep taking on and off to get them all to fit in. God knows what's in them all. DVDs and photos was as much as Joop would say. Talk about sweat. Best work-out I've ever had. Finally left about 10.00. Was worried that there'd be an inspection at the border, but fortunately Joop worked wonders with another wad. Think I might be able to sleep for a bit now.

Sunday 11<sup>th</sup> August

Back in Amsterdam.

My God, how much can happen between one entry and the next. After I'd had a couple of hours kip in the van yesterday, I swapped with Frank so that he could have a nap. On the Frankfurt ring road, Joop drove over what turned out to be a bit of metal. Within seconds, the front tyre exploded, sending us hurtling into the hard shoulder, and a box from the back hurtling onto Frank's head. Then it was Panic-stations City.

Joop managed to stop on the hard shoulder, and leapt into the back. Frank was out cold - I was convinced he was dead, and threw up in utter horror. It went all down Frank's shirt, and seemed mostly water-based, so could've been worse. Joop grabbed a first-aid kit from under his seat - the side of Frank's head was bleeding slightly, and just as Joop was cleaning the cut, Frank came round. Joop told him that he had been sick on impact (what a hero), although Frank said it was funny he couldn't taste it in his mouth. He reckoned he was ok, although his head was throbbing like hell.

After we'd cleaned him up and got him in the front, Joop and I had to then unload virtually all the boxes to get at the spare tyre which was in a compartment under the van floor. Talk about sweat. Eventually, Joop managed to change the tyre, and we were back on the way. Frank slept solidly, but we both kept checking on him - hardly said a word all the way back. Joop got very fidgety as we got nearer the Dutch border, but visibly relaxed when we were finally heading for Arnhem.

As a result of all the palaver, it was 1.00 am when we got back. I thought we'd be dropping the boxes off at the Sexmarkt, but Joop said he'd be passing it on to other suppliers, so we unloaded it at his place. Knackered was not the word. He insisted on driving us over, given Frank's predicament. He flung his arms round us both, thanked us, and told us to let him know how Frank does. Then he got back in the van, looking absolutely shattered, and drove off.

When we got inside, I sorted Frank out with a couple of head-ache tablets, had a quick shower to swill the sweat and grime off, and then flopped into bed. Got up at 2.00 pm. Frank seems as right as rain, and can even see the funny side of it all now, which must be a good sign. Spent the rest of the day lounging around. Sandra phoned a couple of times, wanting to know all the details. When I told her about Frank, she said "Oh Gerard, thank God it wasn't you, I couldn't go on if anything happened to you". Frank was really chuffed when I told him. Anyway, definitely time for bed now. Nothing like a relaxing city break.

Tuesday 13ᵗʰ August

Total exhaustion, the last couple of days - feel as if I'm in a trance. The whole Prague incident seems like a dream. Shop dead busy, so not even managed to get on quietly.

Sandra over tonight - and all over me like a rash. Then she started messing about with things in the flat. While I was out fetching a take-away, she'd totally rearranged the saucepan cupboard and tidied up my underwear draw. Think she thought it'd make my day, but I just felt like messing it all up again. Afterwards, she insisted on having her way with me in the living room, which is all very well, but I wasn't in the least surprised when Frank walks in with Officer Arnold in tow. They both yelped like a couple of teenage girls, which is more than Sandra did. She just said "Evening boys", and carried on, while they went into the kitchen. Frank started making a drink, and I heard him shout out "Oh Gerard, wonderful, you've tidied up the pan cupboard!" It was at that point that Sandra climaxed. Within minutes, we'd pulled on our clothes, and were sitting round with Frank and Arnold talking about microwavable dishes and non-stick pans. Maybe I got hit on the head as well.

Thursday 15th August

Decided to ring mom and dad tonight, just to see if they were still alive and missing me. Managed to ring in the middle of *Home and Away*, so was asked to ring again in twenty minutes, which I did. As usual, needn't have bothered. Mom asked me if I was keeping well. I started to answer, but she said I'd have to excuse her as Mrs Pagett from number 36 had just come to the door. When she came back, I told her I'd been to Prague at the weekend. "Did you have nice weather for it, Gerard?" Dad was re-grouting the shower cubicle, so couldn't be disturbed. Oh well. At least they can't say I never bother with them.

Frank had to leave his computing course early today, suffering with a bad headache. I've told him he should see a doctor just to make sure everything's all right since the bang on the head, but he reckons he just needs rest and plenty of herbal tea. Joop came round tonight to see how he was, seemed very concerned. He stuffed a couple of bank notes into our pockets "for our help" and didn't hang around after Officer Arnold arrived with a couple of roses. He and Frank seem well away with each other. Frank looked delighted as Arnold minced up to him, roses between his teeth. Wonder if he carries on like that at the constabulary.

Saturday 17th August

Unbelievably busy in Sexmarkt last couple of days. Funny how you get to know the regulars. Some come in time and time again, but all you get is a quiet nod. With others, it's "Nice to see you again, Frans, the usual?" Joop must be seriously rich,

God knows what he does with it all, as he's only got his rooms within the hostel (as far as I know).  Probably got some mansion in leafy Bussum or Wassenaar.

Sandra round tonight.  I'd just gone to fetch a beer, when she screamed in the living room - there was a half-eaten Mars bar on the coffee table.  I told her it must have been Frank's, but she didn't believe me.  All she said was: "Gerard, I've warned you about this health plan - why can't you keep to it - do you want to stay as you are?" which really hurt me - am I really so bad or grossly overweight?  I was about to tell her she'd better leave, when she just got up anyway, and said she was off.  I didn't bother saying anything.  What a ridiculous situation!  Why can't she be just a normal person, with normal reactions to things?  After she'd gone, I realized she'd tidied up the pile of cassettes on the floor.  Not really sure what I'm getting out of this relationship.

Monday 19<sup>th</sup> August

Quite a nice day yesterday.  Frank was busy on computer, as into last week of his course, so decided to take myself off somewhere.  Walked to Central Station, and got some info from the Tourist Office.  In the end, got the bus to a place called Marken, a lovely little fishing village by the sea.  Not too many about, as a lot of the Dutch are still on holiday, which means they're everywhere but Holland.  Beautiful weather.  Sat in a cafe for a bit with a couple of diet cokes, then found a quiet spot on the water front with *De Telegraaf.*  Usual stuff going on in the world.  Middle Eastern tension and some woman from Amersfoort choking on her false teeth at bus stop.  It's amazing how much seems to happen at bus stops when I'm not waiting there.  Anyway, lovely relaxing day, and am actually quite tanned now.

Expected Frank to say that Sandra had been on the phone when I got back, but no.  He was lying on the couch when I got in - he'd had to stop working on the computer because of a headache.  Told him he must see a doctor this week, which he's finally agreed to do. Officer Arnold away on some course ('Optimising successful criminal engagement'), so no interruptions, just a pleasant evening after a pleasant day.

Today just another normal Monday in Sexmarkt. Got haircut at lunchtime, which wasn't so clever really, as now have a white mark on neck between hairline and tan. Still no word of Sandra.

Wednesday 21st August

VICTORY DAY!

Amazing! Was sitting having quiet glass of wine with Frank and Arnold tonight (he's growing on me a bit) when doorbell went - BEN! At first, my heart sank, but when he came in, I noticed he'd got his arm in plaster! When I asked him what he'd done, I could've jumped for joy - he reckons his jeep must have had a slow puncture the other week, as he ended up crashing into a bollard when the tyre gave out, and broke his arm in the accident! He was a bit less obnoxious than usual, and said nothing disparaging about any of us for once - he just slipped me a couple of addresses and cash for another painting job tomorrow and left. Who says there's no justice? Who says patience in revenge doesn't get you anywhere? (Does anybody say that?) As the evening went by, though, started to feel guilty - what if he'd got killed? He might've killed somebody else in the collision - how would I have lived with myself? But thank God it didn't come to that. But oh, revenge is very sweet. (People do say that.) Poured myself a large glass of wine after he'd gone, while Frank and Arnold tried to fathom the full extent of my glee - I said I was glad to see the git come a cropper. Arnold wanted to know what it is I've got against him, and what my connection is with him. I made out I helped him out with a bit of translation work, as God knows what the full story about the tax evasion is.

Frank went to see the doctor yesterday. Nothing to worry about, apparently, just told him to get plenty of sleep and be careful. Nice to know six years of medical training aren't being wasted.

Sandra round again last night. Totally emotional, all over me again. "How do we keep letting it happen? We must keep each other, Gerard, I love you, blah, blah, blah." We went to the bar on corner of canal for meal (chicken salad, ordered kindly by Sandra for both of us). I just let her go on and on, about us, about her job, about how we are made for each other, about some flats her mother saw that would be great for us... Came away eventually, having decided that enough is enough. Don't know how I'm going to tell her though. It's just a pointless relationship, apart from the physical side - we're just on two different planets. Will have to work out how to tell her - still remember how hysterical she was after her last boyfriend ditched her, although the circumstances were different. Anyway, feel relieved that I've decided to take action.

Friday 23rd August

**AWFUL DAY**

Well, wasn't too bad until this evening. Frank in relieved mode, after finishing his computer course, and looking forward to setting himself up in Sexmarkt, etc. Went out about 10.00 pm to collect painting for Ben - on the slip of paper, he'd put "Collect after 22.00", so thought I'd be fine. Got metro from Central Station all the way out to Bijlmermeer. Managed to find address in tower block, was handed painting, and made my way back - delivery address in Amsterdam Noord, so decided to get metro back to CS and then bus, but didn't get that far. Got back on the metro, hardly anybody about apart from a group of kids, really loud and obnoxious, so sat as far away as possible in the carriage, with painting under my arm.

After a minute, they made their way up the carriage, and said something I didn't understand. I made the mistake of saying pardon, as when he repeated it, I realized he was being vile.

The three others burst out laughing. One of them started pushing me. I pushed him back, dropping the painting from under my arm, which one of them grabbed - I tried to get it back, but the others pounced on me as I stood up, and started thumping me in the stomach, totally winding me. I fought back, hoping someone might step in, but there was only a woman in her forties in the carriage, and she didn't budge an inch. Can't blame her. I could see her looking at me out of the corner of her eye as they laid into me, desperately focussed on not reacting. One of them had pulled off my jacket while I was struggling and getting thumped. I ended up on the floor, they were rubbing my face in a couple of fag-ends and a dead wasp under the seat. As I looked up, I could see that the one who'd nicked my jacket had opened his flies and was peeing in it. He chucked it back at me, just as the metro was pulling into the next station, where they fled hell for leather, taking the wrapped painting with them. The woman scarpered as well.

Quite a few people got on then. As I lifted myself off the floor, some woman gawped at me and tutted, thinking I was some sort of down-and-out. Staggered back to flat, stomach killing me, stinking of pee, as it'd run off my jacket all over me when the bastard chucked it back at me. People staring at me all the way back. One bloke shouted out "Filthy low-life!"

Frank must've gone out with Arnold, as nobody in when I got back here. Went into bathroom and looked at myself in mirror. My face was deathly white, apart from patches of smeared filth from metro floor and grazes; a bit of the dead wasp still in my ear; my shirt, the blue one Sandra got me, had a big oil stain on it and two buttons had come off; hair all over the shop, wet from sweat and piss. Sat on the toilet staring at sink and just cried. Can't ever remember feeling so alone. Eventually got under shower, and rinsed all the muck off.

Later.

1.00 am now, Frank still not back. Thought about going to police, but pointless reporting it, as daren't divulge any involvement with painting business. The worst thing is that the painting's gone astray, so have just got to wait for the news to reach Ben, and dread to think what'll happen then. Can't deal with any more at the moment. If this isn't judgement on me after the other day, God knows what is.

Sunday 25th August

What a weekend. Can't believe it's only a couple of weeks since Prague. Hardly got a wink Friday night. Frank totally horrified when he saw me Saturday morning. Stomach and chest feel raw, and look even worse. He wanted me to let Arnold report it, but backed down when I pointed out that it might just land me in more bother. He reckoned I should go back to England for a week, and volunteered to stand in for me in shop - that way Ben would be off my back. Thought about it for a bit, but wouldn't achieve anything.

Went down to open up Sexmarkt at 11.30. Ten minutes later, in walks Ben - straight over to the counter, grabbed me by the neck, pulled me forward, so that my ribs grazed against the edge of the counter (absolute agony) and smacked me right in the face, saying he'd never use me again. And then he left as quickly as he'd come in. Now I've got a black eye like I've only ever seen on films. At least he came early on in the day and got it out of the way. People, though, honestly. Must have been ten customers in, and not one batted an eyelid. One git was even asking me how much the blow-up dolls were as Ben thumped me. Mariska had at least rushed upstairs to get Frank, who took over for me whilst I had yet another clean-up session in bathroom. Amazingly, didn't feel too bad at first - just relieved it was all properly over and done with. Then I looked at myself in the full-length mirror - blimey, I was no oil painting before Friday, but I'm a sight-and-a-half now.

Sandra been round all day today. She's been as good as gold, no words of recrimination either. In fact, she's not said too much at all - she's just listened and patted me in camomile lotion, in between feeding me. Haven't had the heart to talk about breaking things off, and not sure it's such a good idea now either.

Mariska played a bit of a blinder as well yesterday. Ben must have put his keys down on the counter before he went for me - she found them there after he'd gone. And sure enough, he was back ten minutes later, while I was still up here, to see if he'd left them. She made out she hadn't seen them. When she told me, she fetched them out of her pocket, winked at me, and said maybe I could think of doing something with them... Will have to think very carefully about this one. Can't afford any mistakes this time.

Tuesday 27th August

Have never been so sore in my life - everything aches and bruised - face, chest, ribs, stomach. If I had much more black on me, I'd pass for an extra in Roots. Eye looks a right mess. Have hardly ventured out of shop the last couple of days. What is it about people that they have to comment? Every sodding customer in the Sexmarkt has had something to say about the way I look. I've heard everything from "Somebody not popular lately?" to "Isn't that you in S & M Extra?" And I've heard a thousand-and-one tips on what to stick on my eye, from raw steak to a used condom.

Have slept badly too - keep reliving the horror of both incidents and waking up in a sweat. Nearly attacked again in the night as well - Arnold walked into the bathroom at 2.00 am and thought I was some sort of disfigured burglar - he was about to grab me round the neck when he finally realized it was me - thank God. He'd come round after I'd gone to bed, so hadn't seen me till then. Frank had told him that some yobs had set about me, and left it at that. Arnold put his hand on my cheek and told me to get some rest.

Sandra round briefly tonight. Yet another family birthday party tomorrow night - another uncle's - but fortunately excused this time for looking such a dreg. Felt a bit hurt when she said she'd be too ashamed to have me with her, but past caring really. She also started on about how we should seriously think about getting a flat together outside Amsterdam in somewhere like Almere new town, and how I should think about getting myself a more respectable and safer job with proper prospects. Eventually she wanted to get back to her flat as somebody called Nelke from her office was calling round with a tableware catalogue. She's decided she wants to start collecting some decent plates for our new home. Couldn't be bothered to respond, especially with stomach throbbing. Think I might call in at doctor's tomorrow, just to be on the safe side.

Wednesday 28th August

Managed to get appointment at doctor's before opening shop this morning. Funny looking bloke with incredible buck teeth - spitting with every word. Not sure people like that should join the medical profession. He asked me if I lived nearby. When I told him, he said a young German had been in recently with the same address, suffering with a nasty head injury - did I know him? I explained that we were flat-mates, and then he looked at me very quizzically. Was I sure we weren't involved in any dangerous sexual practices that were getting out of hand?! Only in Amsterdam would a doctor come to that conclusion! Had to insist that I'd been beaten up against my will before he'd think about prescribing any pain killers. After I'd taken my shirt off for him to examine me, he said: "Mm...nasty. Do you follow a low-fat diet?" When he finally stopped demolishing my self-esteem and passed me the prescription, he handed me a little card as well. When I got outside, it was the SM help-line number! Bet Dr Gupta in Walsall never hands out cards like that. He even blushed when he once asked me if "there was frequency of passing water" when I had a kidney infection. Another world.

Been very morose generally. Maybe it's just a reaction to the shock. Frank knocked on the toilet door tonight after I'd been in the bathroom for half an hour - could have sworn I'd only

been in five minutes. Frank out with Arnold now. He called
in to ask me if he could get me anything before Arnold came
for him, which was nice. They're both as cheerful as nobody's
business, which somehow made me feel even worse. Have
been lying on bed all evening staring at ceiling, indulging in
self-scrutiny. What am I doing here? Shouldn't I really go
back to the West Midlands and re-enter the education system?
Am I just living through some fantasy-based extended break
that's going nowhere? How am I going to get uninvolved with
Sandra? Will I meet someone else if I manage it? What do I
want out of life? Where am I going? Am I safe here? What if
I see those thugs somewhere and they try it on again? Will I
ever manage to lose my stomach? Should I get my revenge on
Ben again and what should I do with his keys? Do I want to
stay in Amsterdam and sell dildos and copies of Benelux
Boobs for the rest of my life?

Friday 30th August

Feeling a bit brighter now. Sandra's been having to work late,
so have only spoken to her on phone. Uncle's party was
wonderful, apparently, as he'd gone to a lot of trouble with
some tasty nibbles. Her relatives had at least asked after me.
But rather than just say I wasn't well, she'd given them the full
humiliating saga of me being jumped on in the metro. This
had caused great amusement, she said. I could've slammed the
phone down. As it was, I made out somebody was at the door,
and then put it down.
    Bertus has been round all day helping Frank install the
computer in backroom and set up the Internet connection.
Heard him speaking German to someone on the phone when
he thought nobody was around, but couldn't quite hear what
he was saying. Something about money. Frank had already
designed the Sexmarkt's home-pages, so we'll be "porning out
to de whole verld", as Bertus put it, very shortly, with Frank on
floppy control. He really is excited about it all. I'm glad that
he'll be around during the daytime, as Mariska never has much

to say for herself. Bertus reckons the Internet will "launch Joop into de mega-buck zone" (God knows where he gets these phrases from) and that we'll do nicely out of it as well.

It's been a week now since I was set about. Still can't believe it. Chest and stomach not quite so sore now, eye still looks bad though. Keep wondering if Ben will turn up again. Keep trying to think about revenge strategy.

Sunday 1ˢᵗ September

Joop's birthday

BIG celebration at hostel tonight! Loads of people there I'd never seen before, but it was obvious that everybody loves Joop. Masses of food laid on, free drinks, not a miserable face in sight - apart from Sandra's. She reckoned the whole affair was vulgar. Bertus farted at one point and shouted: "Quick, stop it before it gets out of de door!!" Sandra raised her eyes to heaven, whilst everyone else collapsed. Was glad when she left early "to be fresh for work". Talk about a killjoy.

I'd got Joop quite a nice book about Britain, full of stunning scenes. In the front, I wrote: "To a great friend, wishing you a very Happy Birthday, gratefully yours, Gerard." When he read it, I could see him filling up, and he flung his arms round me, until I winced with the pain - still very sensitive round my ribs. Then he said he was going to speak to me about the bastard who'd done this to me, who'd regret the day he was born.

Frank bought him one of those funny nail imaging things, where you push something into it, and the nails make an impression of it. It was just after Bertus had flashed an impression of his privates round that Sandra left. Funny present really, but Joop seemed to like it. Bertus had got him the software for the computer in the shop, Sandra got him a basket of men's toiletries. In fact the bar was covered in that many presents that you could hardly put your drink down.

Left about 11.30 with Frank. Joop shook my hand firmly and said he'd be in touch, then winked knowingly. No Arnold tonight, as on duty. Quite nippy as we walked back - gradually heading into autumn, I suppose. Would normally just be starting the school year again now. What a terrifying thought.

Tuesday 3rd September

Felt much better so far this week. Soreness much improved, face starting to heal as well. Great having Frank around in Sexmarkt. He's been dead busy on computer. I've had a look at what he's done and it's incredible. Basically, the whole shop is on the computer. There are various pages with information that you can get by clicking on certain words. Everything we stock has been put under categories, like magazines, DVDs, CD Roms, accessories, etc. If you click on a category, you get a list of everything we have under that heading, with prices, etc. People all over the world can place an order with us by filling in their details and credit card number on screen and then sending it to us by e-mail - amazing. It'll take Frank a few days before he's input all our stock, but he's finished the mags and DVDs. He's also managed to scan in pictures of each item, and there's even a page which tells people about the Sexmarkt, with pictures of me, Frank and Mariska. Under my picture, which is not one I'd have chosen, it says: "Gerard assures you discrete delivery" in four languages. Frank'll really have his work cut out when the orders start coming through. More work for me as well, as I'll have to make sure the wholesalers get the stuff to us more regularly. Difficult to know how to gauge it over the next few weeks.

Sandra over tonight. She was in her "Oh Gerard, I could never live without you" mood until she'd had her way with me. Then she switched to gripe mode - starting by going round the flat hunting for chocolate, accusing me of secret nibbling, as she's convinced I'm not losing my stomach. Fortunately I'd decided to hide the chocolate among Frank's CD collection, so I scuppered her. Then she started on about Joop's birthday party, how vulgar everybody was, how we need to get out of Amsterdam, and how I should start to move away from the likes of Joop and Bertus.

Eventually, she switched back to loving mode, and got upset when she told me she was going to Antwerp for a week on some sort of course from work. Think she thought I was going to be annoyed, but I was actually relieved, and wished her an enjoyable week. When she finally went, she said she'd be thinking about me every day and would miss me terribly. I said I would as well (lying). Closed the door behind her and felt a weight lifting off my shoulders. Had two Mars bars in glorious defiance, but then felt the weight descend again.

Thursday 5th September

Good news! Back in June there was a competition on the back of my low-fat Brekko-Bites - give five reasons why you like Brekko-bites. I'd put: they're low in fat, they're tasty, they're value for money, they're nice with yoghurt and they keep me regular! I'd put the last point in English, as I don't know how to say it in Dutch. Anyway, I posted it off, never giving it another thought, but, lo and behold, I get a letter from them today, telling me I've won! They love the last line in English - they think it's some kind of clever pun, God knows what they think I mean. Anyway, the point is I've won a year's free supply, and the chance to feature in their advertising! I've got to go to the Brekko-Bites' head office in Eindhoven and have the publicity sorted out.

Joop rang this evening - he was really chuffed for me as well. He's asked me to call by tomorrow so that we can discuss how he's going to help me re the whole Ben saga. Intrigued what he's got up his sleeve, won't do any harm to find out anyway.

Arnold over tonight as well. He's shaved his moustache off and looks much better. When I asked him why he'd shaved it off, he said someone had told him it made him look a bit rat-faced. Quite a pleasant evening, drinking wine and listening to music. Bit of a sticky moment later, though, when Frank reached for his Deutsche Hitspop CD and got covered in minto-choc. I made out that it was a complete mystery.

No word from Sandra in Antwerp. I'm not complaining.

Saturday 7th September

Dead busy in shop again yesterday, and today for that matter, so didn't get over to Joop's till midnight. Lot quieter in hostel, though, so good chance to talk. He poured me a jenever, and sat down next to me. Then he wanted to know exactly what had happened the other week, so I spared no details. He listened without interrupting me, and then put his hand on my shoulder, and told me I was a good kid who meant a lot to him. He went on that there wasn't really anything he could do about the thugs on the metro, but he could do something about Ben. I know he's got some heavy contacts, so I assumed that was what he was getting at. He told me he could sort me out with free protection, then winked. I couldn't really fathom the wink, so asked him what he meant, but he just repeated what he'd said and winked again. Then he asked me if I knew what protection was. I said of course I knew. Then he chuckled, saying he didn't really think so. Apparently, people in danger pay him money to arrange for protection. He was amazed I'd never heard of this type of business - sounds very Robin Hoodesque. Anyway, to cut a long story short, he's got 'boys' who can make sure Ben'll never even look sideways at me again, but in my case, I won't have to pay a thing for the privilege.

I know he means well, but I didn't want to let him get himself and other people involved in my problem. So I thanked him but assured him the whole business was in the past now. What a hero, though, and what a bloke to have as a friend. That's Joop all over - looking after people.

I was there till about 2.00 am. He wanted to know all about the Internet stuff, and sounded quite excited. He said it was going to mean big money, and that Frank and I would be seeing our share of it too - nice one! I asked him how he'd managed to sell off all that porn from Prague without putting it through the shop. He just tapped his nose, and said there are things he can't discuss. But then, that's Joop all over as well. After a few more drinks, he shook my hand and told me to sleep well.

As I walked back, I realized I don't really know that much about him, yet he's really taken to me and Frank, and never seems to want much in return - even when we do him a favour he makes it worth our while. Funny really. Suppose some people are just decent by nature.

Normal sort of day today. Frank dead chirpy, as first orders came through on email - from San Francisco and Runcorn. Both orders were worth 300 guilders!! If this is anything to go by, Joop's going to be raking it in. He was less chirpy later on, though, with a terrible headache. Didn't even fancy going out. Probably all that staring at the computer screen all day.

Still no call from Antwerp. With a bit of luck she'll have fallen for somebody else. Bruises fading now, eye still improving. Stomach exactly the same, weight also unchanged.

Monday 9th September

Frank felt a bit brighter yesterday. Arnold on another police course about inter-personal skills development (I pity the tutor), so we decided to make the most of the day and got train to Bruges. Had to change train in Antwerp. Thought how funny it would be if we bumped into Sandra. Anyway, got to Bruges and what a place. Beautiful. Lot like Amsterdam with canals and bridges, but smaller, more intimate, less crowded. Spent the day wandering around, stopping off at the odd cafe for the odd pilsje or coffee. Frank wanted to visit the Memling museum - some Belgian painter. Quite pleasant, really. We had quite a good chat about things. Funny really, I always seem to manage to get things in perspective when I go on a trip - Frank's exactly the same. Asking each other about our lives, we somehow seemed to sort it all out. I asked him how things were going with officer Arnold. He said it was good because it wasn't a demanding relationship, Arnold is just happy to go out and be with him when he can, they never make plans or talk about the future. Very sensible. I told him all about Sandra, how she seems to want to dominate every aspect of my life and take over. Frank said it's time I did something about it - the sooner the better. He's right, of course.

Anyway, walked back to the station about six. Got train from Bruges to Antwerp, where we changed again. As we sat on the Antwerp-Amsterdam train before it left the station, I could have sworn I saw Sandra walking down the opposite platform holding hands with some tall blond bloke. Frank thought it looked like her as well, but they'd gone before we could be absolutely sure. Felt very odd all the way back after that. No call from her last night, or tonight.

Today was really busy in Sexmarkt again. Sixteen email orders! Tried to anticipate demand based on orders so far, so contacted suppliers for extra deliveries, in between the usual business. There was some stroppy Dutch woman in complaining about a blow-up male doll she'd bought. She reckoned he looked nothing like the bloke on the box. The bloke on the box was the tanned, blond, chiselled Baywatch type. When she took the dummy out, I saw what she meant. It had a head like a beach ball with a wig and make-up on. The body was even less convincing, but the groinal attachment was something else. I heard somebody wince over by the 'Bigger Means Better' shelf. "How am I supposed to enjoy myself with this?" was all she kept saying. I managed to keep my calm, and told her that this was a standard product - if she expected a real body, she'd have to go out with a real person. In the end, she shoved him back in the box and stormed out. Honestly speaking. If I'd bought a blow-up doll, I'd never ever go back to the shop to complain about it, even if it did look like something out of Perverts' Playschool. But that's the Dutch all over again - no concept of being embarrassed.

Wednesday 11th September

Got up yesterday with the Ben business on my mind for some

reason, and couldn't shake it off all day. Then I knocked over
the box containing the broken pieces of the angel of hope,
which went all over the floor again. Nearly rang Joop at that
point to take him up on his offer, but then changed my mind.
I'd got into this whole shady business on my own, and I would
do something about it myself. On my lunch break, I went up
to the flat, took Ben's keys from my drawer and nipped down
to his flat on the Van Den Bonkengracht. No sign of his jeep,
so went up to the door and let myself in, checking behind me.
I'd already decided what I was going to do. Wore gloves so as
not to leave any fingerprints. Heart beating ten to the dozen.
Let myself in and had a good look round the flat - very smart,
if a bit minimalist - all black and white and stainless steel, not
very lived-in looking. In fact, very cold and severe, like him.
Looked in the bedroom - all red and black, looking very lived
in, with a mirror above the bed. Walked into bathroom, put
plug in sink, and switched on the tap. After a while, heard the
water spilling onto the floor, so left quietly - still no sign of
anybody. Walked back out onto street, heart still in mouth.
Still can't believe I had the guts to do it, and would love to
have seen his face when he got in. Feel shocked at myself in a
way. Keep thinking about going back and doing something
else, really spooking him, but will have to see.

Had a call from Brekko-Bites. They want me to go to
Eindhoven on Friday for publicity shots, etc, so Frank has
agreed to hold the fort in Sexmarkt. Still no word from
Sandra. Very odd, she must be back by now.

Friday 13th September!

Finally heard from Sandra yesterday. In fact, I gave her a ring,
as I was really curious. She was a bit odd on the phone, quieter
than normal - which made a change. When I commented, she
put it down to tiredness. When I asked why she hadn't been in
touch sooner, she said she'd been overloaded with work since
she got back. Her only comments about the course were that
it had been really tiring. I told her about Frank and I going

down to Bruges on Sunday, and how we'd seen someone who looked just like her at the station. She laughed, but didn't say anything - maybe it was her. I wouldn't care, to be honest, but I'd like to know if she is seeing somebody else. At least it'd give me a good reason to finish. She said she'd ring me over the weekend.

Anyway, got the train to Eindhoven on time this morning. Was expecting something to go wrong with it being Friday 13th, so wasn't surprised when the train stopped in the middle of nowhere for 45 minutes, whilst some problem with the points was sorted out. The Dutch are a right lot when they're delayed. In Britain, there'd be a few tuts and a lot of low-key mumbling, but here it's something else. They were running up and down the carriages, ranting and scoffing, briefcases flying behind them. Hands going up in the air, choruses of "unbelievable, ridiculous." The conductor was nearly lynched by some bloke with a mobile phone and buck teeth. As it was, I finished off a cream slice and leafed through a copy of *Healthy Man Living*.

Eventually, it started off again, but with a massive jolt. In fact, it was so violent, that a case fell off the rack and landed on some old woman with a blue rinse, now tinged red with blood. The woman opposite her pulled the emergency cord, so it stopped again, causing further cries of exasperation. When the conductor came, they decided it'd be best going on to Eindhoven, where he'd arrange for her to be collected by ambulance.

I was still on time, as had left very early, anticipating a delay. Found my way to Brekko-Bites easily, and reported in. A flashy blond called Nienke appeared within seconds and whisked me through to meet the runners-up (who'd all won a six-month supply of Brekko-Bites). They were all quite chubby, and as we sat round waiting, it looked more like a Weight-Watchers Convention than a publicity stunt. Nienke introduced us to some smoothie type called Marc, who looked congenitally smarmy. Marc was the Brekko-Bites PR man, and he went over the order of the day with us. We all had to introduce ourselves in turn (which I loathe) and say how long we'd been eating Brekko-Bites so that they could form an idea of brand loyalty for marketing purposes.

After coffee and cakes (couldn't resist), Marc whisked me off again and said I'd have to have some make-up on my face to disguise my eye (which is an awful lot better now anyway). I thought I'd be taken to a special suite, but Nienke just fetched her foundation out and rubbed it over my face, Marc still smiling. Then we were taken on a tour of the factory, stopping every so often for Otto, the company photographer, to film us marvelling at the low-fat production techniques. Some of the shots will be used in their adverts. God help 'em.

Then there was a sort of prize-giving type of affair, where we were presented with our vouchers by the company chairman, accompanied by great applause from Marc and Nienke, Otto still busily filming. I was the last one up, having won the star prize. The company chairman complemented me on my Dutch (which was nice), but asked me what part of Germany I was from (which wasn't so nice). Instead of saying I was English, I just laughed inanely, by which time he'd moved on anyway, so I didn't get round to correcting him. Then there were seemingly hundreds of photos taken, by Brekko-Bites and the winners, posing with everybody. I had to hold up a big poster which had the words: "With Brekko-Bites everyone's a winner!!" written on it, as Nienke and Marc put their arms round me. Never felt so naff in all my life.

Anyway, made my way back to Amsterdam, and took over from Frank in Sexmarkt. He'd been busy packaging up email orders, so took them off to post office when I got back. Not such a bad Friday 13th, all in all.

Sunday 15th September

Sandra round tonight. She flung herself at me, told me how much she'd missed me, and then started moving plants around in the flat, and checking the cupboard for chocolate bars. After a bit, she took out something square from her rucksack -

a present. I unwrapped it, wondering what on earth it was - hard, square and flat - a set of table mats - well. Pretended I was pleased, and was then subjected to a spontaneous tearful outburst. "Oh Gerard, I've done something awful, please, please forgive me, I must tell you, and you must please forgive me, and not let things spoil our future...." On and on she went. When she'd finally got a bit of self-control back, she confessed that it *was* her on the platform in Antwerp - with another bloke.

His name was Peter and he was doing the same course. They'd had adjacent rooms and ended up having a bit of a fling, even though he's married with two young kids! I could barely speak. I thought I wouldn't have been bothered, but somehow I was furious, although I didn't shout or anything. All I could do was ask her to leave while I tried to come to terms with the shock, and decide how I felt about her now. There were more tearful pleas, but for once I was having none of it, which she could see, so she left sniffling and red-eyed.

After she'd gone, I sat on the couch for a bit. Really can't believe it. What the hell is it with women and me? Here I've been, not having the heart to tell her I want to finish with her, while she's having it away with somebody else, even though she wants us to get married and the rest of it. So even though she really wants me, she manages to reject me, and even though I'm not bothered, I feel utterly rejected. Can't get my head round it. Maybe it's just because it brings the Tina thing back. And the Jane thing before her. And Alison... Felt as desperate as the night I'd been set about. Don't think I'll let on to Frank about this. Have just had half a bottle of wine and put the table mats out with the rubbish.

Tuesday 17th September

It's a funny old thing, feeling spurned. Ended up telling Frank about the whole business after all, and he was very sympathetic. He reassured me that it was probably just one of those things that happened, and that Sandra obviously still loved me. He reckons gay men are always having flings, even when they're in a stable relationship, it doesn't mean anything. The most important thing to focus on was my own feelings towards her, he says. The funny thing is that I had actually started thinking that she did mean an awful lot to me. When I told Frank, he said that I needed to differentiate carefully between my pride, my heart and my true mind. Arnold butted in at that point and said "And your penis!!!" and spent the next ten minutes guffawing at his wit, using the term loosely. Another typical Dutch characteristic - no sense of appropriate behaviour. I asked him if he learned such behaviour on these courses he keeps going on.

Anyway, after going through a brief phase of wanting things and Sandra back the way they were, only better, I started to feel quite angry - how could she sleep with somebody else when she makes out she loves me? Then I started thinking about the health plan, the family birthday parties, the what-to-wear syndrome, the inane chat, the Mars Bar prohibition, the moving things around in the flat, and I thought NO. Enough is enough. We weren't going anywhere I wanted to go before, we certainly won't now.

Decided to go over to her place this evening and have it out with her. Got there at about 10.30 after finishing at Sexmarkt. She was ages coming to the door, and when she did, she was all flummoxed and embarrassed (as much as the Dutch can be embarrassed, that is). All tussle-haired and red-faced. As I walked in, I noticed there were two dirty dinner plates on the table and an empty bottle of wine. She saw me surveying the scene and coming to my conclusions. Before I'd even said anything, she started shouting "Gerard, no, it isn't the way it seems!", and blurbing on to that effect. Talk about a double whammy - what on earth is she on? He could have still been there for all I knew, so I didn't want to hang around. I just said: "Look Sandra, it's obviously not working, and I don't like being betrayed and lied to. I'm sorry, but I don't want to see you again".

She rushed up to me, pleading with me to change my mind

and forgive her. When I asked her why I should bother, nothing could have prepared me for the horror of what she was about to say: "Gerard, please, this thing with Peter doesn't mean anything deep, *it's just that he has such a good body!*" I felt totally and utterly crushed, as much as you can feel crushed when you're apparently the original fat bastard. Couldn't even bring myself to respond to that, so brushed past her and slammed the door behind me.

Walked back home feeling like an utter dreg. Frank and Arnold out when got back in, fortunately, as don't think I could have faced them. I cleared out every bar of chocolate in the flat, including the ones amongst Frank's CDs, and had a glass of water instead of a beer. Then I made the mistake of getting undressed and examining myself in the bathroom mirror. Bad idea. The only good thing to say was that the bruising has gone down. Think I would cry if I didn't feel so angry and hurt. What an absolute git she is. Definitely time for bed.

Thursday 19th September

Felt sorry for myself all day yesterday. Tried to keep reminding myself that in spite of everything, Sandra still appeared to want me, and it was ME who was ultimately rejecting her. It was quiet during the afternoon. Frank was busy packaging up more email orders (obviously going to be a real winner), Mariska was making the most of the chance to dust the dildos down, and I was sitting behind the till, sifting through next month's batch of 'Beefcake Buggers' (God knows who thinks up these names) that'd just come in from Hamburg. The Beefcake Bugger on the front cover was some hard-bodied git called Mike from LA. There was a bit of a write-up inside about how he used to be fat, but got tired of taunts from classmates, so started working out, and now works as a full-time model. Something really clicked inside me at that point. I'm not fussed about featuring in Beefcake Buggers, but with a bit of discipline and will-power, I could lose a bit of weight and improve my muscle definition. Suddenly, I felt as though I'd come out of reverse, and that Sandra had done me a favour. So I've decided to go back to the gym three times a week, watch my diet without being fanatical, and see where it gets me.

Went this morning before work. Frans has apparently left, which is no bad thing. His replacement is a woman called Rita, who didn't really seem that interested (suits me fine). Have decided that weight loss is my priority, so won't bother with the weights yet. Spent ten minutes on treadmill, five minutes on stepper, ten minutes on bike, then another five minutes on treadmill. Absolutely exhausted when finished, so had a warm shower and relaxed in sauna for about ten minutes. Only one other person in there - some blond woman with huge breasts. Had to leave when she started massaging her bosom with some sort of oil. Still had my eyes closed, but even the noise was erotic. Why can't the Dutch just behave modestly? I'd never dream of creaming my genitalia in public, but the Dutch don't think twice about it. If you did it in England, you'd end up in front of the magistrate.

Anyway, the point is that I feel positive, and am determined not to let it all get me down. Frank is very impressed with my attitude and reckons I should spend ten minutes meditating every morning to focus positively on my plan for the day. Might give it a try.

Sandra's kept ringing for me, but have got Frank to say I've been out. Can't see the point in prolonging any relationship with her.

Saturday 21ˢᵗ September

What a funny old world it is. Went to the gym again this morning, same routine as before, and felt quite invigorated walking back. Stood at the pedestrian crossing on the Singel, waiting to cross over, saw that nothing was coming so decided to cross over. Just as I did, somebody boomed "STOP!" behind me. I stopped for a second, thinking there might be a car coming from some unseen angle, realized there wasn't, so carried on again. Again, the booming voice. This time I turned round to see two policemen rushing up to me. One of them told me that it's an offence to cross the road when the red light is on. I thought this was too pathetic for words, and made out I couldn't understand Dutch. He explained the problem again, this time in flawless English. I then made the mistake of trying to say that we don't stick to slavish rules in England and prefer to let common sense prevail. This got right up his nose, as I had to give him details of where I was staying, blah, blah, blah. When he found out I live here, he got really snotty, and said that I would be issued with a fine! "In Holland, jay-walking is a crime, and crime is not a matter of philosophical subjectivity!" was his next comment. Smarmy know-all police git. That's the problem with Holland - they're just all too educated. Honestly, it's just bloody typical - I get fined for going innocently about my own business, but there's no bugger around when I'm severely set about on the metro.

Frank annoyed me by failing to appreciate my point when I got back. "In Germany you may also not cross by the red light". Then he lit a jasmine incense stick for calming.

Went over to hostel tonight for drink with Joop. Frank and Arnold came too, Bertus propping up the bar as usual. Joop always bristles a bit when he sees Arnold - not sure whether it's because Arnold is in the police, or whether he just thinks he's a git. Arnold was going on at one point about some bloke he'd arrested for persistently parking in a non-designated area on the Keizersgracht, when Joop said we'd have to excuse him while he went to feed his goldfish. Bertus, ever the subtle, just slapped his arm round Arnold's back and told him not to be such a boring bastard.

Spoke to Sandra on phone yesterday evening - had I calmed down, could we get back to normal, blah, blah. I told her I was perfectly calm, that I was no longer interested, that she could carry on with her hard-bodied adulterer and I'd appreciate it if she'd stop ringing me. On that I put the phone down. Arnold was earwigging with Frank on the sofa, and said: "Ooh, darling, the tiger's got his claws out!" I told him to shut his face and went to bed.

Monday 23rd September

Have started doing press-ups and sit-ups now first thing in the morning and last thing at night. Sit-ups still slightly painful, so not doing too many. Every time I think of stopping, I keep seeing Sandra's face, and the anger spurs me on. She actually came round last night, but I got Frank to tell her I was out - what is wrong with this woman? Arnold can't see what the big deal is. I thanked him for sharing such rare insight, and told him her unfaithfulness was only a minute fraction of the reason why I no longer wish to associate with her. Frank jumped up to light another jasmine incense stick at that point, but I told him I was perfectly calm already.

Normal sort of Monday today. No word of Sandra for once. Eighteen email orders over the weekend! If it carries on like this, we might have to take somebody else on just to cope with the admin load, processing all the bank paperwork. Still, at least it's all been worth Frank's hard work.

Wednesday 25th September

Had a card from Sandra in post yesterday. "To a friend, who's dearer to me than he knows" was the message on the front - yuk. Inside she'd written:

*"Gerard, I know you find it hard right now to forgive me, but I know in your heart you're a forgiving person, and that our love will overcome this. In spite of what I've done, I love you and I want to share the rest of my life with you. I'm sorry about what happened, and I know you need time. When you feel ready, please call me, and I'll arrange for us to see one of those flats in Almere - yours forever, Sandra"*

Nearly choked on my Brekko-Bites - the sheer nerve of this woman! Ripped it up and threw it away on my way to the gym before work. Had a really good session, felt the pounds falling off me. Nobody in the sauna afterwards either, so felt totally liberated and threw my towel to one side.

Friday 27th September

Have decided to start growing a moustache to add character
and mystery to my face. Nobody has commented yet, so far so
good. Will be glad when it's fully grown, though, so I can get
all the comments out of the way - almost puts me off growing
it. But no, I won't be psychologically daunted.

Had another communication from Sandra in post this
morning:

*"Gerard, hope everything is ok now. Have made an appointment with
estate agents for 11.30 in Almere tomorrow morning - give me a ring
tonight so we can arrange where to meet.*
*Love, Sandra"*

Talk about taking things for granted. Decided to ring her to
put the record straight once and for all. I told her that it was
wrong of her to assume that I'm just going to "come round"
eventually, as I'm not. I told her that we were finished, and
that I don't want to hear from her again until I'm ready -
maybe in time we could be friends again. Didn't think she was
listening at first, as there was no reaction. Suddenly there was
horrendous sobbing and pleas of "Oh forgive me, darling,
please!" I felt like some sort of heartless git abusing a
desperate woman, but knew it was more than my life was
worth to go soft on her. Anyway, she went in the end, still
sobbing. Just hope that she'll leave me alone for a bit now.

Sunday 29th September

Not so busy yesterday in Sexmarkt. Definitely get the feeling
that autumn's on its way now, not so many tourists knocking
about either. Still, the email orders are coming through like
nobody's business, so nothing to worry about.

Moustache developing quite nicely now. Gives me a look of
a young Tom Selleck, even if I say so myself. Frank's finally
noticed, as did Arnold when he called round tonight. Frank
reckons it deepens my masculinity, Arnold just smiled inanely,
so I'm assuming that's a compliment. He was a bit down for

once, as he's normally a bit hyper. Frank told me later he'd been working on some sort of disturbing abuse case.

Tuesday 1st October

Amazing - no word from Sandra, so assume she's got the message. Every time the phone rings, I keep expecting it to be her, bracing myself for another scene. Maybe she's just resigned herself to having it away with her married man.

Feel I'm making good progress at the gym. Still doing usual routine, and it seems to take a bit less out of me each time I go. Got chatting to a nice-looking woman in the sauna today. She started telling me all about her new diet - eating as much protein as you like, but cutting out carbs altogether. I told her I might give it a try. She looked at me as though she was really surprised, and said she couldn't imagine that I'd want to lose too much weight. Then she winked at me and said everything looked to be just about the right size. I sort of choked, smiled and mumbled a flustered response.

Fancied a coffee before I left, so went over to the bar area, and noticed her sitting on her own, combing her hair. Decided to go and sit next to her. Reckon she's in her early thirties. Long blond hair, still damp from the sauna. She ordered another coffee and asked me what my name was. She's called Else. She said she's seen me there before, and asked me what I did. I told her I managed a shop in the Red Light area, which she thought must be fun. She works part-time as a tour guide for one of the boat companies that do trips on the canals. Had quite a good chat, and as I left, she gave me a really nice smile and said she'd look forward to seeing me again. Have felt really perky all day - am sure the moustache is working already.

Thursday 3rd October

Frank's not feeling a hundred percent again. He's lying in his room at the moment with his essence of tranquillity candles lit and Arnold humming the theme tune from *Hill Street Blues*.

Sandra still keeping away. Went to the gym this morning, and hoped I'd see Else. Was disappointed when I left and hadn't seen her. Not that I want to rush into anything, but a bit of something to boost my ego wouldn't go amiss - something to make my heart beat a bit faster.

My God, Arnold is still humming *Hill Street Blues*. Feel the need to escape for a bit of peace.

Later.

Arnold now humming *Cagney and Lacey*. Very nippy out tonight. Just had a brief stroll down canal - looks so beautiful at night, with all the reflections from the neon signs. Popped into the bar at the bottom for a mineral water. Not many people around. Could hear some American tourists arguing about the capital of Denmark - one said it was Carslberg, another said Denmark was the capital of Sweden. Was about to go over and put them out of their misery when some big bloke walked in. I'd seen him somewhere before, but couldn't think where - then it dawned on me. He was the one I'd seen in the scuffle with Joop over at the hostel bar the other week. As he walked in, the barman looked as nervous as anything, and disappeared into the back. This bloke just followed him through. I tried to make out what they were saying, but could only hear raised muffled voices. After a bit, the bloke walked out, as menacingly as he'd walked in. The barman emerged looking flummoxed, with his bow-tie pulled over to one side - very dodgy. Must remember to mention it to Joop.

The Americans had moved onto working out whether Helsinki or Oslo was the capital of Luxembourg, so I decided to leave at that point.

Saturday 5th October

Been in a funny sort of mood the last couple of days. Been thinking a lot about being back in England - no doubt because of my dream the other night. I dreamt I was back in Walsall, living with Phil and Jan, and teaching at the comp again. It was a really weird dream. At some point, I went into a pub with Phil, and my old head of department was serving behind the bar. He asked me how much longer I was going to be away, and said it was time I stopped messing about and got to grips with the real world. I turned round, and one of year 9 French groups were sitting there. Jan was amongst them, and told me to get on with it - they'd been waiting nine months for their next French lesson. I panicked, and started asking them what they did in their spare time in French. Nobody answered, though - they all jumped up and started talking amongst themselves, a few of them rushed up and started swearing at me. Mom and dad were suddenly there, tutting, saying they'd have to get back to make sure they'd set the video. Phil started berating me for my lack of classroom management skills, at which point my head of department rushed in with a copy of the National Curriculum, a pack of flash cards and a Rennie. I looked over to the door, and saw Ben gesticulating for me to come outside. Then I saw Joop and Bertus behind him, who started laying into him. I turned round and noticed I was still in a pub really. Over at a table in the corner, Frank and Arnold were having a drink with Sandra. Sandra urged me to come and finish my drink so that we could get home. When I asked her what home, she jangled some keys in front of me. At that point, I woke up sweating. Can't seem to shake off the strangeness of it all.

The really stupid thing is that it's made me feel as though I'm just filling in time here before I go back - very unsettling. In one way, it feels as though I've lived here half my life - the job, Frank, the flat, Joop, the business with Sandra (still no word from her - fingers crossed), etc. On the other hand, it hardly seems any time at all, like some sort of extended holiday.

Wonder if there is a point that people get to when you know that this is how your life is going to be. Do you get up one morning, feeling settled? Even if I had a wife, a kid, a mortgage, etc, I still think I'd wonder whether I was in the right life, and whether I shouldn't be moving on to something else.

Went to the gym this morning, thinking it would shake me out of the mood. No sign of Else, unfortunately. Didn't feel like going out tonight, so sat in and watched TV. Daft programme where ordinary people do impressions of their favourite singer. Think I'll go to bed now - maybe a good night's sleep will see me right.

Monday 7th October

Feeling fine again now. Funny how you can be so affected by a dream. Frank noticed I was a bit odd, so told him all about it when he asked. He made some herbal tea to calm my emotions, and put it down to the recent upheavals and shocks. Then he got out his dream interpretation book and sat leafing through it. When I asked him if he could work out what it all meant, he said it all seemed to point to an underlying anxious insecurity (which I could've told him), and then went and fetched me some more herbal tea. He persuaded me to let him demonstrate a meditation routine which he's convinced will bring me inner peace. Sat cross-legged on the sofa for twenty minutes letting the essence of my being transform my negativity into useful energy, as Frank explained. Just as I was communing with my astral plane, some workmen started on a pneumatic drill outside, so it was back to square one.

Otherwise, things much the same. Sandra still keeping away, shop still quite busy, especially with the email orders. Felt quite flattered when Frank showed me one enquiry - some woman called Linda from San Diego wanted to know if there were "any blow up men with Gerard's fine face". At least somebody out there loves me.

Wednesday 9th October

Went over to Joop's last night. Bertus came in just after me, doing his trousers up - he'd been next door to the brothel. "De urge just took me," he said. Joop much amused by it all.

Joop really liked my moustache, and said all real men have moustaches. Bertus said he hadn't realized they could do eyebrow transplants, and made his way to the toilet.

Gave Joop a quick low-down on business in the shop, he seemed very pleased. Am not surprised, though. Last month we turned over 200,000 guilders - quite amazing. He also wanted to know how things were, and whether I'd had any more trouble with Ben. I said all was well. Mentioned that bloke to him who I'd seen in the bar down the canal last week, the one I'd seen at Joop's too. He came over all confidential, shifting back and forth and looking round carefully, like he does when Arnold's about. One of his collection boys, apparently. It turns out that there are one or two clients who are quite happy to enjoy Joop's protection, but are not that keen on paying for it, so Joop has to occasionally send somebody round to make sure that they cough up. He must be sitting on a goldmine - God knows what he does with all this money. And all he does is spend day and night in the hostel bar. Not much of a life, really. Still, he always seems happy enough. Something to be said for being content with your lot.

Friday 11th October

Sandra rang yesterday. Thought it was too good to be true. Could we meet up, go out for a drink or even have a meal together - just for old time's sake? I said it was still very much early days, and would rather leave it a while, but I would still like us to be friends. God knows why I said that. It's not that I don't like her, but I've not really missed her. On the other hand, it does seem a shame to have absolutely nothing to do with her ever again. I don't know. Anyway, will have to see what happens.

Still no sign of Else at gym. It was the same girl serving at the bar, so I asked her if she knew someone called Else. She'd apparently been in earlier. Shame. Thought about trying to spot her down by the Central Station on one of the tourist boats, but thought better of it. Not sure I want to pursue anything either. Maybe it's just better as a thought, a possibility. Maybe that's when relationships are at their best - when they're just a vague emotional possibility. The virtue of unrequited love - it never has to die or diminish.

Anyway, amazing news tonight! When Arnold came round, he said he'd seen Ben down at the police station, and was curious as to how we'd got to know him exactly. I explained about having done a Dutch course with his ex-girlfriend originally, and that he knew I was English, so occasionally asked me to check letters for him (don't want him knowing the full story). Anyway, when Arnold recognised him, he asked a colleague, who explained he was in on suspicion of drug dealing! They reckon he's a big-time dealer, but never manage to get any hard evidence against him. Arnold said they even searched his flat recently (which he said was absolutely soaked - he'd been away for a few days and had left the tap on - the neighbours had noticed water coming from under front door, but didn't think it was any of their business, so didn't bother reporting it – typically Dutch again. When Ben got back, everywhere was sodden, and it still hasn't dried out!) They'd acted on a tip-off, but there was nothing to incriminate him, so they'll have to release him fairly soon. What a villain, though. And then there's all the paining stuff, which the police probably have no idea about. I really hope he gets his comeuppance.

As Arnold was talking to me, he was a bit odd – hard to put my finger on really – bit more like he was the evening he picked me up for loitering. Not sure he totally believes me about the letters' business. Not that it matters. Fantastic hearing that my feeble revenge plan was successful, though. Have it!!

Saturday 12th October

Terrible news today. Had a phone call from Jan - Phil got knocked down by a car yesterday afternoon and is critical in hospital. Can't believe it. There's me gloating over Ben coming a cropper, while Phil's in a coma. How can you be going about your business one minute, probably thanking God it's Friday, and the next you're in hospital, not knowing whether it's the last one you'll ever see. Poor Phil. Feel as though I've turned my back on him this year.

Went over to Central Station to book ticket back, have got to go over and see him. People walking around with ice-creams, tourists with cameras, house-wives with shopping, gangs of teenagers with walkmans on, playing the fool. Felt sick and angry at the same time, looking at them. Not one of them would even raise an eyebrow if Phil died. Hope to God he pulls through.

When I got back, there was a letter for me on the mat - the fine for jay-walking had come through from the police - 60 guilders. Filled in the enclosed money transfer slip and cried my eyes out.

Sunday 13th October

Hook of Holland - Harwich ferry bar

Spoke to Jan again last night, she reckons he's stable but still not out of the woods. Frank was fantastic yesterday, a real tower of strength, cooking, sorting out the Sexmarkt. Surprise visit from Joop last night. Turned up with a box after Frank had rung him to ask him if he could sort some cover out for me. Hearing I was going back, he wondered if I could drop off some 'merchandise' at a shop in Soho! Was disgusted at first at his lack of sensitivity - a friend of mine could be dying, but never mind, how about dropping off some DVDs on the way? Even for the Dutch, that's tactless. He could see he'd shocked me, so made out he hadn't realized how badly injured Phil was, and gave me a big hug, saying he was sorry. But if I was interested, there's a £1000 in it for me! The shop owner would give me £5000 for the DVDs, I could keep £1000 for the delivery. £1000! A grand to invest in my future.

Started to disgust myself at that point, suddenly there I was revelling in the prospect of cash while Phil might have been breathing his last. Then the risk dawned on me as well - porno smuggling must be a crime in Britain. Joop said it was just standard Dutch hardcore, and the worst that would happen IF I got caught would be that the DVDs get confiscated and I get a fine/a warning. He told me to trust him, and I must admit, I find it hard not to. So here I am on the ferry, one case full of porn, a head full of fear, and a conscience somewhere, telling me I should be having thoughts for the well-being of my old best mate, not my own scalp at Harwich customs. Phil wouldn't believe this if I told him. Hope I do get to tell him about it.

11.00 p.m. - Walsall

Arrived at Harwich, feeling one stone lighter. Felt like I was wearing a T-shirt saying "GUILTY - STOP ME NOW", and sure enough, they stopped me. Customs officials are incredible. They stand there in uniforms with their 2 GCSE's, like defenders of some superior empire relishing the prospect of exercising their rubber glove powers, exuding quiet smarm. They can't even speak normally: "What is the duration of your residence in the Netherlands, Sir?" "Are you in gainful employment, Sir?" "What is the purpose of your current re-entry to the UK?" I was too nervous to be cocky, so explained about Phil, and think they thought I was going to get upset, so they ushered me through quite quickly then, no doubt fearing they'd have to deal with blubbing.

Got onto boat train to London, full of Southerners and Dutch tourists. And suddenly I realized I was back. People on platforms wearing brown and grey; crimplene and anoraks had come into their own once again. Spotty youths selling over-priced and under-quality 'station refreshments' (any beverages or pastries for yourself with that, Sir?), kids eating crisps and throwing fish and chip wrappers on the floor. And somehow I could imagine people getting back home from the pub and talking about Barry's new extension, Rita's holiday in Majorca, the mother's back trouble, and how scampi and chips down the Red Lion repeats on you. It dawned on me suddenly how there's something incredibly mundane about Britain that I'm not aware of in Holland, although it must be there. Mundane but comforting.

Got to London, which dispelled any sense of mundanity. Not keen on London - feels more foreign than Amsterdam, it's far too big, busy, and everybody's got a chip on their shoulder because they all think they're where it's at. Managed to find the shop in Soho. What a joke. Cosmopolitan London, with what must be the tamest sex shops in the world. I've seen more explicit greengroceries in Holland. Anyway, some greasy-haired Cockney called Malcolm had the DVDs off me in the back, and gave me five grand in fifty quid notes, which I carefully counted out.

Packed the money carefully in bag, then made my way to Euston for the Birmingham train. At New Street, there could be absolutely no doubt I was back. Pure Midlands. The accent, the concrete, the drab city-scape. I love it and loathe it at the same time. Arriving in Walsall was unreal. The most alarming thing was that NOTHING had changed. I even recognised an old bloke waiting at the bus stop when I got off. He said "Oroight mate", as though it was just another normal day in Walsall, which I suppose it was. Weird.

Everything still exactly the same at Jan and Phil's except there's a baby there now but no Phil. Phil woke up this afternoon apparently, and is on the mend, so was delighted to hear that. Will go and see him tomorrow. Jan's got the baby with her in her room, so here I am, diary on lap, in my old room - but thank God not in my old life.

Monday 14th October

It was so weird waking up this morning. Lay there for ages looking at the wall paper; every stain held a memory, the pattern in the carpet was like a catalogue of worries scrutinized in another life.

Jan's been very friendly, motherly even, am sure she's sorry about the way she behaved in Amsterdam. Anyway, called in to see Phil. Took him a few car magazines and some chocolate. What a state - legs and arms in plaster, his face all bruised and swollen, patches of hair missing. Hell of a shock, felt quite choked. But he's going to be all right. He was confused at first, couldn't understand what I was doing there. I told him I'd come over to see him, and he started crying. I sat there, holding his hand, feeling even more choked, till he calmed down. Poor Phil. If this isn't "die gebrechliche Einrichtung der Welt", God knows what is. Chatted about this and that, but he kept drifting off, must be the painkillers he's on. In the end, I said I'd keep in touch more often, squeezed his hand and walked out with Jan. Glanced back at him lying there, all wired up and alone, machines going 'beep'. The old truism about us only having one life came into my mind, and I thanked God that I was finally doing something with mine.

Tuesday 15th October

Amsterdam

Miraculously back home again. Got off early this morning, was on ferry by midday. Had thought about calling in on mom and dad, but couldn't be bothered. Spent most of the time kipping, so got to Hook of Holland in no time, and relieved not to have any reason to fear customs. Who of course stopped me. Same types as in Harwich, only surlier and blonder. Went through all my luggage, found the five grand, and wanted to know all about it. Started sweating at that point. Said it was money from my bank account which I'd closed as I was now living in Holland, etc. They wanted to know what bank account. I gave them my Lloyds number, and think they were just trying it on to see how I'd react. Anyway, after keeping me waiting for ages, faffing around with my passport and residence permit, they let me go, and that was that. Got on boat train, and back in flat in no time, the last few days seeming like a dream. Frank delighted to see me, no news here. Rang Jan, and Phil still doing ok. All's well that ends well.

Wednesday 16th October

Have taken it easy today, feel exhausted. Joop came over tonight, delighted the delivery had gone ok. He put his arms round me and called me a super kid. I handed him the four grand and he kissed me. Thank God they didn't search my stuff in Harwich, as I wonder now how lenient they would have been. Told him about what happened in Hook of Holland, but he said they'd have just been going through the motions. Must put my grand in the bank tomorrow.

Frank tried to get me to go to a club tonight, but haven't got the energy, so he's gone with Arnold. I stayed in my room before he came round, as can't be bothered making small talk. Lay on the bed listening to him humming *Hawaii-Five-O* in the other room, while Frank finished spiking his hair.

Friday 18th October

Feeling more normal again now, but have had a few panicky moments. Frank says it's post-traumatic empathy with Phil, brought about by the unpalatable realization of our own futile mortality. I said I thought it was the shock. He's got me doing a meditation routine, which does seem to help a bit. It involves lying on your back and raising your legs over your head, and then just trying to let your mind go blank. Frank manages to hold a tranquillity candle between his feet while he's doing it, it takes me all my time not to fall off the bed. While we were doing it tonight, the window-cleaner suddenly appeared outside, and stood there shaking his head, his shammy going from side to side. Nosey git.

Saturday 19th October

Fairly quiet in shop today for a Saturday. Miserable drizzle all day, so most people probably couldn't be bothered coming out. Loads of email orders yet again, though. It was quite nice this afternoon, quite homely really. I sat most of the afternoon with Frank, packaging and addressing merchandise, while Mariska manned the till. When we started on the magazines, I said to Frank: "You stuff and I'll lick", at which point everyone turned round. It's actually quite a pleasant shop, really, with all the bright flesh-tone colours and the upbeat tunes coming out of the video cabins. It's also very hard not to smile when you look round and see people puffing and panting and fiddling with dildos - and that's only Mariska unloading the van.

Monday 21st October

Frank's under the weather again with a cold. The flat smells like some sort of Turkish massage parlour, with all kinds of exotic oils spreading out from his bedroom. Arnold was round pampering him last night, humming *Cagney and Lacey* again, and walking round with a towel on his head, as they were both at the deep inhaling.

Arnold said that Ben was released a few days ago, as they couldn't come up with any hard evidence against him. What a shame. Thought about going over to Joop's tonight for a change, but felt quite tired myself, so spent the evening reading. Have started reading a Dutch book called *The Evenings* which is about a kid who's being driven mad by the banality of life in post-war Holland.

Wednesday 23rd October

What a brilliant book *The Evenings* is turning out to be. Was up till 3.00 a.m. reading it this morning, so consequently felt shattered all day. It's the sort of book that makes me think that I could write as well, although I'm not sure I'd have the discipline or the imagination. It's one of Frank's favourite

Dutch books, although he says he's not that fond in general of
Dutch literature. When I asked why, he said that most modern
fiction is about the German occupation during the war.

He's been quite quiet since yesterday, in fact. I finally
persuaded him to go to the doctor's, just to be on the safe side.
He didn't have much to say when he came back afterwards,
but he looked a bit better all the same.

Spoke to Arnold on the phone earlier when he rang for
Frank (who couldn't be bothered going out tonight). He was a
bit curt with me, I thought, but then I'm never too sure with
the Dutch.

Have got to a bit in *The Evenings* where the kid is doing
something very strange with a toy rabbit. Frank said there's
another famous Dutch book where a teenager does something
very questionable with a live chicken. Wonder what
Shakespeare would have made of all this.

Friday 25th October

Went to the gym yesterday for first time in what seems like
ages. Felt as though I'd never been before, and struggled to do
a steady ten-minute jog on the treadmill. Looked round all the
time I was there in case Else was about, but no sign of her
until I'd changed and was leaving. I noticed her at the
opposite end of the gym laughing with some bloke who looked
like a Beefcake Bugger. She didn't see me. Another vague
dream dashed. Some days, my spirits ride on dreams like that.
Bit worried about Frank, who's not entirely over his cold, and
still seems a bit quiet.

Sunday 27th October

Frank still a bit down, he says he's just tired. Mariska and her
friend Hetty have been helping out in the Sexmarkt, quite busy.

Tuesday 29th October

Felt very wintery the last couple of days, biting wind. Bloke from upstairs came down to ask if we'd had any trouble with our hot water, as theirs keeps going cold, apparently. Fortunately we haven't, but hope this doesn't mean the waterworks are dodgy here in winter. Can't be as bad as they were in Phil's house. Been doing the stock reorders today, it's just unbelievable how much merchandise we manage to shift. Five email orders came through within the space of one minute last night while Frank was on-line. Amazing. Some people contact us with really sick requests, though, I couldn't even write them down.

Called in for a drink at Joop's tonight after closing, as needed his signature on some of the orders. When I walked in, that bloke I'd seen in the bar down the canal was there again, and I noticed him handing over yet another wad of cash. Very odd.

At one point I asked him whether he intends to run the hostel for the rest of his life. He laughed, twizzled the ends of his moustache, and said he'd be moving on within the next five years. Turns out he's got this plan to buy a villa in the South of Spain (where he's got loads of contacts, of course) and retire. That's obviously what he's doing with all his cash - saving it till then. Then he started laughing again, this time in a sort of secretive way, and asked me to guess how much money he'd made from the Prague trip (he never actually uses the word porno). I suggested around 3000 guilders, which made him roar - 60,000! Don't know whether to believe him. I asked him again what sort of porn it was, but all he would say was "Gerard, porn is just porn!"

Anyway, Joop reckons Bertus has been after me for an escort job coming up. Will give him a ring tomorrow. Left at 12.30, and walked along the canals, which never fail to thrill me at night when it's so quiet, gables and bridges reflecting in the moonlight. Went flying on a used condom by the toilet on the corner, though.

Friday 1st November

Was walking back from gym yesterday (Else not there) in teeming rain, when Ben went past me in his jeep, driving through a puddle which soaked me from head to foot. He obviously realized it was me, as he tooted his horn. Git.

Quite busy at work, as there's a 'team' been in the back filming since yesterday morning. The film is about two busty, lusty sisters who live alone, and is called *The Repairmen Are Coming*. There've been mechanics, service engineers, electricians, carpenters and all sorts traipsing through in overalls all day long. Bit of a commotion this morning when one bloke came rushing out ranting and raving - turns out he was a real plumber, come to look at the neighbour's water tank. Thought it was strange, as he was the only one with a spanner.

Bertus called round in the middle of it all - helping himself to the phone in the shop. Annoys me how he just helps himself when we're busy. Anyway, he's got an assignment for me tomorrow night - some Ukrainian businessman. He was full of apologies (which surprised me) for the lack of work he's put my way, but I told him again that I have less time now anyway, and don't need the cash so much either. That was a mistake, as he immediately negotiated a reduced rate (which didn't surprise me).

Frank seems much better again now, although still a bit quiet. He's reading a book called *The Herbal Way Forward* which I suppose is enough to make anyone quiet. Arnold's been over tonight again. He sat there reading *New Approaches in the Force*, quietly humming *Hart to Hart*. When I asked if either of them wanted a hob-nob, they both said "Shush!" I leafed through *CIAO BELLO* for a bit before coming to bed. If this isn't the social high life, God knows what is.

Saturday 2nd November

Letter from Jan today - Phil's doing much better now, and might be coming home soon. Really glad about that.

Mariska got her friend Hetty in tonight to cover for me while

I went out on Bertus' escort assignment tonight. She seems a
very pleasant girl, and quite chatty compared to Mariska. She'd
brought her 'Millennium Tapestry' with her to do in the quiet
moments. It's a big thing like the Bayeux Tapestry, only with
all the key developments from the birth of Christ up to the end
of the 20<sup>th</sup> Century. She aims to get it done by 2000 but has
only just finished three metres on the Romans, so I'm a bit
dubious.

The Ukrainian businessman was a ball-bearings manufacturer
from Kiev. Little bloke who wouldn't have looked out of
place in Llandudno. I met him at The Happy Thai Restaurant,
very nice meal, but conversation like extracting teeth.
Afterwards, he asked me if I could give him a tour of the Red
Light Area - what a surprise. So off we went. Thought he
might loosen up a bit, but he just loped along, red-faced and
quietly sweating. He shook my hand outside a brothel and
thanked me for a most pleasurable evening. I replied the
pleasure was all mine, as he stepped into Maison Matilde and
loosened his tie. Wonder what he normally does of a Saturday
night in the Ukraine.

Monday 4th November

Yesterday was a beautiful day, chilly but sunny. Frank and
Arnold went to Utrecht where somebody was giving a talk on
the benefits of homeopathy. I declined the invitation. Have to
draw the line somewhere. Was determined not to pootle
around the flat on my own, and since it was such a nice day,
decided to jog down to the Central Station and go on one of
the tourist boats. Walked up and down a few times, trying to
spot Else, and after about ten minutes, I noticed her on a boat
that was about to leave. Rushed over, bought a ticket and got
on. She recognized me straight away and waved like I was a
long-lost friend. As she reached over for the microphone, she
told me not to disappear at the end, beaming from ear to ear.
Then she gave a 45-minute commentary in four languages,
sparing no details on gables through the ages, during which I

wondered whether I might not have been better off going to the homeopathy talk.

But no. When everybody else had got off, she said that was her last tour for the day. I asked her if she'd had anything to eat. She hadn't, so I suggested getting something. And sure enough, she said it was a great idea! Off we went to a brown cafe near the Central Station. We chatted for ages about things, life in Amsterdam, and so on. She asked me whether I'd been to all the museums yet, as she could get me some free passes, one of the perks of working in the tourist trade. Turns out she's 28, grew up in Arnhem, studied psychology but hasn't been able to get a job, so is just biding her time on the tourist boats, as she loves being in Amsterdam. She wanted to know all about me, and seemed genuinely interested. Her eyes never stopped smiling at me. She got through about ten cigarettes in a couple of hours, bit of a nervous disposition, I reckon.

As she stubbed out a cigarette, her wrist popped out of her sleeve, and I noticed it seemed a bit twisted. She saw me staring (which made me feel awful) and said that she suffers from arthritis in her joints (at 28!). Sometimes it's quite painful, but going to the gym helps keep them supple, and there are people with far worse things to cope with, she reckons. Turns out she's on the Dutch Arthritis Charity committee, and helps out with all kinds of fundraising activities.

Anyway, I'd lost all track of time, so had to rush off eventually to take over in the Sexmarkt. When I got up, she looked a bit disconcerted, and asked when I was going to the gym next. I said Tuesday, and she smiled, saying she'd look forward to seeing me there. Rushed onto the tram on a high, and haven't come down yet. All day today, have kept thinking about her, and can't wait to get to the gym in the morning. As I handed some bloke the change for a pair of handcuffs and a suspending harness kit tonight, he said, for no apparent reason: "You know, there's nothing more beautiful than love, is there?"

Tuesday 5<sup>th</sup> November

Spent ages at the gym this morning, nearly totally dehydrated in
the sauna at the end, but no sign of Else all the time I was
there. Came away feeling literally wrung out. Up one minute,
down the next. Always seems to be the way. Why do I always
let myself get so carried away? Don't know about 'love at first
sight' with me, it's more like 'naive and unjustified over-elation
at first sight'. Maybe she thought I was boring, or put off by
the arthritis thing. Sat listening to Frank's Barbra Streisand
love tapes tonight, indulging in self-pity, but not sure it was
such a good idea, as feel ten times worse now.
Wednesday 6<sup>th</sup> November
Got up feeling a bit more stoical about it all this morning,
plenty more fish in the sea and all that. Loads of people in and
out all day today, so not had much time to dwell. Talk about
miserable, though. Some people look as though they're
spending their last guilder. Some scrawny bloke, who looked
about as cheerful as a wet weekend in Widnes, took five
minutes counting out the exact change in 10 cent pieces for
this month's Beefcake Buggers, before shoving it inside his
anorak and zipping it up. Would have smiled at him, but
didn't want to give him the wrong idea. Should count my
blessings, really.

Friday 8<sup>th</sup> November

Arnold came round tonight, looking very pleased with himself
as usual. He disappeared into Frank's room, where I could
hear what sounded like heavy discussion going on, interspersed
with long periods of silence, and then angry outbursts of "For
God's sake!" and much worse. So God knows what's going on
there. Wonder whether Frank has been trying to ditch him.
That could account for his glumness of late, as it's never
pleasant trying to end a relationship, as I know with Sandra
(not heard anything from her for ages now - probably still
having it away with her hard-bodied git-face lover). Arnold left

in a huff after a couple of hours, looking all red-faced and less pleased with himself. I knocked on Frank's bedroom door and asked if he was all right, but he just shouted he was, and wanted to get some sleep now.

Saturday 9th November

Went to the gym today, still no sign of Else. Maybe she just forgot, or had to work - there could be all sorts of reasons, I suppose. Each time I heard the buzzer go as someone walked in, I looked round, hoping to see her. When I weighed myself this morning, after another vigorous session, the scales read 79kg! I'd thought my belt was getting a bit loose, and there's the confirmation. Bucked me up no end. Thought of strolling down to the Station and trying to spot Else on one of the boats, but don't want her to think I'm stalking her, especially if she's not interested. Nothing sadder than a spurned lurker.

No Arnold today. Frank's not mentioned him, and still seems a bit sullen. When I asked him if he was okay, as he was extremely quiet, he smiled, started crying, and then reached for some kind of homeopathic pill. He said he was fine, and all the better for having such a solid friend in me. When I asked if it was anything to do with Arnold, he said not really, smiled, and picked up *The Herbal Way Forward*. He's on Basil at the moment (the herb).

The most amazing news of the day is that I've had a call from Sandra! Was beginning to think I'd heard the last of her, not that I'd have been bothered, of course. Had quite a pleasant chat. She says she ended her affair with Peter, as things had started to get very awkward at work (serves them right). Besides which, she was riddled with guilt (took long enough). She went on a bit about people from work (who I don't even know), her family (they'd been to an aunt's birthday party) and some shell-suits that she'd got cheap on a market outside Amersfoort. Eventually, she asked me how I was and what I'd been up to. Had trouble thinking what to say at first, and then started to tell her about Frank and Arnold, but she interrupted me and went on about somebody from work.

Then she said she'd love to meet me "for old time's sake", as "we've been through such a lot together", and "time heals all wounds", and finally, "good friends should always be there for one another". Sandra is proof that the Dutch wouldn't be able to speak a word of English without pop songs and American talk shows. Anyway, I agreed to meet her tomorrow afternoon at Bar Scorpio, as I couldn't think of a reason not to.

Nobody seems to have noticed my weight loss yet. Might as well have half a Mars Bar.

Sunday 10th November

Suppose Armistice Day is quite appropriate for re-establishing the bond of friendship between myself and Sandra. She was already there when I walked into the bar, and I was surprised how nice she looked. Her healthy red hair (seemed darker than normal), fresh-smelling perfume and tight jeans. Her blouse was quite tight as well, emphasising her chest, and I noticed her face was tanned. I asked if she'd been on a sun-bed, but apparently she'd had a mishap when she used some sort of long-lasting henna on her hair, and ended up improving her complexion as well.

She started telling me the same things that she'd told me on the phone last night, only in more (unwelcome) detail. I sat there, my concentration drifting off, thinking how only a week ago I was sitting in a bar with a woman who could've become an interesting part of my future, and a week later, I'm in another bar with an uninteresting woman from my past. I came to when she started saying things like "Oh Gerard, you mean so much to me, I hope we'll always be there for each other", and "Who knows, maybe in time you'll learn to love me again". This was followed by "But I'll be patient, only time will tell. I've learned my lesson well, but I'll be there, waiting, if you decide you can love me". I ordered some peanuts and said we should concentrate on moving on. I expected her to try pressurizing me, as she looked aghast, but all she said was

"Do you realize how much fat there is in peanuts?"

In a way, I was almost relieved when I had to leave to do my shift in the Sexmarkt. When I was leaving, she said she felt "we've come a long way" and was so glad "we've been reunited in friendship", and that "love will always win the day". I said "That's as maybe, but there are dildos that won't sell themselves if I don't get a move on". She didn't say anything to that, but just smiled at me in a kind of forlorn way as I walked out. I can really do without all this.

Hetty was helping Mariska out in the shop again when I got back, and had just started embroidering the Vikings. Mariska was quietly refilling the shelves with copies of "Danish Assblasters". "Plus ça change", I thought.

Tuesday 12<sup>th</sup> November

Went to the gym yesterday morning, and joy of joys, Else was there! As soon as I saw her, I felt my heart racing. At the same time, I could feel fear and humiliation pulling it back down, as I braced myself for the realization she'd probably rather carry on with the dumb-bells than with me. As soon as she saw me, though, she rushed over, I was staggered at her eagerness. She said she was so glad to see me and suggested getting a coffee at the bar before I started. My heart beat was straight back up by this point.

Apparently, when she'd got back home that Sunday, there was a message on her answer-phone from her dad, saying her mother had been involved in a car crash and was in intensive care at the hospital in Arnhem, where she spent the rest of the week. Her mother's on the road to recovery now, though, in spite of a broken leg, arm, chest injuries and a fractured skull. Her voice started to break a bit then as she tried not to get upset. I reached up and rubbed her arm. She looked really touched and held my hand for a moment, while she apologized for being silly. My heart-beat was doing more than the beefcake bugger's on the treadmill by this point. Anyway, she'd more or less finished her work-out, and had to get off to work, but spurred on by the sense of rapprochement (like that word), I suggested meeting up in the same cafe as before on Thursday evening, to which she agreed! In fact, not only did she agree, she positively enthused. I was almost light-headed now, and was struggling not to lunge at her there and then. Then she squeezed my arm as she left to get her things. Some bloke on the pec-dec must have been watching, and said something about me having "my hands full with that one." He was a big, muscular, hairy bloke, so I just said "yes" and went to get changed. Jogged with ease on the treadmill for thirty-two minutes.

Frank still on the quiet side, Arnold still keeping away. When I've tried to get him to open up, it's obvious he doesn't want to. He'd left his diary on the table tonight, and I noticed he'd written "Arzt" by tomorrow's date. Funny, as he doesn't exactly seem ill, in spite of his quietness. Maybe he'll tell me tomorrow.

Wednesday 13th November

Frank was up quite early sorting out email orders, and seemed ok. He didn't let on he was going to the doctor's, but said something about nipping to the shops. That was at eleven o'clock this morning. It's gone half past eleven at night now, and he's not been back yet. Very odd for Frank.

Thursday 14th November

Frank didn't come back last night and there's been no sign of him all day. Rang Joop this afternoon, but he was as clueless as me. I even rang Arnold, who wasn't in, so I left a message on his answer-phone, asking him to ring me if he knew where Frank might be. It's funny, as he hasn't taken anything with him, and it's not like him not to say anything to anyone, especially me. Hope nothing has happened to him. I also rang the doctor, and was told he'd left after seeing him yesterday morning. Can't work it out at all. Don't know whether to notify the police. Maybe I should leave it a day. With a bit of luck, he'll be back any minute.

Anyway, had a wonderful evening with Else tonight, although had Frank at the back of my mind all the time. She was wearing an amazing blue dress (long-sleeved), which, with her blond hair and blue eyes, made her look like a Nordic princess. Very easy conversation. She'd even brought me the museum passes she mentioned the other week. When she asks something, it's as though she really wants to know the answer, which I find rare these days. She says she loves my sense of humour, which she calls "the English sense of humour". What a great thing it is at times to be English. She's got a funny habit of swinging her elbows around when she starts laughing - don't know if it's to do with the arthritis.

In the course of conversation, she got onto previous boyfriends, and said she had the impression that most of them were only attracted to her because of her breasts, which, once revealed, made them lose interest in her. I said how awful I thought that was (suddenly feeling ashamed of myself), and then she just came right out with it - was I attracted to her? Lost the power of speech for a second or two, grappled to produce a non-fatuous response, but ended up saying "Yes, I am".

Of course, she asked why. I joked that there were two big reasons, which got her doing the elbows thing again. Then I knew I'd have to try and be a bit deeper, and went on about her easy-going charm and sincerity, which made her smile. There was a bit of a silence at that point, after which she asked me why I hadn't asked her if she was attracted to me. I felt myself blush, and before I could say anything, she said, "Well, I'm going to give you the answer anyway, Gerard. Yes, I am attracted to you, your wit, your smile, your honesty". I was totally bowled over by that, and felt my face lift the room temperature by another 10 degrees.

I was just as shocked when she said that she'd rather we didn't go to bed together for a while, as she'd like us to get to know each other properly first. I told her I wasn't expecting to anyway, which led her to ask me what the longest was I'd been without sex. I said twenty years, which made her roar with laughter again, elbows flying about uncontrollably. I didn't let on that I wasn't joking after her reaction. Anyway, we ended up kissing as we left the bar, which suits me fine. After a while, I noticed somebody loitering a few doors away, staring at us, but whoever it was ran off down the canal. We said we'd meet back there on Monday night, as she's off to Arnhem at the weekend for an 18th Century arthritis fundraising day that she's organised - guess the weight of the Frisian cow, dike vaulting, Edam rolling and the clog race.

Got back to an empty flat. Looked all round for signs of Frank having been in, but nothing. In fact, starting to get quite worried. Had a Bounty, thinking of Else.

Friday 15th November

Still no Frank. Kept expecting him to walk into Sexmarkt all day while I was down there. Even Mariska seemed quite concerned, but was sure he'd turn up, so haven't contacted the police yet. What on earth is he doing? Where is he? Why didn't he say anything? I just don't get it, it's not like him at all.

Saturday 16th November

Still nothing from Frank. I slept quite badly last night, hoping to hear him coming in. Spent the day going from bar to bar, wandering round the canals, down at the station, looking round the gay clubs. It's another world, the gay scene. One bloke covered in leather and a huge moustache in Guy World thought he'd seen someone matching Frank's description going into the 'dark room' at the back. I said I'd go and have a look, but then he said "Don't go in there unless you want cock," which stopped me dead in my tracks. Apparently, blokes go into this unlit room on the understanding that they can do anything to anyone, and have it done to them as well. He said he'd go and check for me. Eventually, he wobbled back out in just a G-string, only to say there was nobody in there called Frank, only a Hans, Dik, Frans, Arie and Mike. I took him at his word and left.

Have hung around the flat the rest of the day. Keep getting up and having a look outside, but no sign. Wonder if Frank ever goes into dark rooms. The mind boggles.

Sunday 17th November

Still no Frank. Thought about ringing his parents, but can't believe he'd just go to Cologne and not say anything. Don't want to alarm them either.

Have spent today doing the same as yesterday, scouring the bars and clubs, all much quieter on a Sunday. Went back into Guy World and saw the same leather bloke as yesterday, who reckoned I must be 'on the turn' and should try ten minutes with him in the dark room just to see. Politely declined, and decided it was time to try another tack - the police.

Saw the same policeman who'd dealt with me last time - Van Arlen. He realized who I was when he took my details. He showed about as much concern as if I'd gone in saying bread's gone up half a guilder, but that's the Dutch police for you. Filled in a few forms, which he scanned, and then he asked me how many people I thought went missing in Amsterdam each year? Hundreds, apparently, and that's only the Dutch ones. He then passed me a bundle of photos of missing foreigners last seen in Amsterdam, just in case I'd seen any of them. One of them was Annika, Ben's girlfriend. In shock, I nearly admitted I knew her, then thought of Ben and decided it'd be best to act ignorant. "Know her?" he asked. I made out that she just reminded me of someone, but don't think he was convinced. Walked out, realizing I might have got out of the Ben web more lightly than some, and that Van Arlen was obviously not going to send out a task force to track Frank down. Then he shouted in Dutch "No doubt see you again soon!" Hilarious.

Came back feeling flat and anxious. Did Ben do something

to Annika?  And Frank, where the Hell are you?

Monday 18<sup>th</sup> November

Monday 18<sup>th</sup> November, I'll not forget that date in a rush.
Woken up at 2.30 am by Frank's bedroom door opening - he's
back!!  Dashed out of bed, and he stood there in his doorway,
looking totally knackered and dejected.  When he saw me, he
ran over to me, put his arms round me and started sobbing.

  He was sorry he'd just gone off like that, but didn't know
what to do.  He very carefully lit a couple of meditation candles
and then blurted it out .... he's got a brain tumour.  I collapsed
onto the settee – what the....????  He'd had some tests and
scans a few weeks ago, as he kept feeling under the weather.
Had an appointment at the hospital on Wednesday to discuss
the results but couldn't handle it.  After mooching round the
Red Light Area for a bit, he went to the Central Station and
bought a ticket to Copenhagen (because he'd never been there
before - funny thing to do, but what *do* you do?).  Anyway, he
pootled round Copenhagen for a day, and then decided to
come back, stopping off at his parents in Cologne (should have
rung them after all).  Apparently, they were great - calm,
supportive, and of course, concerned.

  Anyway, after a lot of talking, he started to feel stronger - at
least he knew now what the matter was.  The doctors want him
to have an operation remove it, and his parents kept telling
him that it was bound to be a success, especially with all the
medical advancements being made, radiotherapy, drugs, and so
on.  So eventually, he decided it was time to come back, face
things and carry on.  Then he got up, made some herbal tea,
and asked me what I'd been up to.  I couldn't speak for a
while, as it started to sink in.  My best mate tells me that he
may have a life-threatening tumour, makes a cup of tea, and
asks me what's been happening.

  Hardly slept when I went back to bed, so felt exhausted all
day.  Frank has seemed full of beans - he sat there packaging
up rubber butt plugs and suspenders as though nothing has

happened.  At one point I heard him crying in the toilet, but I
didn't go over as I wouldn't have known what to say.  What
can you say?  Got to stay positive though and hope.  Feel really
trivial writing about anything else now.  Wished I hadn't
arranged to see Else tonight, as I feel wiped out.

Wednesday 20th November

Wished I hadn't bothered going now.  I wasn't much in the
mood for chirpy conversation in a smoky bar, which just ended
up making my eyes even sorer.  To make matters worse, Else
had brought a friend along.  My heart sank instantly.  Why had
she brought her along?  Couldn't she face the thought of being
on her own with me?  Was she just having me on the other
night?  I felt really stupid.  Her friend was a really striking
statuesque woman, big full lips covered in red lipstick, big dark
eyes, and I'm saying nothing about the bulging breasts.
Alarming.  On top of all that, she's an interpreter for some big
import-export company.  I don't know what it is, but put me in
the company of intelligent, successful and beautiful people and
I just sit there feeling totally overawed like some sort of
medieval cabbage chopper.  Else kept trying to engage me in
conversations, but it felt as if I was listening in from an
underwater box.  The Frank thing was whizzing round in my
head all the time, and I was whacked out.  After about an hour
I excused myself, saying I thought I was coming down with
something.  I told her I'd probably see her in the gym at some
point, and swallowed the lump in my throat.  Think I sensed a
sort of sadness behind her smile, and she pulled her sleeves
down to cover her hands, right up to the finger tips, but the
tide had pulled me back too far by then.  As I walked back, I
could have sworn somebody was following me, but each time I
stopped to look round I couldn't see anyone.  Maybe I'm going
round the bend.

  For some reason, I didn't fancy going straight back to the
flat, so decided to stroll over to Joop's, as haven't seen him
much recently.  When I got there, I looked through the glass

door and it seemed quite busy. I could see Bertus propping up the bar and laughing, Joop pulling pilsjes, and a couple of prostitutes from the brothel next door touching up their make-up. The sight of it all just depressed me even more, I felt a sort of hopelessness descend. So I turned straight round and walked back.

Had another long chat with Frank about it all. He'd got more candles on the go than ever, and was eating his way through a packet of tofu. God knows how I'd cope if it was me, but he seems quite calm, and keeps talking about how successful the treatments are these days, and the clever teams of scientists all over the world working night and day to make advances. I wondered if the bang on the head on the Prague trip could have caused it? The doctors think it's unlikely, Frank said, but who knows?

Drifted through yesterday and today, feeling just on the edge of depression. The weather hasn't helped at all - grey, drizzly, biting wind. Have kept lapsing into self-scrutiny, asking myself what I want, where am I going, rereading bits of La Rochefoucauld. Can't be bothered writing any more.

Friday 22ⁿᵈ November

Feel a bit brighter now. Still keep having thoughts about what I'm doing and what I want out of life, and still not sure I know the answers, but for some reason it's not depressing me any more - maybe because I've had more sleep. Haven't been to the gym yet, and haven't seen Else either.

Frank still seems 'all right'. To look at him, you'd never know, of course. Heard him crying in his bedroom again last night. He doesn't want anybody to know, so has sworn me to secrecy. Been saying my first prayers in years – what can you do?

Thought I'd caught some bloke shoplifting in the Sexmarkt today, as he was fumbling round by the dildos, and I was convinced he'd shoved one down his trousers. When I approached him as he was about to leave, he became totally indignant.  He dropped his trousers to convince me, fortunately there were no other customers around, and the bulge was amazingly all his own.  "Satisfied now?" he asked me.  "*I* would be," said Frank, before I could apologise.  Had to make Mariska a cup of tea.  Thank God Hetty wasn't around, we wouldn't have wanted that on the Millennium Tapestry.

Sunday 24th November

Decided to go round to Joop's last night with Frank.  Frank seems ok, though every now and then I look at him and can see he's trying really hard to be upbeat, but there's a sadness and fear behind his eyes.  It's pointless me saying anything, but he knows I'm here to do what I can.  He rang Arnold with the news, but the rat-faced git just blurted out he's met someone else...a plumber from Purmerend (how many plumbers are there in Holland?!).  He apologised for the poor timing (!) and wished him well with the op, as and when.  Another huge blow for Frank.  I knew Arnold was a git from the moment he took down my particulars.

Anyway, Joop was pleased to see us.  He'd trimmed his moustache so that it was less walrus-like, and looked as though he'd lost a bit of weight from round his stomach, lucky git.  He wanted to know if anybody had been into the shop asking 'questions', but wouldn't be more specific than that.  Funny really.  He also seemed a bit on edge, which isn't at all the Joop I know, except when Arnold was around (he told Frank he was well rid of him).  I told him about meeting Else, and Sandra and I being back on speaking terms.

Frank wasn't overly talkative.  Understandably. When Joop asked him what he'd been up to, he just said "Nothing special."  When we asked Joop what he'd been up to, he tapped his nose and said "Nothing special either".

Went to the gym this morning.  78 kg!  No Else - a shame.

Monday 25th November

Went to the gym early this morning, but no sign of Else until I'd nearly finished. She looked as if somebody had switched her lights on when she saw me, even if I say so myself, and I was delighted to see her, especially in her breast-defining leotard. God, I sound like such an immature perv at times. When she asked if I'd been there long, I made the mistake of saying no, and agreed to wait for her to finish, which was another hour. I ended up doing all the exercises again, and am as stiff as a board now. Anyway, she suggested having a sauna, the thought of which forced me to privately acknowledge that I am an immature perv, so I said I was still a bit under the weather and declined. We ended up having a coffee instead. She wanted to know how I was now, what I'd been doing and when we could meet up again. I just wanted to ravish her there and then, but as it was, I just went on for a bit about being busy in the shop. She said she hoped I didn't mind her friend being with her last week. They'd bumped into each other outside the bar, so she couldn't avoid inviting her for a drink. Then she said she'd been quite disappointed because she knew she wouldn't have my undivided attention!

She even admitted wondering whether I'd changed my mind about her the other night; I told her I'd wondered if she was trying to put me off by bringing a friend along, but she laughed and said the Dutch aren't that subtle, which I should have realized by now.

I suggested going out for a meal on Wednesday night, to which she said no. I felt really stupid then and must have looked it as she started laughing, and said we should stay *in* for a meal - at her place. She wrote down the address on a beer mat, and told me to take some 'protection' along, as she didn't think she could wait any longer, and would just have to face the consequences if I went off her! I just thanked God I wasn't in the sauna at that point.

Tuesday 26<sup>th</sup> November

Have hardly been able to concentrate on anything all day.

Sometimes I really need to grow up. Head keeps spinning at the thought of it all. Could have done with working in a newsagents' today, as there's absolutely no distraction from sex in the Sexmarkt.

Wednesday 27th November

What can I say? Perfect day. Beautiful meal, beautiful conversation, beautiful woman, beautiful body, beautiful bedroom, total physical abandon. She'd even wrapped up a little present for me - a box of Belgian chocs. What a woman. This has got to be the answer - never mind where am I going, what are my ambitions, where do I want to be in five years. This is living, and there's no question about it. Just that cloud of worry about Frank behind everything....

Thursday 28th November

Still feeling groinally driven. Miserable winter's day, but don't care. Am seeing Else again tomorrow night. Even though I know it's early days, I've got a really good feeling about this relationship and about Else. There's a basic stability about her which I really like. With Tina and Sandra there was always that hint of the unbalanced. At the same time, I don't want to get carried away, as I've been there before. Frank keeps reminding me to take it one step at a time. I think my jollity has rubbed off on him a bit, as he seems just like his old self now. He's taken up embroidery, though. He says he got the idea from Hetty's tapestry. Suppose it's therapeutic if nothing else. Date for his op has come through – early January.

He was saying how pleased he is that I've met someone and got a bit upset while he was talking. I tried to console him when he asked "Do you think I will live to have another boyfriend?" Sometimes words just totally let you down.

Friday 29th November

Virtually counted the minutes all day today. Had to keep
telling myself to calm down and take things coolly. Else came
over here tonight. Brilliant evening. Frank and Else hit it off
straight away, which pleased me, and before long he was
showing her his cross-stitch. After a bit he took himself off to
the cinema, which was nice of him. Another evening of
indescribable joy followed, although I'm paying the price now.
There's no cream or ointment anywhere in the flat, so have
used some of Frank's hair gel, seems quite soothing so far.

The sex thing apart, it's fantastic being with her. It's ok to
talk, it's fine not to say anything, and when we do talk, it's
interesting. She said she knew I was lying the other night in
the bar when I said I was coming down with something. I
didn't want to get into the Frank story, so said I was having a
bit of a downer. She says she has them too now and again,
especially when the arthritis gets very painful. Apparently,
there's a chance she might not be able to use her hands at all in
ten years or so, but she tries not to dwell on it.

As we lay there, she asked me if I'd called her last night. She
said she didn't think it was me, as whoever it was wouldn't say
anything - she could just hear them breathing. Very odd. I
was almost offended that she could even suspect it was me, but
she said she knew it wasn't, she just wanted to mention it.

She went about an hour ago, as she wants to sort a few
things out before she goes back to Arnhem to see her parents
for the weekend and take part in a charity run. I'm going to
have to be careful, as I started feeling panicky as soon as she'd
gone. I must try and take things more calmly, I don't want to
let myself get hurt, especially with Christmas approaching.
Don't want a repeat of last Christmas.

Saturday 30th November

Been in groinal agony all day, throb is not the word. Don't
think the hair gel was a good idea. Kept having to reorganise
myself very carefully in the shop. A few people asked if I
needed a hand. In fact, everybody seems quite cheerful at the

moment, I dare say it's with Christmas approaching. I'd
ordered a whole range of Yuletide items for the shop, which
have all been selling like nobody's business: novelty Xmas
knickers (crotchless with holly), snowman dildos, a range of
mags from Copenhagen called "Skandasantasex", and a
selection of DVDs in the series "Last year's Christmas party",
which are basically orgies surrounded by Xmas trimmings.

Frank said he could tell instantly that Else is exactly right for
me. He reckons he could detect an aura of tranquil
benevolence about her. Know exactly what he means. He's
been going all-out on the email orders today, which have been
phenomenal. Think it's a good thing for him to keep busy.

Sunday 1st December

Had a surprise visit from Joop today in the Sexmarkt.
Couldn't believe it, as he seems to spend every minute behind
the bar at the hostel. He slapped me on the back, pinched my
cheek and rubbed my hair in a sort of manly affectionate way,
and then did the same to Frank, who was just as surprised to
see him. Frank then spent the next few minutes spiking his
hair back properly. Joop said he was glad things were going so
well in the shop, and was sorry we hadn't seen much of each
other of late. For a second, I thought he was going to get a bit
emotional (very odd), his mouth went all twitchy, but he just
inspected the Xmas porn and said what a good choice I'd
made with the blow-up Santas. He couldn't stop long, but
wanted us to go over to his place on St. Nicholas Day (5
December), as this is almost more important than Christmas
for Dutch families, and he feels we're the nearest thing he's got
to a family here. We were staggered. Big burly Joop
organising a 'family' do, whatever next. Frank's eyes went all
watery, and I felt quite touched as well, so we agreed. He
wants to take us out for a meal beforehand, and then go back
up to his flat for presents and drinks. Marvellous! Will have to
think carefully about presents.

Just had a phone call from Else! She's back from Arnhem,

having come second in the charity run and saying she'd missed me. She hoped I didn't mind her saying that. Mind! When she said good night on the phone, I could hear her smiling, and I realized instantly that Else is not just going to be a run-of-the-mill girlfriend.

Monday 2nd December

Went to the gym this morning - 77.5 kg! Just call me Mr Abs! Was really bucked up by that, and did 40 minutes on treadmill.

Rang Phil, who's back home now and making good progress, thank God. Had a frightening thought that I seem to be a health jinx on my friends this year! Anyway, Phil wanted to know if they'd be seeing me over Christmas. Told him I wasn't quite sure what my plans were. Decided to ring mom and dad, as it's been ages since I've been in touch with them. They could phone or write to me, of course, but they never seem to bother. I'd been wondering what they were doing for Christmas, as I had thought it might be nice to go back to England, but they've booked a Christmas coach trip to somewhere in the Tyrol they can't pronounce. Only spoke to Dad, as Mom was out shopping in Dudley with Phyllis from next door. Started to tell him how well things were going for me, but he cut me short, saying he didn't want to run up my phone bill, and hopefully they'd see me in the New Year. So that's that then.

Frank must have noticed I was having a 'Pascal moment' after that, as he kept asking if I was all right. I didn't have the heart to tell him, plus he's got enough on his plate. And blimey, I'm a grown man now anyway. I asked him what he plans to do at Xmas - going to his parents in Cologne. He asked me what my plans were. I said I hadn't thought about it yet. I'd be more than welcome in Cologne, he added. I said that sounded great, went into the toilet and shed a few tears - honestly, what a fart I am at times.

Went over to Else's tonight. Heaven. She cooked chicken salad, had George Michael on the stereo, and lights on dimmer.

I can't get over how we never run out of things to say. She's incredibly knowledgeable as well - history, architecture, psychology (which she studied of course), but is very down-to-earth. She said she'd love to write a novel, a thriller of some kind, but doesn't know where to start. She also talked about her ideas for setting up a dating agency, which sounds brilliant to me. She'd be brilliant at the personality profiling. Wouldn't mind getting involved myself. Who knows?

After a while, she asked me about my previous girlfriends, but I was deliberately vague. Didn't want to expose my shambolic dating record, and couldn't really be bothered getting into the Sandra saga, so thought I'd come off better by being a bit enigmatic, and just said "I'd rather not wade through the muddy waters of my past with women". I could tell she was intrigued and impressed by the way she kept gazing into my eyes. There were moments while she was talking that I just drifted off into total adoration. She started to tell me about her last boyfriend at one point, but it felt really weird somehow, so I said I'd rather the past stayed in its place, and felt totally overawed by the Richard Gere-ness in my voice.

When we'd finished eating, I couldn't hold back any longer, driven totally by the desire to consume her. She said she thinks I'm fantastic, that she can't believe how good things are between us so fast. I didn't say anything, playing it cool, but just hugged her even harder. Just before I left she had another funny phone call - very odd. I was glad I was there, though, as at least she knows for sure it's not me now.

Tuesday ³ʳᵈ December

Totally ordinary day, apart from the fact that I'm in love. Can't stop thinking about Else, the things she says, her face, the mole on her cheek, her body, her husky voice, the way she runs her hands through her blond hair, and even the elbow thing. Have hardly any appetite - don't even fancy any chocolate, amazingly. And I've got another huge box she bought me the other day - must get her something next time.

Wednesday 4<sup>th</sup> December

Ditto!

Thursday 5<sup>th</sup> December - Sinter Klaas

Weird old day - nice, but weird. Had the day off, as Sexmarkt only open this morning, Mariska holding the fort. Went round the Bijenkorff department store with Frank looking for presents. Everywhere packed, nightmare. After hours of struggling through hordes of shoppers with less manners than Londoners with itchy piles, I finally emerged with some presents: an aroma-therapy kit (for Frank), a scarf and moustache trimmer (for Joop), and *The human mind and emotions – socio-neural interchange re-visited*, by the acclaimed American psychiatrist Everhard B. Jones-Frankenthaler Junior (for Else).

  Had a quick coffee afterwards with Frank (who still hadn't got any presents but had made friends with a bloke on the aftershave counter), and then went off to meet Else for lunch in Bar Scorpio. Heaven. She was over in the corner when I walked in, and looked more gorgeous than ever, staring out over the canal, smoking a cigarette. Had a sandwich, though not really hungry again, and sat there chatting and holding hands across the table. The sun was shining in through the window behind her, and made her look like some sort of erotic angel. She was thrilled with the book, and kissed me passionately in front of everybody, but I didn't care, in fact I was really proud. I got a book as well - a novel entitled *All Good Things*, by Dutch writer Willem van de Pompetronk. Never heard of it, but Else thinks I'll like it. She'd had another weird call last night, apparently, and an awful anonymous letter in the post, which called her everything from ugly tart to whore of Babylon. Strong stuff. I'd have been frantic, but she seemed more bemused than upset. The whole thing is bizarre.

  Anyway, went over to Joop's this evening, and he took us to a fantastic fish restaurant on the Utrechtsestraat. Was amazed to see Joop in a collar and tie, very smart. Chatted about the

Sexmarkt, what an incredible year it's been, and so on, but somehow the conversation seemed a bit stilted. Frank was a bit quiet, but I put that down to the health worries. It's bound to prey on his mind, I know it does on mine. Can't quite put my finger on Joop, really. It's not that he wasn't chatty, it just felt as though we weren't meshing, somehow. Maybe it was just me.

Eventually, we strolled back to Joop's, and actually entered his flat for the first time - wow, what a pad - the last thing I'd have expected above the hostel - three flats knocked through, everything electronic, metal or leather, total amazing luxury. Not much furniture though. Frank and I just looked at each other in amazement as we went in. Unbelievable. One of the bathrooms (!) has three bidets and a shower the size of my bedroom! Joop poured us out some jenevers, and we got our presents out. Frank gave me another copy of *All Good Things* (didn't let on, talk about Sod's law, though) and Joop a jumper with leather zig-zags in it. They both seemed quite pleased with my presents.

We sat silent for a minute, waiting for Joop to produce a couple of packages, but nothing. Just as I was coming to the conclusion that the meal must have been his present, he said it was time for our presents now. Brilliant, I thought. Mine was in the bedroom on the left, Frank's in the bedroom on the right. We'd have to go in and get them. Suspense or what. Frank and I looked at each other, not knowing what to expect. And I don't think we would ever have guessed. Frank opened his door first, and over his shoulder I saw some dark-haired bloke in a G-string sitting on the bed. A split second later, I opened the other door, and saw a buxom orientally-attired woman. Prostitutes for Christmas. What can you say? Joop came over to us, told us to enjoy, and that he'd be back in an hour - some business to attend to. The doors closed, and, an awkward moment followed – though the thought of being pushed to unimaginable boundaries of physical experience was appealing, I was sitting on a full stomach, and only just about winning on the trapped wind front. Plus, Else – there was no way. So I suggested a back massage which was actually beyond belief, and eventually I plopped out of the bedroom like a lump of lubricated jelly, at which point I also lost the trapped wind battle. Frank emerged wobble-legged two minutes later. We lay on the floor and laughed and laughed and laughed like I don't think I ever have before. The sort of laughter that extends your life by about five years. Joop came back before we'd got up, and said it looked as though we'd received a reasonable service. No Christmas present will ever surprise me again.

We chatted and laughed a bit more over coffee, feeling totally 'enmeshed' now. Out of the blue, Joop said he wanted us to know we mean a lot to him, that we are good kids, and that he'll always think that. I felt a bit embarrassed, Frank went over and hugged him. It suddenly felt as though it was time to go, so we got up and made for the door. I was amazed when he grabbed us both, hugged us hard and then quickly closed the door on us. Frank said Joop had tears in his eyes, but I couldn't tell.

As we walked back, we laughed and chatted about the evening. Frank seemed totally lifted by the whole experience, he bounced along the canals in his woolly green cardigan. Seeing him like that was as good as being given another present. And somehow, I feel as though I love Else even more now.

Friday 6th December

Feel quite worried about having been massaged by a prostitute. Didn't bother me at first, but can't help wondering whether I might have caught something. Is that possible? Am I being ridiculous? Keep checking myself for growths, but so far so good.

Saw Else tonight, I could barely control myself. Afterwards, she told me how impressed she was by my obvious experience. I just smirked and put the kettle on (I really do need to mature). She said how wonderful it was being with me, and started crying. I rushed over with a cup of tea, wondering what on earth was up. I stroked her hair away from her eyes, but then she started laughing and hugged me. The weird ways of women. She said her last boyfriend never made her a cup of tea, he only ever talked about TV and his work.

She also wondered whether I'd like to spend Christmas with her family in Arnhem, as she'd hate to think of me on my own, and would love to spend the holiday with me. It's funny, really. If Sandra had said that, I'd have been filled with dread. But coming from Else, I was overjoyed. I said I wasn't sure what was happening yet, but thanked her, and said I liked the idea.

Walked her back to her flat, very cold night, even snowed a bit. When we reached her door, somebody had sprayed BITCH in red letters on the steps. There are some right weirdos about.

Saturday 7th December

Two identical packages for Frank and me in the post this morning. Opened mine, not knowing what to expect, and fetched out a huge wad of cash - 5000 guilders!!! Frank had exactly the same. With each wad there was a note which said "Take care of yourself, Joop". What an all-round brilliant bloke he is. Rang the hostel to thank him, but Rita the cleaner said he wasn't around. Rang a few times today but he's still not there - dare say he's seeing to 'a bit of business.' God knows why he's sent us so much money, especially after Sinter Klaas. And sending cash through the post! Will put it into my account first thing on Monday.

Marvellous evening over at Else's. I took her a bunch of roses, which made her cry. When she was putting them in a glass vase, she dropped the whole thing on the tiled floor, glass, water and roses everywhere, so more tears. Her wrists have been quite painful recently, she said, and sometimes the pain makes her clumsy. When I said the roses didn't matter, the tears became uncontrollable, but eventually she calmed down, as I stroked her head. She's just so wonderful.

There was a Bond film on the TV, so we lay on her sofa together watching it, after I'd cleared the mess away, incurring multiple finger pricks from the roses in the process (Else doubled up in hysterics by now). She reckons I have a look of Timothy Dalton, and I was inclined to agree, until, horror of horrors, in the break there was a Brekko-Bites advert WITH ME IN IT!! It was one of the scenes filmed in Eindhoven, and made me look more like a cross between Les Dawson and one of the Kray twins. Horrific. Else was majorly impressed and said how wonderful it was to have a boyfriend who was a secret TV model.

Later on, when I kissed her good night on her doorstep, a stone flew past my ear and hit the door frame. Frightened the life out of us. We looked round, but couldn't see anybody. I kept looking over my shoulder all the way back, but no sign of anyone. Can't work this out. Who on earth could have anything against Else? Or is it me? Wondered if it might be Ben's idea of a joke, but don't think so. Very odd. It's starting to unnerve me now.

Sunday 8th December

Could hardly sleep last night, it was all playing on my mind. Got up early, forced myself to go to the gym, kept thinking about the stone incident and how awful I looked in that advert. Felt better by the time I came out. Tried to ring Joop and thank him for the mysterious donation, but he still wasn't around. Must have gone away for the weekend.

Anyway, Frank, me and Mariska all down in Sexmarkt this afternoon, as anyone would think Christmas was some sort of annual mass orgy as opposed to a religious festival, going by the number of customers we've had in today. When I finally had the chance to go up and get a coffee, I couldn't believe it - we'd been burgled!

There was glass and newspapers all over the floor, it was a right mess. The TV had gone, so had Frank's CD player. I rushed into my bedroom and felt under the mattress to see if the 5000 guilders were still there, which, thank God, they were. I ran down after Frank, who was horrified, but relieved to find his money still under his bed too. Frank had us doing some breathing exercises to calm down, then rang the police, who arrived after about an hour. Amazingly, it was Van Arlen again (the Amsterdam police must be seriously understaffed). "Your friend turned up in the end, then? Seem to attract trouble, don't you?" Git. There was another younger 'officer' with him, who was obviously at the cutting edge of policing: "Looks like a break-in to me."

They reckoned it was probably drugs-related opportunism, said it was unlikely they'd get whoever did it, and suggested we think about security measures. The younger one went upstairs to ask the neighbours if they'd seen anybody suspicious, but they hadn't. And that was that. I thought there would at least have been somebody in an overall dusting round for fingerprints. But that was that. Van Arlen said he'd no doubt see me before Christmas (still hilarious), the younger one asked me if I was the bloke in the Brekko-Bites advert (splitting my sides). Frank was appalled by their laissez-faire attitude, and said he could see why the police spend so much time on self-development and inter-personal skills.

Anyway, we cleaned up the glass from the broken window, and stuck a plastic bag over the gap. Will have to get somebody in to repair it tomorrow. Thank God they didn't find the money. Shame about the TV, although at least I'll be spared the further humiliation of seeing myself on any Brekko-Bite adverts.

Monday 9th December

Hardly slept a wink last night. Kept thinking about some git walking about the flat, looking through my things. The wind kept blowing the plastic bag in and out, which sounded like somebody moving about, so I must have been up about ten times just to make sure. Frank was doing the same at one point, frightened the life out of each other.

Took the 5000 guilders to the bank first thing. Tried to get Joop all day, firstly to thank him for cash, and secondly to ask him if he knew any glaziers, but still not around (God knows where he is), so had to fall back on Yellow Pages. Decided to ring a company which sounded quite good - twenty years' experience, trained and qualified fitters, all wearing hard helmets and clean work overalls (concealing manly chests according to Frank) in the advert. Two hours later, a sixteen year-old lad with a fag behind his ear and a hammer turned up with a bloke in smeared dungarees carrying a jar of puttee. Still, they had the glass in in no time, and left us some leaflets on security locks. Frank reckons we should wait till we speak to Joop, as he's bound to know someone who could do it for us.

Told Else the news when she rang. She'd got some bad news as well - her bike had been vandalised when she went back to it after a full day of doing boat tours.

Somebody had cut through all the spokes in both wheels. Feel I'm moving into another Pascal period.

Wednesday 11th December

Still don't know what to do for Christmas. Don't know why, but the thought of it depresses me. Maybe it's just because it's mid-winter. Maybe it's just because I had a Christmas card from mom and dad wishing me all the best for Christmas. Not even "all our love". Frank seems a bit fragile again as well. He had seemed to be bearing up quite well, or so I thought, but he's come down with a bad cold now, and I'm sure it all plays on his mind when he feels weak. There's the constant smell of scented candles around the flat now. Still saying my prayers.

Extremely busy in Sexmarkt. Tried to get hold of Joop again, as need to check some orders with him, but nobody's seen him. Rang Bertus in the end, who said that he had no idea where he was. He sounded a bit standoffish.

Sandra called last night. Could hardly think what to say to her. She wanted to know whether I'd like to spend Xmas with her family! I said I wasn't sure what I was doing, but thanked her all the same. Then she wanted to know what I'd been up to, where I'd been, why I hadn't been in touch, and if there was still a chance that we could get back together, as she'd hate to lose me, and still hopes that we could make a go of things, etc. I didn't say anything about Else. Blimey, and I thought all that was behind me. I said I'd be in touch before Christmas, and lied that someone had rung the doorbell just to get off the phone. Haven't said anything to Else about this.

Friday 13th December

Else's had two more awful letters. She's getting very upset by it all now, but swears she can't think of any reason why anybody would be harbouring such a grudge. Spent the whole night over there last night. We talked about reporting it all to the police, but I couldn't bear to see Van Arlen's sniggering face again, and they'd probably do bugger-all anyway.

I know it's early days yet, but marriage keeps coming into my mind. She's just so wonderful. And we just get on so well, I can't believe it. Suppose it's because we share the same intellectual interests. But it's still more than that, somehow. On top of it all, there's that feeling I got when I saw Maria, that check-out girl in Milan. Maybe it doesn't matter where you're both from, what you have in common, what you do or anything, as long as you have that undeniable gut feeling. Have decided to spend Xmas with Else's family, though feel nervous about meeting them. She's absolutely delighted.

Saw Ben when I was doing the shopping this afternoon. He was on the opposite side of the canal. My heart sank, and I was dreading him seeing me, so rushed up an alley in the Red Light Area and hung around for a few minutes, breathing heavily with the shopping, until a prostitute told me to "sodomieter op", as I was putting the punters off. Charming. When I went back out, there was no sign of him.

Frank seems a bit better, fortunately, but still no sign of Joop - he must have disappeared off the face of the earth. Hope he hasn't had some sort of terrible diagnosis as well...

Sunday 15th December

Just Frank and me in shop yesterday, as Mariska off with the flu. Frank went on line every three hours to check the email orders, and each time there were about ten new orders. In between manning the cash desk I helped him make them up. At least half of them are for England, which surprises Frank, as it doesn't fit in with his 'stiff upper lip' image of us. Half of Surrey must have Santa dildos by now. The whole county must be buzzing like mad, there'll probably be posh gits complaining about it affecting property prices.

Sandra called again last night, asking if we could meet up. I said I was exhausted (which was true), and that I'd give her a ring some time (which wasn't true). She wanted to know whether I'd decided about Christmas, so I said I was going back to England. She was sorry, of course, but insisted we meet up "for old time's sake", especially with it being the festive season. I promised I'd ring her this week, but really don't want to, especially after tonight.

Met Else after she'd finished work on the boat. They're doing candle-lit Christmas tours of the canals, so we decided to go along. Marvellous - there was even a meal on board. I've never had such a wonderful evening. Total and utter romance. The water sloshing gently, the Christmas lights, the candles, the wine, and the most beautiful girlfriend I've ever had, running her fingers through her gorgeous blond hair, when she wasn't holding my hand.

The tour took us down the Van den Bonken canal where Ben lives. As we approached, I could see flashing blue lights near his flat. And I would never have believed what I saw then - policemen escorting the man himself, handcuffed at that, into one of the cars! It's obviously fate, I was meant to witness the moment of his demise, what a total and utter triumph.

Everyone on the boat seemed slightly unnerved by the scene, but I couldn't have been happier. I was totally overcome by emotion, and told Else that I loved her (have never told anybody else that), and tears welled up in her eyes. She pulled my hand to her chest, and said what a fantastic Christmas it was going to be, especially since she loves me as well!

We kissed over the table, and I only noticed that a buttered roll had stuck to my stomach when I sat back down. Else roared with laughter, elbows all over the place, but I just smeared some of the butter on her cheek, which made her laugh even more. Can things really stay this good?

Monday 16th December

Have been on a high since last night, knowing that my love is reciprocated, and that Ben the git is probably behind bars. And all is well.

Tuesday 17th December

Still desperately need Joop's signature on some orders, so went over to the hostel this morning. Couldn't believe it - it was all barred up! Went back to the flat and rang Bertus straight away. He wasn't in, so I left a message asking if he knew where Joop was. He only rang back tonight. Apparently, Joop's had to go away for a while, and that's all he would say, and for us to carry on as normal in the shop. And one last thing - if the police turn up, we were to say nothing about escorting, the Prague trip, Ben and the deliveries. Bizarre - why should the police turn up? I never mentioned anything to Bertus about the deliveries either, so assume Joop must have told him, but can't think why. Joop obviously knew he was going away, that must be why he gave us all that money. Just can't understand why he didn't say anything. Frank reckons there must be a good reason. Don't like the sound of all this.

Going over to Else's now. Am spending the night there, as she's taking part in a sponsored  silence for arthritis, and I won't see her again now till Christmas Eve.

Wednesday 18th December

Don't know where to start. One day things are fine, the next the whole world is turned upside down. Can't believe it.

Last night was the most perfect night of my life. Have never come close to feeling so loved, so in love, such warmth and happiness. Left Else this morning on Cloud Nine. Had been in the Sexmarkt for about two hours when Arnold walked in. Assumed at first he'd come to make peace with Frank, but no. He'd come to take Frank and me in for questioning. Frank and I both laughed, even Mariska laughed, but then three other policemen came in behind him. He said he was sorry, and really looked it, so we followed him out in disbelief.

We sat in the back of the police car, asking him what the hell it was all about, but he wouldn't say. He apologized to Frank about the way things had ended between them again but said it was just as well, given what's now come to light. Can't describe what went through my mind waiting in the car till we got to the station. And it didn't get any better.

We were led into a room where two detectives were already sitting down with various papers. They had reason to believe that we were involved in the distribution of illegal pornography. I laughed at that point, saying that we work in a sex shop in Amsterdam, so what would they expect. One of them said they were talking about ILLEGAL pornography. They'd managed to intercept some child pornography and DVDs from Bosnian war camps, as well as torture DVDs and magazines filmed in Eastern European prisons.

I went cold. Frank's head sank into his hands. Then we just looked at each other. Joop had obviously had some inkling of this, hence his sudden departure. Frank started explaining about the Prague trip, and we both insisted that we'd assumed it was just stuff for the shop. We also insisted that there was never anything like that on sale in the shop. One of the detectives said he hoped we were right, as it wouldn't help our case if they found anything. At that very moment, the whole shop was being gone through by police, and the licence to operate was to be revoked pending the outcome of the investigation.

They took Frank away at that point, went over and over the whole business with us again individually, left us on our own for hours at a time, and then went through the whole business again. Where was Joop now, who was his contact, where exactly had we gone, etc, etc. Eventually, they must have realized we were telling as much as we knew, and they let us go at ten past five.

We got outside and just stood there. Frank asked me to hug him, I didn't refuse. Thank God I wasn't on my own. We just can't believe it. I don't know what to feel worst about - Joop getting us involved in such awful stuff, being such a mug as to let him, the shop being closed down, losing our jobs (will we get them back eventually?), or what'll happen to the flat. And Joop. How could he knowingly get involved in all that? Surely he couldn't have known *how* awful it was, I can't believe that.

Frank's having a lie-down. I had a walk round the shop, which looks like a bomb's hit it. The computers have gone, the police took them to check for illegal files, according to Mariska, who rang to ask if we were all right.

I feel totally winded. Can't even begin to describe the layers of disappointment I'm coping with. Frank looks destroyed. If I wasn't in love underneath all this, I think I might be throwing myself in front of something big and heavy. It was just all going too well.

Thursday 19th December

To think that this time last year I was coming to the end of another dull term and contemplating the staff Xmas do down the Berni Inn. And a year later, I'm being made redundant by the sex industry and contemplating marriage in my private moments, in between helping police with their enquiries.

Took me two hours to eat a bowl of Brekko-Bites this

morning. Frank and I just sat there, discussing what to do next, in between bouts of stunned silence. Frank keeps meditating to try and process the shock and disappointment. This is all he needs on top of the health worries. I've rediscovered Mars Bars, love or no love. Frank's talking about staying in Cologne when he goes for Christmas, and wants me to join him. He's sure I'll find a job there, says I could easily get a job teaching English, but not sure I want to go down that road again. Don't think I'll be able to afford the flat on my own though, especially without an income. Maybe Bertus can put some escort jobs my way, but the thought of it all sickens me somehow. But if I leave Amsterdam, how will I carry on seeing Else? Have I used up my happiness ration or something? So many times, I've thought I've been onto something, and before long it's gone wrong, fizzled away or ended. Does it only happen to me?

It's just all been so good here. It's been fun, stress-free (mostly), a change, it's been so me. Signor Cosmopolitano's element. And now it's hello uncertainty, hello the dole maybe, goodbye Frank, Joop's already gone, the hostel and the shop have closed down. I just can't believe it.

Frank says what gets him the most is knowing that he's helped distribute such sick material, and might easily have ended up in court or worse for it. He can't believe how Joop could have knowingly exposed us to that risk. And leaving us to face the flack. The pit of my stomach keeps hitting the floor. I wish Joop was here so we could ask him about it all.

Am worn out with wondering what to do. Can't ring Else as don't want to jeopardise her sponsored silence. Just hope that Sandra doesn't call, as I'd promised to ring her this week. Need her like a hole in the head.

Friday 20th December

Supposedly the shortest days at this time of the year, but they feel like the longest in history. Slept badly again last night, so got up early, and was still on my Brekko-Bites when Arnold arrives again. Could I accompany him to the station yet again? Just me this time. Not before I'd spent twenty minutes throwing up, but he waited, worst luck. He wouldn't tell Frank what it was about. Frank came with us and waited for me the whole time.

I was taken through to Detective Van Arlen, whose first words were "Here we are again!" He then launched into a tirade against me. How they could do without devious and subversive foreigners like me in Amsterdam. I pretend to be some innocent, yet there's a catalogue of misdemeanours to my name. He reeled them all off: helping to import and distribute obscene illegal pornography; manager of a sex shop; working as a male escort; picked up for late night loitering (Arnold had obviously logged that, what a git); arriving at the Hook of Holland with £5000, allegedly withdrawn from a Lloyds' bank account which customs officers had been unable to trace; sporadically large deposits in my Dutch bank account; wasting police time with false claims of disappearance and possibly even staging burglary for false insurance claims; even the jay-walking offence was mentioned; hardly a clean-living person. I started to object about the jay-walking, but threw up on the table, and couldn't stop convulsing for ages. When I'd just about recovered, he went on.

Yes, I was very clever. That innocent face, hiding a criminal brain, which, despite my implication in various issues of an international dimension, made me clever enough to cover my tracks. But this time I've slipped up. How did I know Ben Verbraak? I thought Arnold must have dropped me in it again at first, but Van Arlen said there was no use denying I knew him, as they've got Ben's little black book, and my details are in it, together with dates and symbols of some kind. Plus Officer Arnold Smit has confirmed his presence at my dwelling. Cheers Arnold, just as I'd thought. They also had a statement from an American Interpol officer alleging some link between me and Ben - can only think that that must have been Tom, my first escort assignment.

I was in too much of a state to pretend to bluff, so I explained the full story, about how I'd got involved with him through his ex-girlfriend, and had been semi-forced into delivering paintings for him. I said I didn't know any more than that, as Ben would never give answers. Detective Van Arlen then said it seems that I go through life not asking enough questions, and suggested I might want to alter this aspect of my personality in future.

Did I know what the paintings were of? Who they were for? They kept on at me to remember all the addresses I'd ever delivered paintings to, and I had to pinpoint them on a map. I was shown photos of buildings and people, did I know them, did I recognize them, when had I been there....This went on for hours. Did I know anything about a German bank account in Ben's name, with regular telephone transferals from the Sexmarkt number? Why had I stopped helping Ben? I explained about the delivery mishap when I got beaten up on the tram, and Ben subsequently assaulting me. Van Arlen just sniggered and went on. The police had apparently managed to intercept some of the paintings. Did I know what was in them? I kept swearing that I had no idea, I thought they were just paintings. Eventually, he told me they concealed laundered money, drugs and illegal pornography, and were all part of some elaborate international distribution network. They know that Joop was the porn supplier and Ben a key player in its distribution. But so far, I was the only link between the two - for some reason, they were satisfied that the two men did not deal directly with – or weirdly, even know (dark contacts?!?) one other. Someone had to have established the link though. If it wasn't me, did I have any ideas?

After hours of gruelling desperation, fear and vomiting, Detective Van Arlen said I'd been helpful and they were satisfied I was not the link. I was now free to go, but should watch myself in future, especially now it might get out I'm a grass. I went to stand up, but fainted flat out. The next thing I remember was Frank shoving some kind of scented capsules up my nostrils, telling me to relax. The indignity of it all in a police waiting room. Thank God he'd waited though. I truly felt as though I'd been to hell and back. I told Frank how I'd had a vision of my future at one point, where I was looking at a ten-year stretch with a maniac homosexual bruiser as a cell-mate. "So it wasn't all bad", was all he could say.

And as if all that wasn't enough, as if the stress of the last week, not to say year wasn't enough, as if it wasn't awful enough just having to go a few days without seeing Else, never mind anything else happening, who should a couple of police women be bringing in, but Sandra! The very last person I wanted to see. When I asked her what she was doing there, she looked at me coldly, slapped me across the face, and called me a lying, deceiving bastard!

I sat straight back down, and so did Frank. Arnold was still mooching about, and I saw him talking to the police women. Then he came over. Apparently, she'd been taken in for assault. Assault on a woman called Else van Kampen! Else!! Frank was about to shove more capsules up my nose, but there was no way I could black out at this, I'd got to hear what was going on - Sandra had attacked Else outside her flat with a brick two days ago!

Suddenly, the penny dropped. The phone calls, the graffiti, the stone, the watching - the stupid bitch. Else had been out cold for a day, and is still in hospital now. When she came round, the police wanted to know if she had any idea who might have attacked her. She explained that her last boyfriend, a plumber called Jaap (!), had been two-timing her with an "unhinged, obsessive type", who'd once caught them in bed together. She was the only person she could think of, and so she gave the police Sandra's details. And when the police went round, Sandra blabbed it all out straight away, as if she was really proud of herself. And to think that she and I finish, and I end up seeing the same woman her ex had cheated on - amazing. No wonder she bears a grudge, but I would never have had her down for all this.

Arnold said he was sorry about the way things had gone, but it was over between him and the Purmerend plumber, so if Frank was interested in hooking up again? In a sudden move, Frank shoved a capsule up Arnold's nose with surprising force, for which Arnold said he could have him on an assault charge, but didn't. We got a taxi back here, and I rang the hospital straight away - Else is doing fine. There's so much going round in my head, I don't know what to think of first. Between the shock, the worry, the horror, the tension, the amazement and the general confusion of it all, I really don't know whether I'm coming or going.

Frank's got some food on the go, and I can hear him opening a bottle of wine. Don't think that'll be the only one tonight.

Saturday 21st December

Have only got out of bed today to eat a boiled egg and use the toilet (not at the same time). My head has been spinning, aching and thumping. My stomach has been churning and aching. My mind has been plagued by horrific flashbacks, fear and uncertainty. In between I've had hours of total numbness. I can't cope with much more. Frank has brought me drinks in and tried to get me to meditate, but I've just not had the energy. Thank God he's here, though. And thank God Else is all right. Thank God she's there, even if she is in hospital. Thank God she loves me. And thank God for Cadburys.

Monday 23rd December

Well, it really does look like the end of an era. What a week, what a year. At least I feel calmer today. I went to see Else in hospital this afternoon. Hell of a blow to the back of her head, no wonder she was out cold for so long. In the fall, she must have landed on her wrists, as they're both broken. The doctors were very concerned about them healing, given the weakness already there. Poor thing. She told me all about Sandra, and I told her all about her as well. We ended up laughing until she had to stop because of the pain in her head. Didn't tell her about the rest of the business in the week, just that the shop has had to close down, the owner having absconded. The whole week just smarts like a massive cut. Keep thinking I

190

should be going down into the shop, and then remembering it's closed down. Out of losing my job, the police nightmare, and poor old Else, I think the worst thing is my disappointment in Joop. It's a sort of piercing, stabbing disappointment - it wrenches at my stomach, makes my eyes well up and my head spin. It goes away briefly and then comes back because I can't make it right.

But after everything this week, it was fantastic seeing Else. I wanted to tell her that I love her more than I've ever loved any other person in my whole life, but I just stroked her hair with one hand, and ate a muesli bar with the other.

Frank's spent the day packing. He says he just needs to get away from it all, make a clean break. He can't deal with it while it's all so close. He keeps talking about Joop and welling up as well. He's even eating things without reading the additives information on the packets. Says he'll be glad when it's tomorrow, but wants me to come with him. Says I could easily travel up to Amsterdam at weekends to see Else, it's only two-and-a-half hours on the train. He also thinks it might be dangerous for me to stay - if word gets back to Ben that I've grassed him up, he's bound to have contacts on the outside. I told Frank the last thing I need right now is him putting the willies up me, which I realize with hindsight was a silly thing to say to a German homosexual. Maybe I should go with him. Else comes out of hospital tomorrow, so we'll definitely go to Arnhem to spend Christmas. I can't work out what to do beyond that. Most of me just so badly wants things back the way they were that I can't contemplate anything else.

Haven't bothered sending any Xmas cards. Rang Bertus a few times, but his number's been disconnected. All I get is the recorded telecom message saying "number unobtainable". Sounds to me as though he's jumped ship too. Wonder how he figures in all this.

Christmas Eve

Surprisingly, I don't feel too bad right this minute in spite of

everything. Maybe all the hardship is toughening me up. God
knows. Whatever else happens, though, whatever else I do,
I've got Else and Frank, and I've still got a flat to live in
Amsterdam. A job will come along somehow, whether I'm
here, in Cologne, Istanbul or Wolverhampton. Maybe I should
talk to Else about going into partnership on a dating agency. I
don't know. I might leave the flat, but there are always other
places. Keep thinking about Bill Bixby at the end of each
episode of the Incredible Hulk. Forced to move on every
week by terrible circumstances, but always stoic, and always
surviving. But then he could draw on super-human strength
when it counted. Six months down the gym haven't quite
done that for me yet, but no matter - things change, people
cope.

Towards the end of every year, I always try to guess what the
next year will be like, and in the past, my diary forecasts have
been frighteningly accurate in every dull detail. I didn't do one
for this year, and could never have guessed what lay ahead,
good and bad, in my wildest dreams. The bad have been
desperate: getting beaten up, getting involved with Ben,
Frank's tumour, the trouble with Sandra, Phil getting knocked
down, the police wrangles, Joop disappearing. Joop....

But the good have been bloody brilliant: Else, Frank,
Amsterdam, learning Dutch, the travelling, Brussels and Gaby,
the adventures, the fun and the laughs, the variety, the feeling
of living. Milan, even Prague, even Joop.... The humdrum
emotional vacuum has well and truly had the air let in, and I've
certainly been breathing. And in spite of the last week, I think
I'm actually looking forward to Christmas for the first time in
my life. So probably a good time to shove my diary in my case,
forget about self-scrutiny and recent events, and get myself
sorted for Arnhem and Else.

Have just picked up a postcard off the mat - nothing written
on it, apart from our address, but it's postmarked Malaga and
has FELIZ NAVIDAD printed on the front....

Anyway, Merry Christmas, Signor Cosmopolitano. Enjoy
your life. Keep moving, keep going, and despite the cracks -

never give up hope.

Printed in Great Britain
by Amazon

81496117R10113